THE DIONYSUS HEIST

A FORENSIC WITCH NOVEL
BOOK 1

SHANON ERAMI

Dionysus... the Master of Illusions, who could make a vine grow out of a ship's plank, and in general enable his votaries to see the world as the world's not.

— E.R. DODDS, THE GREEKS AND THE IRRATIONAL

CONTENTS

1

STRANGE DOINGS AT THE PALACE HOTEL

Detective Sergeant Victoria "Rab" Rabinowski got the call ten or so minutes after one in the morning: a robbery at the Palace Hotel. She clicked her tongue when she ended the call. It was her first case since transferring back to the Robbery-Homicide division, and it was a simple B&E.

She got ready quickly, exited her apartment building, and crossed the street where her service car – an old, battered, black Crown Vic with a super-charged engine she nicknamed "Bruiser" – was parked. She drove down Nob Hill as a sinister, miasmic fog drifted into the city, making a turn onto Market Street, a cigarette smoldering between the fingers of her left hand, and turned on the flashers as she cruised down.

Rab drove towards New Montgomery Street, seeing the Palace Hotel come into view. Spotlights running along the hotel's first story illuminated the dark tan bricks of the façade. Above, the hotel's bright antique sign cast spectral halos in the thick fog.

She pulled up to the entrance and got out. Long, copper-red hair streamed down from a dark gray beanie. Cynical, brilliant blue eyes scanned the area as she pulled on the last remains of the cigarette before tossing the butt down onto the sidewalk and stamping it out. She opened her hoodie to adjust the gun in her shoulder holster: a classic M1911 forty-five. Strange symbols were engraved on the barrel plate. A black obsidian handle shimmered in the cascading lights of the hotel's marquee. In its center was etched the outline of a slithering dragon.

She strolled into the bright golden marble and crystal lobby, surprised by the number of cops hanging around. They guided her to an elevator bank. She got on one and pressed the button to the sixth floor, then clipped her badge onto her belt.

Two uniforms were waiting for her in the hallway. They nodded in salutation before directing her to Room 612. It was a corner suite, and opulence was the operative word. The sitting room was large and beautifully decorated with framed oil paintings, antique furniture, and luxurious lighting. A vase of colorful ranunculus stood on a table in the center. To the right were doors that opened to the bedroom, enticing Rab to enter.

With lavish dark carpet and varnished wood, the creamy white curtains were pulled back, offering views of downtown San Francisco. A warm, inviting king-size bed, ideally made with Egyptian cotton and silk sheets, stood nearby. The only things out of place were the cops pacing around and a large antique traveling trunk in charred, jagged pieces near the bed.

Rab walked to the trunk, which looked like something exploded inside. Its bronze lock lay mangled and twisted on the floor, and wood splinters punctured the wall behind it. The two halves of the trunk yawned open, revealing inscriptions etched along their edges. She crouched down to examine them, feeling them delicately. They were severely scorched.

"Good seeing you, Rab," someone said behind her. She looked around and grinned. Lawrence Matt, Captain of the SFPD Robbery-Homicide division, stood near her, a tired, relieved smile on his lips. He had a few new wrinkles around his eyes. Silver began its encroachment on his temples. But he still had a youthful countenance, like Obama before his first inaugural.

"Hey, buddy," Rab said in a calm, friendly tone. "It's been a while."

"It has. So, it's true. They let you transfer back to us."

"Well, it's not like the powers-that-be had much of a choice, I guess."

"That's a fact. You've been good?"

"Every day." She pointed to the trunk, "I missed quite a lot. What's the story here?"

Matt squatted down with her. "The owner's name is Selene Archambeau, from Savannah. She was returning from some gala at the Fairmont before midnight when she heard a loud bang inside her room. She ran in and saw these dark figures standing near the remains of her trunk."

"That was brave of her. And very dangerous."

"Especially with the caliber of people we're probably dealing with."

"What do you mean?"

"According to Archambeau, when they spot her, they vanish into thin air with the loot."

"Witches?"

"That's what I'm thinking." There was a hint of disgust in his voice. "Probably crank hexers. They've been operating in the area recently."

"You found anything?"

Matt shrugged. "No, not yet. We're waiting for your new partner."

Rab glanced at him, "You're partnering me with a forensic witch?"

"She's new to the force and could use your guidance."

"Great, I'm stuck playing the babysitter again." She stood up and placed her fists on her hips. "What was in it?" she asked.

Matt joined her. "Get this: the Cup of Dionysus."

Rab's face slackened from surprise. "Whoa, no way! Serious?"

"Very."

"I thought it was a myth."

"It's as real as the sun and moon, according to the American Cyathomancy Society."

She smirked. "So, can you see the seventeen living rings of the universe inside? Does it overflow with the wine of eternal madness?"

"Sorry, Rab. Can't help you there."

"Okay. Wait. Why was this Archambeau lady carrying it around with her?"

"Ms. Archambeau was scheduled to be at some Dionysian thing at the Legion of Honor since she's one of the head initiates. The cup needed to be there, she told me."

Rab studied the trunk once more. Behind her, a gang of uniformed men were chuckling. Lawrence Matt turned towards them. "Oh, Christ," he muttered.

"What?" Rab said.

"Looks like your new partner's here."

She turned to the suite's sitting room where a woman stood. She was wearing a long black dress and hooded coat, black ankle boots, and a messenger bag slung over her shoulder. A weather-worn, wide-brim, rough wool alewife hat sat crookedly on her head. Curling black hair came down the length of her back. She looked around with bright, intelligent brown eyes behind a pair of cat-eye glasses. "Wow," Rab said. "Usually, forensic witches are much subtler than that."

"Give her a break. She's a rookie," Lawrence Matt said. He approached her with his hand out, "Harriet June? I'm Captain Matt."

She adjusted her messenger bag and shook his hand, "Pleased to meet you, Captain." She sounded excited, tempered with abundant nervousness.

Rab had joined him. She nodded her head at Harriet. "What's going on?"

"You must be Sargent Rabinowski," Harriet said. "I was told we were going to meet here."

"You can call me Rab." They shook hands as well.

"Alright," Matt said, "now that you two have met, we should start this investigation."

"Right," Rab said. "Come on, June. Follow me."

"Where are we going?"

"We're going to interview Archambeau."

They were told Selene Archambeau was sitting in a vacant room across from her suite. Outside of the door was a man in a professionally tailored black suit. He was in his fifties, with graying brown hair and gold-framed glasses perched on a thin aquiline nose. He smelled of lavender and honey. "Can I help you?" he asked tersely when the detectives approached. Rab showed her badge, as did Harriet.

"I'm so sorry," he said, sighing. "I didn't mean to be rude. It's been a very stressful night."

"Understandable," Rab said. "And you are?"

"I'm Tobias Gregarian, the manager of the Palace Hotel."

"Okay, Mr. Gregarian, no worries. We'll investigate this robbery and maybe save your employer's reputation. Is Ms. Archambeau inside?"

"Yes, she's been waiting for you."

He unlocked the door and stepped aside. Selene Archambeau was sitting on the edge of the room's bed. She was handsomely matriarchical, with feminine and masculine features. Most likely sixty years old, with fierce green shimmering eyes. Her silver and white hair was pulled tight into a bun behind her head. She wore a stark white high-collar blouse with a long black woolen skirt and a long silver necklace with a pendant around her neck. Her skin had a pale gray pallor, which contrasted strongly with her rouged lips. Harriet detected a subtle smell of earth and trees and flowers in bloom.

"Ms. Archambeau," Rab said, "I'm Detective Rabinowski, badge number four-five-seven, and this is my partner Harriet June."

"Good evening, detectives," Archambeau said, her voice rough and froggish, lacking the music of a Southern accent.

"Our captain told us part of the story. But could you tell us what happened to you tonight?"

Archambeau looked annoyed, "I have to repeat myself?"

"Please, it'll help."

"Well, it happened in an instant. It was around midnight, I believe, and I was returning to my room when I heard an explosion from outside my door. I ran into it. It was dark. But I saw the shadows of two or three hoodlums standing near what was left of my trunk. They quickly turned towards me; one had the Cup of Dionysus in his hand, and they evaporated."

"Did you hear anyone utter an incantation before they vanished?" Harriet asked.

"Can't say that I did."

"I noticed the etchings on the inside of your trunk," Rab said. "What are they?"

Archambeau shrugged. "I'm not sure, detective. They were there when I bought the trunk."

Harriet studied Archambeau.

"Thank you for your help, Ms. Archambeau. We'll be in touch." She and Harriet exited the room. Mr. Gregarian spirited himself inside and closed the door. They stood in the middle of the hallway. "What do you think, June?" Rab asked.

"Something *is* going on here. Weird vibes."

"For sure. And Archambeau?"

"She's the weirdest one here. I can't tell why, though."

"Yeah. She skeeves me out a bit. But we're not here to judge the vic. It's time to figure out how our thieves pulled this off. Are you ready to go to work?"

"Oh, one hundred percent."

Harriet took the lead back to the suite's bedroom. She placed her messenger bag on top of the bed and opened it, pulling out a glass vial filled with a dark, viscous liquid, a piece of chrysocolla, two candles, a stick of incense, and a Bic lighter. "Can someone kill the lights?" she asked as she lighted the candles and incense. A uniform flipped a switch, and a dull, eerie illumination filled the bedroom. She placed the candles on the nightstands and held the smoking incense in her left hand. She put the chrysocolla on top of the shattered trunk. Then, she hopped on the bed, opened the vial, and dipped her finger into its liquid. She wrote elaborate symbols on the wall above it, flipping the vial upside down to wet her finger. Rab watched the work with great interest. She hadn't noticed Lawrence Matt and other officers gathering behind her. "What's going on?" Matt asked quietly.

"I don't know," Rab said. "This is my first time seeing a ritual like this one."

When she was done, Harriet hopped off and handed Rab the incense. Before taking her coat off, she pulled a silver instrument that looked like a tuning fork from her coat pocket. Rab saw tattoos of delicate birds and leaves going up her arm like in a whirlwind.

"What did you use to write all that, Harriet?" Lawrence Matt asked.

"*Du sang de porc. Ne le dites pas aux enfants,*" she answered.

"What?"

"What are you looking for?" Rab asked.

"The thieves had to have used some pretty dirty magic to get in and out with the cup. This ritual should help locate some of it."

Harriet focused on the silver tuning fork, whispering an incantatory formula. The air in the room was alive with an eldritch, storming energy. The candles' flames flickered wildly. The incense became rich and overwhelming. The symbols on the wall oozed upwards, their liquid collecting on the edge of the ceiling. The liquid raced around the ceiling's corners, over the bedroom's door jamb, and into the sitting room. Harriet quickly followed it, with Rab close behind her. They ran into the outside hallway, the liquid progressing swiftly along the ceiling. Then, it disappeared through a wall at the end of the hall.

"What?" Harriet said exasperatedly.

"What happened?" Rab asked.

"It just disappeared through that wall!"

"Can it do that?"

"It can't defy physics!"

Harriet went up to the wall and placed her tuning fork against it. "That's so wild," she said. "I can still feel it."

"The magic?" Rab asked.

"Yeah. But... how?"

Rab stood in front of the wall and gently knocked on it. A hollow echo came back. She pulled out her gun and slammed its grip against it. The echo was louder. "Stand back, June." Rab used her gun to hammer a hole into the wall, pulling apart the drywall until an empty door frame was revealed. "Well, there you go," she said. "Your magic just seeped right through the gaps."

"There was a door behind the wall?" Harriet said.

Rab pulled apart more drywall, making a larger entrance.

"What was that for?"

Rab turned to her after finishing her work, "Who knows? I'm sure there are many weird doors all over this place."

They stared through the darkened frame. Rab pulled out her cell phone and turned on its flashlight. Dusty concrete stairs ran down into a shadowy labyrinth. Harriet held up her tuning fork. "It's down there," she said. "Very much alive."

"Alright," Rab said, "Let's chase it down."

2

THE WRAITH OF THE
BOOTLEGGER'S TUNNEL

Their walking kicked up a thick cloud of dust and mildew. Harriet stopped in the middle of the stairs, covering her nose with her hand. "God!" she shouted.

"You okay?" Rab asked.

"Sensitive nose, sorry."

Her cell phone flashlight guided Rab until they reached the mouth of a sizable tunnel, seven feet wide and seven feet high. It was deathly quiet. Their soft breathing was thunderous. Rab and Harriet could hear the blood pumping in their ears. And it was so dark that Rab's light couldn't penetrate more than a foot ahead. Rab turned her flashlight's beam back up the stairs, where darkness shrouded them. "Should we head in?" she asked.

"The magic is in that tunnel," Harriet said. "We can't lose it."

"Alright."

They entered slowly. Harriet leveled the tuning folk, chanting, and focusing. "I wonder, why so many?" Rab asked, almost to herself.

"What?" Harriet said.

"Archambeau said she saw two or three thieves during the heist. Why have a gang for something that could be a solo act?"

"Not sure. Having a lookout, I guess."

"But that's splitting the loot multiple ways. I wouldn't call that ideal."

"Maybe the ringleader has plans for the others. Rogue witches can be ruthless."

"You're thinking we should keep an eye on the bay for bodies?"

"Not a bad idea. Not a bad idea at all."

"God..."

They walked several feet before Harriet felt something. "Hold up," she commanded.

"Anything?"

"Yeah. I feel something. An energy. Oof, it's a big one!"

"What do you feel, June?"

"It's powerful. And... sad? Confused?"

"The energy? Is it a witch's?"

"I don't know."

Harriet stood in place, gathering more of the energy into herself. Rab walked further on, shining her light around. She was well ahead of Harriet when she heard something rustle near her. She focused the light on the direction of the sound. There was nothing. And for a moment, the tunnel's peace resumed. Then, the rustle returned and morphed into a moist skitter. The air around Rab became cold and bitterly electric. The hairs on her arms stood up. Her heart beat rapidly. Dread seeped into her bones. Instinctively, Rab drew out her gun and held it up with her light. The sound suddenly stopped. The tunnel was still again. She couldn't hear Harriet. "June?"

Out of nowhere, a viscous vaper materialized before her, collecting into a hoary bulbous mass, its flanks undulating wildly. A low, rumbling, vicious growl came from the mass before congealing into a humanoid shape. It screamed as it reached for Rab. She shouted, gritting her teeth, and fired a couple of shots into the mass.

Harriet heard the shots. "Rab!" she screamed.

"Over here!"

She rushed to her partner. Rab was holding her smoking gun, the beam of her cell phone's light pointing toward the ground. As Harriet stood next to Rab, she saw a ghostly apparition of a man spread out on the floor. His face was a mix of deep shock, fear, and a touch of anger. He was in a three-piece suit with a high collar and tie. Thin white hair topped his head. His eyebrows were bushy. An eye drooped slightly.

"My goodness!" the apparition shouted. He had a Midwestern lilt.

"A ghost?" Harriet said.

"More like a ghoul," Rab said with a quivering voice.

"You could have killed me, young lady!" the apparition continued.

Harriet and Rab looked at each other. Harriet shook her head. Rab turned back to the apparition, her brows furled, "But... you're already dead, man."

The apparition blinked rapidly, "I am sorry. Come again?"

"You're a goddamn ghost, dude!"

The ghost's face twisted angrily. "Watch the language, Calamity Jane! I am a god-fearing man."

Harriet stepped closer, leaning towards the ghost. "My partner is right, sir. You are deceased."

"That is impossible! Very impossible! I cannot be dead!"

The ghost stood up and tried to dust his clothes, finding no material to brush. He studied his hands in the cell phone's light, seeing they were translucent. He shot a look of silent horror at Rab and Harriet. "I'm dead?" the ghost whimpered. "How could I be dead? How?"

"It's pretty easy to get there," Rab said, holstering her gun.

"What year is it?"

Harriet told him. The ghost expressed complete bewilderment. "One hundred years! I have been dead for one hundred years!"

"Who are you?" Harriet asked.

The ghost composed himself enough to appear insulted. "Do you not know who I am?"

"No," Rab said. Harriet shook her head.

"Why, I am Warren G. Harding."

The two detectives were silent for some time. They appeared deep in thought, but it was mostly a façade to give the Ghost of Warren G. Harding some time to calm down.

"Sorry. No clue," Harriet finally said.

"Doesn't ring any bells," Rab answered.

He leaned closer to Harriet and Rab, his hands held out. "President Warren G. Harding?"

"President? President of what?"

"Of what!" he shouted. "I am president of these United States!"

Harriet inched to Rab, "When the hell was Warren Harding president?" she whispered. Rab shrugged.

The Ghost of Warren G. Harding was crestfallen. "Do you truly not know who I am?" he asked.

"Sorry," Harriet said shyly.

"The only presidents I know are Reagan, the elder and younger Bush, Clinton, Obama, and Biden," Rab said.

"Obama?" the Ghost of Warren G. Harding said.

"See what you can find, June. I want to go home."

Harriet raised the tuning fork and went back to work. The Ghost of Warren G. Harding paced while tapping his fingertips together. "How could it be?" he repeated to himself. "Of everything I've done, all I've accomplished... gone, in a flash, like lightning in a summer storm. Alive and full of vigor one moment, a wraith the next." He stopped; his eyes darted around. "Just as maw maw warned me about, but I didn't believe her! My god! Dead and forgotten? Does no one know who I was?"

"Can you calm down, Warren?" Harriet asked. "You're messing me up."

"Who are you both?" The Ghost of Warren G. Harding demanded. "What are you two doing here?"

"I'm Harriet, and she's my partner Rab. We're investigating a robbery."

"Investigating?"

"Yeah. We're police officers."

"Police officers? But you're women!"

"Great observation skills there, Warren," Rab said, leaning against the tunnel's wall, making sure the phone's light was leveled with Harriet.

The Ghost of Warren G. Harding watched Harriet as she chanted and concentrated on her tuning fork. "I might not have been a detective in life," he said, "but I don't believe this is how you collect clues."

"Sure, not for a hump crime," Harriet said. "But this is how it works for my kind of crime."

"What kind of crime is that?"

"Witchcraft."

His eyes grew large. "Witchcraft?"

"Yup. Witches might have been involved in the robbery. I'm trying to find out how they did it."

The Ghost of Warren G. Harding glared at Harriet nervously, "Are you a witch?"

She nodded. "Been a witch my whole life."

"I don't understand it. I don't," he tremored, backing away slightly. "Witches, warlocks. They were suppressed in my time." He walked in a circle, his hands on his spectral hips. "Suppressed!" he thundered. "Just like the anarchists, the communists, those heathen Wobblies! They were not given any succor. Not even the Quakers gave them an inch!"

"Do you mind, Warren?" Harriet shouted, the tunnel's walls shaking. "I'm trying to work here!"

He backed further away from her, a hand to his chest, his eyes rolling about, sputtering, "Are you going to hex me?"

She shook her head. "Can't hex the dead, Warren. That's not how it works."

"Anything?" Rab asked impatiently.

"No. Other than Warren's goddamn whining. I've lost the magic." She studied the tuning fork.

"So, what now?"

"I don't know."

Rab checked her watch. It was 2:20 a.m. "Alright, let's call it tonight. Let the crews collect what's left of the evidence, and we'll hit it again at first light."

"Sounds good."

"I'll drive you home."

Rab scanned the light around her. The tunnel became a black void that had taken on an infinite dimension. "Do you know where we are?"

Harriet peered through the darkness. "Not sure."

"Okay, it's no problem. It's a tunnel. I think our best bet

may be forward. We have to run into something on the other side."

"Sounds good."

Harriet and Rab started in that direction. The Ghost of Warren G. Harding followed close behind them. Rab felt his cold presence on her neck and turned towards him, "Whoa, where do you think you're going?"

He blinked at her. "I... I don't know. It's strange. I feel compelled to follow you."

"Huh?"

"I don't know! It's like I'm being pulled by a magnet attached to you!"

Rab looked at Harriet, "What is he talking about?"

"How should I know?" Harriet said.

"Don't you know?"

"Not every witch knows about the laws of the infinite!"

"Isn't there something you can do? I don't want some stuffy old dead white guy following me around!"

"Stuffy? Old?" The Ghost of Warren G. Harding whispered.

"I'll look it up when we get out of here," Harriet sighed. "I'm sure there's some way to get this chicken to the other side."

They continued into the darkness until Rab's light illuminated another set of stairs. "Oh, thank god," Rab said before they started ascending. At the top of the stairs was a steel door. It was coated with dust and cobwebs and spotted with rust. Rab started hammering it with her gun, calling out. Harriet joined her. After a few minutes, they heard a padlock twisting open and the rustle of thick chains. The door flew open, and an intense light blinded them. A tall, imposing figure stood before them. "What the hell are you two doing there?" the figure demanded viciously. Rab did the only thing she could think of and showed her badge. The figure backed up, "I'm so sorry, officer! I didn't know."

"Don't worry about it," Rab said, "let us through."

Rab, Harriet, and the Ghost of Warren G. Harding stepped into a cramped room. An ice machine hummed electrically in a corner. To their right was a shelf racked high with glass bottles. Cardboard cases were stacked to their left. The figure had been transformed into a man in his mid-forties, with sandy brown hair and green-gray eyes, wearing a white button-up shirt and black necktie. "Where are we?" Harriet asked.

"The House of Shields," the man said.

"Where?"

"The House of Shields, from across the street of the Palace."

"The bar?"

"That's us."

She pointed to the tunnel's exit, "*That's* the bootlegger's tunnel?"

"Well, what's left of it. How did you two get down there?"

"Long story," Rab said.

The man looked behind them and saw the ghost. "Warren G. Harding?" he said.

The Ghost of Warren G. Harding was happy, with a big grin. "You know who I am?" he asked.

"Yeah! Legend has it you had your last drink here before you died in '23."

Harriet turned to him and, sounding accusatory, said, "A drink? With Volstead on the books?"

He gibbered incoherently.

"It's not like the Harding Administration was the most law-abiding presidency in our history," the man said, "at least until recently."

"Can we get out from here?" Rab asked.

"Yeah, yeah. We're just closing up. Boy, it was good I was down here doing inventory when y'all were knocking."

"For real."

Rab, Harriet, and the Ghost of Warren G. Harding left the basement and entered the main barroom. It was lighted up, with its vintage accouterments and tabletops gleaming. From the window near the entrance, the neon sign outside was still burning. Before they left, the two detectives looked at the wall from the far end where an oil portrait of President Warren G. Harding hung.

3

AN EXQUISITE BIOGRAPHY

I t was seven o'clock in the morning, and Harriet was busy with research. When Rab dropped her off at home earlier, she tried to sleep. But excited thoughts kept creeping into her mind. After a half hour of jittery eyelids straining to close, she went to her bookshelves, running through reference books and other tomes to find any knowledge that could assist with solving the heist. But all she ran into were dead ends. Yet she kept reading until the sun began rising. She decided to get ready for work.

Her home on the corner of Fell and Buchanan Streets was a modest one-bedroom apartment on the bottom floor of a Victorian. It was decorated as one in her station would: crystals, celestial objects, various jars of herbs and substances, a bronze mirror, an antique brass telescope pointing out of a living room window, and shelves and shelves of books. An oversized, comfortable leather chair stood in the middle of the living room beside an exquisitely maintained altar. Every room was verdant with plants that grew healthy and large.

Harriet made her way to the kitchen to prepare breakfast. The excited clicks of her dog Ditzy running on the hardwood floor followed behind her. A brown Chihuahua-Dachshund mix, Ditzy was militantly brave on her leash but deathly afraid of plastic bags roiling in a breeze. In the kitchen, she got up on her hind legs, front legs pumping, whimpering, begging to be fed. Harriet picked up Ditzy's bowl and poured her food. "Kibbies, baby!" she whispered, setting the bowl back on the floor. Ditzy sniffed it and ate with a loud, crunching relish.

Harriet made a pumpkin spice latte and went to her refrigerator to take out a pint of Greek yogurt and sliced strawberries. She paired the food with honey and granola. The latte and parfait were delicious.

She dressed, slung her messenger bag over her shoulder, and walked to the living room to get her alewife hat. Putting the hat on, she looked at a picture frame near the altar. The photograph in the frame was deeply faded, a bit singed on a corner, but the shadowy outline of a person was visible. Harriet's face softened from concern.

The streetcar rolled loudly down Market Street, its bell ringing rhythmically. Harriet found a seat near the rear doors and settled in for the ride, pulling out a book from her messenger bag. *The Phantasmagoria of the Shou-Earth* by Nicola KV Dawn, the first book of the *Inheritor of the Shou-Earth* series, was recommended by a friend who knew how much Harriet enjoyed speculative fiction. It is the story of seven teenagers – Peter, the twins Greta and Gregory, Louie, Eveline, William, and Susanna – who are whisked away from their humdrum lives in the suburbs by a honey-hued djinn named Im'vu to the Shou-Earth, a pyramid-shaped dream-like simulacrum of the real world. The teens find the Shou-Earth a strange, exciting place. Yet, there is a weird undercurrent of foreboding coursing through the air, as if a danger that was still a nebulous dream of a nameless adversary is taking shape. Harriet was finishing the chapter concerning Peter, who, prompted by a vision in the Cave of the Ninety-nine Names of All-Mother, began his search for the legendary Star-Lighted Astronomer in the Tower when the streetcar reached her stop.

As she got off the streetcar, she nearly ran into a man on the street. He was dressed spartanly and gave off a Puritan vibe. He glared at her, then forced a pamphlet into her hand before disappearing down the crowded sidewalk. Harriet saw the image of the Reverend Tommy Marlow of the Youthful Jesus Missionary Pentecostal Church smiling grimly back at her. His black and silver hair perfectly coiffured, eyes stern, his message urged the recipient of the pamphlet to attend his revival and listen to his live radio program from Daly City, followed by an obscure psalm. She crumbled the document and threw it away.

THE ROBBERY-HOMICIDE DEPARTMENT in SFPD headquarters was abuzz with activity. Detectives and uniformed officers spoke on phones, met in groups to discuss clues and possible motives, or hammered away on keyboards, finishing their reports. Harriet headed to her desk, catching snatches of conversation as she walked through the office floor.

One detective to a uniform: "Are you sure it was a poltergeist..."

Another detective to his partner: "His neighbor attacked him with a kitchen knife?"

"No, with a crucifix. A really crude one..."

A lieutenant on the phone: "Wait, what? What the hell happened to his blood? A desangie curse?"

"Was there another mauling last night?" a woman in uniform asked her deskmate in disbelief.

"Yeah, down in Twin Peaks, a bad one too..."

Harriet reached the desk space she would share with Rab. She was sitting there with a cup of coffee steaming near her, her face buried in her hands. The Ghost of Warren G. Harding was pacing nearby, mumbling incoherently and wringing his hands behind her. "Are you okay, Rab?" Harriet asked.

She sniffed and looked up. She was visibly exhausted, with dark circles under her eyes.

"Bad night?"

"Oh, June, I was here at five this morning."

"Why?"

"This guy here can make some noise. I couldn't sleep." She jabbed a thumb behind her toward the Ghost of Warren G. Harding. He was nervously offended.

"I keep telling you, Victoria, I tried to keep it down when you first asked," he said.

"Fuck me if that was you trying."

He continued to defend himself, "I was thinking, Victoria! I was troubled with a myriad of thoughts. You must give me that grace."

"Well, next time you want to think, do me a favor and don't. The pacing and muttering were nuts!"

"Sorry, Rab," Harriet said.

"It's alright." She looked intently at Harriet. "Any ideas on how to push him along?"

"Sorry, I hadn't had a chance to look into it."

"Ah. That's cool..."

Harriet opened the Palace Hotel case file, perusing Ms.

Archambeau's statements and Captain Matt's notes and flipping through photographs of the suite and the destroyed trunk. Other than that, the technicians and specialists found nothing. She started from another angle, focusing on the etchings on the trunk's wood.

"Okay, here he is," Rab said.

"What?" Harriet responded.

"Warren G. Harding's biography."

"Oh."

The Ghost of Warren G. Harding leaned over Rab's shoulder, mesmerized by the monitor on her desktop. "What is this?" he asked.

"A portal into the world. Alright, Warren Gamaliel Harding. Gamaliel? The twenty-ninth president of the United States, from Ohio, died midway through his term in San Francisco."

"From what?" Harriet asked.

"Officially, from a heart attack."

"That would explain my chest pains," he whispered.

"Huh. Says here he died in his suite in the Palace Hotel," Rab continued. She stopped and thought for a moment. "Wait. I remember hearing that if you're a ghost, you stay in close vicinity of your place of death. Is that right?"

"I heard that too," Harriet said.

"So, what was he doing in that tunnel and not his suite?"

The two detectives stared up at him. He blinked. "I am... I'm not sure," he stammered.

"Do you remember anything of that day?" Harriet asked.

"Bits and pieces, here and there. Not the full picture, I'm afraid."

Rab returned to her desktop monitor. "Huh. Warren's administration was one of the most corrupt of that time. A few members of his cabinet were jailed. Teapot Dome.

Whoa, and our boy here had a sex scandal after his death!"

"Now, wait just a minute!" he exclaimed, his eyes darting around.

"Oh, I have to hear this!" Harriet said, grinning while resting her chin on her knuckles.

"Yeah, there's a picture of his wife after learning about his affairs. He might've had a few illegitimate kids with a mistress. Huh, there's a list of his mistresses on here." Rab stopped, looked him over, and turned back to Harriet. "Him? A list?"

"What does that mean?" he asked.

"Not gonna lie, Warren. You were not the most attractive man in the world."

"Maybe it was the equipment?" Harriet said with a wink.

"I will not be talked about this way!" he shouted.

"We'll talk about you in any way we see fit, bud," Rab said.

"Yeah. You don't have any moral high ground to stand on here, Warren," Harriet said.

The Ghost of Warren G. Harding sulked around Rab's desk. Rab saw the pictures Harriet was studying. "What are you thinking?" she asked.

"I have a working idea. I'd like to know where Ms. Archambeau bought her trunk and what these etchings are. If anything, we can rule them out from the crime."

"Sounds good."

Lawrence Matt approached their desks, carrying a manilla folder. He looked exhausted. "Morning, Cap," Rab greeted. Harriet followed.

"Morning, everyone." He noticed the Ghost of Warren G. Harding standing by Rab's desk and jumped away, shouting, "What the hell is that?"

"He's the ghost of President Warren Harding," Rab said. "We ran into him last night during our investigation."

"President? President of what?"

The Ghost of Warren G. Harding's eyes grew large and reflective as if sad.

"It doesn't matter, Cap," Rab continued. "What's up?"

Lawrence Matt cleared his throat, sat the folder on Rab's desk, and opened it, motioning for Harriet to join him. She got up and stood close.

"Just a few incidentals," he said, pulling out a sheet of paper and handing it to Harriet. "This has all the contact information for the top brass of the North American Society of the Dionysian Rites, Archambeau's organization. If you need anything from them, call these numbers."

"Where's Archambeau?" Rab asked.

"She jumped ship this morning and took the earliest flight out of SFO. We won't be dealing with her, just NASDR from now on."

"Ms. Archambeau's assistant is on this list," Harriet said. "She's not off limits?"

"I was told she would assist in any way with the investigation."

"Holly Hemlock," Harriet read out loud. "Some name. That's good. I need to get in contact with her." She pulled away from the group and took her cell phone with her.

"Did you find out anything more last night, Cap?" Rab asked as she perused the documents in the folder.

Lawrence Matt shook his head gently. "Same old dead ends," he said.

"What about the night staff? Anything suspicious?"

"It was a skeleton crew. No priors among them, as far as we found."

Rab was reading through a document, then stopped. "Who are these maintenance workers on this roster?"

Matt's brows knitted together. "Maintenance workers?"

"Yeah. Javier Baruch and Jeremiah Lucian Jackson. They were on the schedule for last night. Did they show?"

"We didn't find any maintenance workers in the hotel."

She leaned back in her chair, staring at the document in her hand. "Interesting. Okay. Well, let's start with these guys. See what we can dig up." She moved herself closer to her desktop and opened a tab. Her fingers flew across the keyboard.

Harriet returned to their desks. "Anything?" Lawrence Matt asked.

"No. Ms. Hemlock didn't pick up. I left a message to get back to me."

"Here we go!" Rab said excitedly.

"What's up?" Harriet asked.

"Two hotel maintenance workers were scheduled to work on the night of the heist, but they weren't there when we made the scene. Check this out: one of them has a rap sheet."

Rab pointed to Javier Baruch's record. Twenty years ago, he was sent away for grand theft auto and possession of an unregistered firearm. "There you go," she said.

"Hm. That's a red flag," Harriet said. "God, he was sixteen but charged as an adult."

"His public defender got him a pretty sweet deal, though."

Harriet crossed her arms. "That's still a lot of jail time for a minor."

"And it could've hardened him," Rab said.

"Or he could've grown up."

"Sometimes people don't change, no matter how much time they spend in jail."

"Does it say he's a witch?"

"I couldn't find anything on that. California is one of the states that doesn't note an inmate's magician skills."

Rab's cell phone buzzed on her desk. Harriet saw her notice the 415 number on the screen. She reached out and pressed the side button to stop the buzzing. "Not important?" Harriet asked.

"It's no one."

"Okay. So, who is the other maintenance worker?"

"Jeremiah Lucian Jackson, age forty-three. He has no record. Just an address and his driver's license." Rab thought for a moment. "We have to talk to these guys, June. Hear what they have to say for themselves."

"I see that you two are on top of the case," Lawrence Matt said. "I'll leave you to it."

4

THE MAINTENANCE MEN

Javier Baruch lived in Bayview. His apartment was in a three-story, weather-beaten building on a grassy hill overlooking the decommissioned naval base. Rab pulled Bruiser close to the entrance and parked. Her, Harriet, and the Ghost of Warren G. Harding stepped out and headed to his apartment on the first floor. Harriet knocked on the door, and a waifish boy greeted them. He had a thin face, a small button nose, and large slanted eyes. His hair was dark, wavy, and uncombed. He wore a Disney tee shirt and green sweatpants. The crusted smear of chocolate ice cream was around his mouth. He smiled brightly at the three.

"Hello!" Harriet said, smiling and leaning towards him. "And who might you be?"

"Freddy!" the boy said with an excited voice.

"Hi, Freddy. My name is Harriet, and these are my friends Rab and Warren. Is your daddy home?"

Freddy nodded vigorously.

"May we talk with him?"

The boy disappeared inside. In a moment, a man

stepped to the front door. He was husky and medium-height, with a bulbous nose on a broad, pockmarked face and very thin black hair. He looked exhausted, with sleep's crust still caked on the corners of his light brown, almost hazel, eyes. He wore a Giants tee shirt and purple sweatpants.

"Can I help you?" he asked, then cringed when he saw the Ghost of Warren G. Harding.

Rab and Harriet showed their badges before he could say anything. "I'm Detective Rabinowski. This is my partner, Detective June."

Baruch scrutinized them. "This about the robbery?"

Rab nodded, "You heard about it?"

"Hard not to. Monnie won't stop texting the group chat about it."

"Who's Monnie?"

"Monica. She works the front desk. Why are you here?"

"We're following up on a few things. May we come in?"

He shrugged. "Got no choice, don't I?"

Baruch led them inside the apartment. It was a cramped two-bedroom. The living room was small, with barely enough space for a worn-out loveseat and coffee table. A flat-screen TV hung on the wall next to a colorful illustration of *el Santo Nino de Atocha*. Freddy watched a children's show on the floor when his father and their guests entered. "Go to your room, Freddy," Baruch commanded.

Freddy obeyed with no complaint. Baruch sat down on the loveseat and turned off the TV. He pointed to the Ghost of Warren G. Harding, "So, seriously, what's up with the goofy-looking ghost? Is he a cop or something?"

The Ghost of Warren G. Harding's face was twisted by offense, and he was about to say something, but Rab stopped him. "He's a result of our investigation," she said.

"Cool, cool. Hey, listen, I ain't got nothing against ghosts, personally. We all gotta be reminded of death, you feel me?"

"Is your wife home?" Harriet asked, changing the subject.

He leaned forward in his seat, his face solemn. "No. She's in the hospital."

"I'm sorry. Is it serious?"

"She has COVID and is on a ventilator. I'd say it's serious."

"Is that why you weren't working the night of the robbery?" Rab asked.

"Yeah. I have no one to watch Freddy. My manager understood. There should be a note somewhere."

"What did your group chat tell you about the robbery?" Harriet asked.

"Just that a guest was robbed, something really valuable was taken. That's it."

"Did anyone tell you that witches were probably involved?"

Baruch scratched the back of his head. "Everyone was very hush-hush about it. Just told me the basics, but, like, I didn't need to know more than that. It's not my business." He turned to Harriet and stared at her hat. He jerked his chin towards her rudely. "Is that why you're here?"

"What do you know of your co-worker, Jeremiah Jackson?" Rab asked.

"I mean, we work together," Baruch said. "But it's not like we hang out together after clocking out." He stared at her, his face conveying impatience. "Why do you ask?"

"Do you know about any proclivities of his?" Harriet asked.

"Procliv... what?"

"Does he have any hobbies or interests?"

"I mean, who doesn't?"

"Does he practice any magic?"

He glared at her, his eyes steely, and said, "I ain't never seen him doing piff shit if that's what you mean. Besides, if he does, I ain't getting involved. I don't fuck with piffs."

Rab looked at Harriet. Her face was strictly neutral and professional. "What about you, Baruch?" Rab asked.

"What about me?"

Rab gestured amusingly with her hands. "I'm just saying. Sometimes, temptation can get the better of us. You figure out something clever. I mean, you have full control of the utilities of that hotel—water, air, maybe electricity?"

Hate radiated from Baruch like heat waves. "You looked at my record?"

"You think we wouldn't?"

He stood up in front of the detectives. He licked his lips. "Look, I was stupid, okay? I was what, sixteen? I did my time. I've put my past behind me."

"You didn't answer my partner's question," Harriet said coldly.

"God fuckin' damn it, no!" he shouted. "I'm not putting *my* family through any more fuckin' bullshit than what we have already!"

Rab, Harriet, and the Ghost of Warren G. Harding stood still and said nothing, not wanting to antagonize Baruch further. "Is that all?" he demanded. "Can you go now?"

"That's all," Rab said. "Thank you, Mr. Baruch."

They returned to Bruiser and drove off. "You alright?" Rab asked Harriet when they stopped at a traffic light.

She was seething, staring out the window. "Not the first time. Won't be the last time. I'm hoping Baruch's involved somehow. I want to bust his ass, toss him in the can, and throw away the key."

"I must've missed something," said the Ghost of Warren G. Harding. "Did something happen?"

"Don't worry about it, Warren," Rab said, turning to him, "but whatever you do, wherever we are, don't let me catch you using the word piff in public, okay?"

"Let's check out Jackson," Harriet said. "I want to get this day over with."

"You got it, Harriet."

JEREMIAH LUCIAN JACKSON sat in the living room of his apartment with one long, skinny leg over the other. He was tall, thin, impeccably dressed, dark-skinned, and handsome, with a small, well-maintained Afro. His arms crossed his chest as he slumped back in his chair. He had the countenance of a man who knew what to do when being hassled by the police. He stared at Rab and the Ghost of Warren G. Harding with brilliant, hostile eyes. Harriet paced around the room, looking at the bottom corners of the walls.

"You were scheduled to work last night. Is that right?" Rab asked.

"Uh-huh. But I had an emergency come up. I needed to take care of that," he said, his voice deep and rich.

"What was the emergency?"

"That's private."

Rab looked over to Harriet. She was studying a figurine and a small leather pouch on a bookshelf, her hands in her dress pockets.

She continued, "I understand, Mr. Jackson. But we must account for every hotel staff member to exclude them from suspicion."

Jackson's eyes narrowed.

"You and Javier Baruch were scheduled to work last night but didn't show up. We need to know why."

"Did you talk to Javi?"

"We did earlier. He was taking care of his kid."

"Hm. If you must know, I was attending a meeting."

"Hardly an emergency."

"What constitutes an emergency to you?"

"Fair enough. Has anyone told you about the robbery last night?"

"Some valuable magic thing was stolen. I think it was a chalice or whatever white person thing."

"Did you and Mr. Baruch talk about the theft?"

"Why should we? It doesn't concern us."

"Do you have any reason to believe that Mr. Baruch might've been involved?"

Jackson stared at Rab intently, a slight twitch on the corner of his mouth. "You're thinking that because of his record, right?"

"You know about it?" Rab asked.

"I'm the senior man in the crew. I have to know about it."

"So, what do you think, Mr. Jackson?"

"That Javier's responsible?"

"Yeah."

"I don't think that's an appropriate question."

"We're looking at all angles, Mr. Jackson."

His nostrils flared. "The hell you are. Let me tell you one thing, miss. Javi is a good man, a good father, and a good worker. He's repeatedly said how lucky he was to have this job. He'd never do anything to screw it up."

Harriet cleared her throat. "Do you practice magic, Mr. Jackson?"

Jackson glared at her coldly. "Do I what?"

"I'm just wondering."

"Now *I'm* under suspicion?"

"Please answer the question."

He leaned towards her. "It's 'cause I'm Black, isn't it?"

The detectives and the ghost didn't say anything. Jackson leaned back into his chair. "Hm-mm," he muttered. "We have anything more to talk about? Or is that it?"

"I think that's it," Rab said. "Thank you, Mr. Jackson."

They were outside Jackson's apartment building on Hyde Street, the dying orange light of the setting sun scattered through a canopy of trees. A cable car rattled by, its bell ringing. Rab took out a cigarette and lighted it. "Mr. Jackson seemed upset with us," said the Ghost of Warren G. Harding.

"Can you blame him?" Rab said, smoke streaming from her lips. "Two white ladies and a dead president walking into his apartment and asking accusatory questions. I'd be hostile, too." She turned to Harriet. "What do you think?"

"He's holding something back," Harriet said.

"Yeah?"

"Yeah. There were the things in his living room."

"What things?"

Harriet pulled out her cell phone, opened the camera app, and showed pictures she had taken clandestinely. "The corners at the bottom of the living room's walls had symbols drawn on them. I paced around and realized they were set up on the north, south, east, and west."

"What do they symbolize?"

"I don't know, but the figurine on his bookshelf is part of *Vodun*. It's the same thing with the pouch next to it. It might be a *gris-gris*." She hefted her phone. "Old magic. Powerful magic. He's practicing, I guarantee it."

Rab, Harriet, and the Ghost of Warren G. Harding got

into Bruiser. Rab started the engine. It roared. "I say we call it a night. We've been hard at it all day," she said.

"Yeah, I'm beat," Harriet said. "I've been up since four in the morning, and I can't keep my eyes straight."

"You and me both, June. I'll take you home."

There was a buzz coming from Rab's hoodie pocket. She pulled out her cell phone. Harriet noticed the same 415 number from earlier. But she said nothing as Rab shoved the phone back into her pocket and pulled into the street.

AFTER DROPPING HARRIET OFF, Rab and the Ghost of Warren G. Harding drove up Nob Hill, finding a parking spot on Sacramento Street. They walked into Rab's old brick apartment building, heading to the second floor. Her studio apartment, though small, was comfortable. A Murphy bed was locked in place on one side. A boxing mannequin with a nasty scowl stood by the windows overlooking San Francisco. Haunted house souvenirs from across the country were placed all over. Horror movie posters in clean frames were hung reverently along the walls: *Friday the Thirteenth*, *Poltergeist*, *the Nightmare on Elm Street* series. Robert Englund grinned menacingly from one side. Tony Todd, standing powerfully, glared from the other.

Rab made herself comfortable, dressing in a tank top and shorts. She went to her refrigerator and took out a tall plastic flask containing a pink liquid. She popped it open and had a hearty drink.

"What is that?" asked the Ghost of Warren G. Harding, genuinely curious.

"Dinner," Rab answered.

He scowled, "You people have milkshakes for supper?

Whatever happened to a steak and roasted potatoes, and a slice of apple pie and a piece of cheese?"

She stared at him judgmentally. "Apple pie and a piece of cheese? Listen, I swore I wouldn't judge you too much since you're from the last century. But that's too fucking weird, man."

"Well, I can say the same thing about you, Victoria. How can a milkshake be your supper?"

"It's not a milkshake. It's a protein shake. It has all the protein of a steak without the murder and enough vitamins to count for your daily intake."

The Ghost of Warren G. Harding sat on Rab's sofa, "I simply can't understand it."

Rab picked up the remote control of her TV and turned it on. She flipped through a list of streamers until she opened one and started a show. "Here, watch this," she said. "And please don't talk for a bit?"

He stared at the screen, mesmerized, as she slipped on a pair of boxing gloves. She started punching the mannequin until it rocked back from its base, its head smacking against the wall. She briefly sustained her punches' momentum before switching to a new attack style. After an hour, she was tired, but it was the proud exhaustion of disciplined training. She cracked her neck and took off the gloves. "I'm taking a shower, Warren. You stay where you are, okay?"

He turned to her from the sofa and pointed at the TV. "This... whatever it is, a program?" he said, flummoxed.

"What about it?"

"Americans, traveling abroad, and meeting their foreign sweethearts... and, and... they are betrothed, sight unseen... and they have *ninety days* to wed? What is this?"

She shrugged, "Mindless entertainment?"

"Entertainment? How is this not white slavery?" he

shouted. "Or... brown slavery? Asian slavery?" He sputtered, "How is this modern romance?"

"I wouldn't take it too seriously, Warren. Most of that shit is scripted."

The Ghost of Warren G. Harding wanted to add an addendum to his moral outrage, but Rab disappeared into the bathroom and started running water.

5

IN SALTU LEO NOCTE DORMIT

Minovia, her skin the color of fallen sparkling Sakura leaves and eyes like shimmering pools of magenta starlight, leaned over Susanna as she rested from a long trek on the grassy bank of a languid, turquoise river flowing through the glen of a sylvan forest. Her luminous smile dazzled the young girl hypnotically. Susanna felt the heaviness of her eyelids, but their heft was a pleasure that absorbed every fiber of her being.

"Don't worry, young one," Minovia whispered sensuously into Susanna's ear, producing a silk pillow out of thin air.

"Who are you?" Susanna asked.

"I'm your vigilant watcher. Your protector. Your friend. Minovia am I."

Minovia gently lifted the young girl's head and placed it on the pillow, soft red hair fanning over its golden tassels. "Rest, just rest," she continued. "Leisure is a strength, you must know. It is your strength. And through it, you will be a champion."

The music of the trickling river and the breeze cutting through the treetops lolled Susanna into a doze, her breathing slow and gentle. Minovia ran her hand over the girl's forehead, *cooing and shushing, her loving countenance not betraying the machinations grinding away in her...*

"Hey, Harriet."

She looked up and saw Rab and the Ghost of Warren G. Harding approaching their desks. "Hey, Rab," she said. "You look rested."

"Yeah, got some sleep finally. I think Warren and I have reached a détente."

"She forced me into the closet," he said dejectedly. Harriet snorted.

Rab sat at her desk and saw the book Harriet was reading. She pointed to it and asked, "Is it any good?"

"Have you heard of Nicola KV Dawn?"

"Can't say that I have."

"She's a bit of a nutcase with words but mostly alright." Harriet put the book down. "I was doing a little research when you dropped me off."

"Yeah? Research on what?" Rab asked.

"The symbols in Jackson's living room. They're connected with a family's Orisha, divine spirits. Jackson placed them on the north, south, east, and west as protection."

"Protection from what?"

"I don't know. But what he laid down is strong magic."

"What about the other things in his living room?"

"The leather pouch is a *gris-gris*. But he could be using it for luck or to ward off evil. But other than that, I don't know."

Rab sighed, "But it would make sense that it's to ward off evil considering the Orisha symbols, yeah?"

"That's true."

"Makes you wonder what he's trying to protect."

"Or be protected from."

An officer approached them, "Sergeant Rabinowski, there's someone here to see you and Detective June. He's in the lobby."

"Us?" Harriet asked. "Who is it?"

"He said he's here for the Palace Hotel case."

The detectives and the ghost entered the headquarters' lobby, where they saw a man sitting and waiting. He had one leg crossed over the other, his arms hanging over the neighboring chairs' backs. He was thin, whitish-blond hair with black roots styled messily to the side. He had a delicate face, thin stubble, and inquisitive honey-brown eyes. He wore a tasteful white patterned shirt, a loose black tie, and slim-cut jeans. He smiled as they approached him.

"Detective Rabinowski? Detective June?" he asked, getting up.

"That's us," Rab said, offering her hand, with Harriet following suit. The man shook both. He studied the Ghost of Warren G. Harding, not reacting. "I think this is the first time I've met a phantom on the police force," he said.

"Well, young man, this is not the first time someone confused me for a team member," said the Ghost of Warren G. Harding, grinning shyly. "But to say that I'm honored for such a distinction is an understatement."

"He kinda latched onto me," Rab said. "How can we help you?"

"Ah, I see. My name is Beaumont Hart, and I'm with the Coronado Detective Agency."

Beaumont brought out his wallet, pulled out a business card, and gave it to Harriet. She looked at it. The agency's name was in gothic lettering. In the center was an image of a searching eye topped with a radiant crown and surrounded by a golden laurel wreath. Below Beaumont's name and title was the agency's motto: *In Saltu Leo Nocte Dormit.*

"I've heard of Coronado," she said. "It's one of the best witch sleuthing agencies in the business."

"We're the only best witch sleuthing agency in the business," he said with a smile.

"So, to what do we owe the pleasure of your visit, Mr. Hart?" Rab said.

"I'm sorry, detective. I'll get to the point. The North American Society of the Dionysian Rites recently hired my agency. And I've been assigned to the Cup of Dionysus case. I learned you two were the leads, so I wanted us to meet."

She was taken aback. "We've only recently started work on the case. Why did they hire a private dick?"

Beaumont sighed. "You know how Bacchae are. They're impatient and impulsive. They want results the day before yesterday. Especially for the cup's recovery. The membership is freaking out big time, I hear."

"I figured," Harriet said.

"This is a 'use all resources' kind of thing for them. It isn't a dig against the SFPD."

"We understand. Well, we're here. What do you need from us, Mr. Hart?"

"You can call me Beaumont. Would it be possible to examine Serene Archambeau's trunk?"

They led Beaumont to the evidence storage room and showed Archambeau's trunk to him. He examined the remains, running a finger along its edges. He studied the etchings intently. "You've noticed these, yeah?" he asked.

"We did," Rab said. "Archambeau said they were there when she bought the trunk."

"I'm still trying to reach out to Holly Hemlock, Ms. Archambeau's PA," Harriet said. "I figured if we could find out where she bought this thing, we might get a lead on what they do."

"Yeah," Beaumont said to himself. "It's weird. They look like runes."

"That's what I figured. But they're odd, unlike any I've seen online or in my books."

"For sure. Maybe they're Nordic runes, Scandinavian runes, Baltic, something like that."

"Can you read them?" Rab asked.

He shook his head. "Unfortunately, I can't. They're pretty burnt up, and even if they weren't, Runic magic isn't my thing."

"So, we're still in the weeds then," Harriet said.

"Hm." Beaumont placed his hands on his waist. "My agency has a resource we can tap into, an expert."

"Yeah? Who?"

"He's a professor out in North Carolina. It's his field of study."

"That would be helpful."

"I'll let you know when I find out something. Do you have any leads?"

"The only thing we have are two maintenance workers. One has a record, and the other may have magic skills."

He looked at Harriet. "Magic skills? What kind of magic skills?" he said.

"We were interviewing him yesterday at his apartment. He had all kinds of *Vodun* wards and paraphilia in his living room."

"I see. Is he a part of any *Vodun* societies?"

"Not sure. I hadn't thought to look into that."

"Maybe not a bad place to start." Beaumont pulled out a cell phone from his pocket. "Would it be alright to take pictures?" he asked. "For our expert?"

"Go for it," Rab said.

He took pictures of the trunk at all angles, including the

etchings. When he was satisfied, Beaumont thanked Harriet and Rab. "Good luck, detectives," he said. "And good hunting."

"You'll tell us if you run into anything that would lead us to the cup, right?" Rab asked.

Beaumont smiled gently. "It's part of our contract that we assist the police if any operative has a viable lead in an important case, and this case is significant."

6

THE HOUNFO AND THE LIBRARY

Harriet was reading something on her desktop's monitor rapidly. "Oh, wow," she muttered.

"What you got, Harriet?" Rab asked.

"I'm on the San Francisco coven registry..."

Rab interrupted, "Isn't that going to get us in trouble? I thought that was privileged information."

"Not anymore. The registry was made public after last year's election. You know, in case some witch or coven causes trouble."

"Okay, so what did you find?"

"There is a J. Jackson associated with the Tranquil Mawu Society."

"What's that?"

"A *Vodun* benevolence organization. It's very well respected among the African American community."

"Huh. If that is Jackson, it's like you said. He's practicing."

Harriet shook her head. "No, says here he's a layman in the society."

"What does that mean?"

"Some covens and societies welcome humps to join if they will respect their practices and protect them from outside interference. If this guy is Mr. Jackson, it means he's a non-practicing member of Tranquil Mawu."

Rab stood up from her chair, "Maybe we should go and chat with the folks of Tranquil Mawu and gather some intel."

"We should be mindful," Harriet said. "*Vodun* practitioners are very suspicious of police, understandably so, considering our history."

"Slow and gentle, that's my motto."

They drove down Third Street, parking near the corner of Oakdale Avenue. The Tranquil Mawu Society was in an excellently preserved nineteenth-century building with shining adornments. Rab, Harriet, and the Ghost of Warren G. Harding walked inside and to the receptionist's desk. The young, bespectacled receptionist was studying a manuscript intently on her desk, writing notes in a leather notebook. She looked up as the three approached; a delicate jade necklace around her neck shimmered in the office light.

"Can I help you?" she asked.

Rab and Harriet showed their badges. The receptionist's eyes grew hard.

"Is your head priestess in?" Harriet asked.

"Yes. Our *Manbo* is available. What's this about?"

"We have a few questions regarding a layman of your institution. May we speak to her?"

The receptionist picked up the front desk's telephone receiver and made a call. When someone answered, she spoke in crisp Haitian Creole. "She will be with you in a minute," the receptionist said, hanging up.

"Thank you."

They stood in the middle of the reception area and

waited. Harriet was admiring a mural dedicated to the African diaspora on the wall opposite her when a tall, stately woman in a pristine multi-color gown and head wrap emerged from the hallway and walked towards them. "Detectives," she said. "I'm Chanteuse Kind, *Manbo* of Tranquil Mawu, San Francisco. Welcome to our *hounfo*."

"Thank you for seeing us, *Manbo* Kind," Harriet said. "Our apologies for intruding."

"No intrusion at all, young witch." She saw the Ghost of Warren G. Harding. "President Harding's ghost, I see."

His face lighted up, a giant smile on his face. "Do you know me?"

"Of course," she said politely yet coldly.

"You know, madam, in my time, I spoke on behalf of your people at every chance I got."

"All the while your marines and banks were killing and plundering my people in Haiti, Mr. Harding? What of the profit members of your administration made during that time?"

Rab glared at him, "What did you do?"

He gibbered for a second.

Manbo Kind raised a hand. "How can I help you, detectives?"

"I'm hoping you can identify a layman of the Tranquil Mawu Society," Harriet said.

"Is this layman in trouble with the law?"

"I can't say."

Manbo Kind nodded her head gently, not breaking eye contact with Harriet. She smiled, "I understand, detective. Unfortunately, I can't assist you."

"Why not?" Rab asked.

"It's my responsibility to protect the practitioners and devotees of Mawu. The Tranquil Mawu Society has been a sanctuary, a safe space, from hostile forces for centuries. We may not have the resources most mainstream covens have, but this is something we do: dedication to our people. I am sworn to this."

"Even if it means protecting a criminal?"

"It's not up to us to judge anyone, detective. The consequences of one's actions will come down on them sooner than later. Now, if you believe our layperson is involved in the crime you are working on, you know what to do. You require my assistance? Get a warrant. Is that all?"

"Yes, *Manbo* Kind," Harriet said. "Thank you for your time."

They made their way out of the building and towards Third Street. "Why did you let her walk all over you, June?" Rab said.

"She's right, Rab. The *Manbo* must protect those under her care. We're running into her place demanding she give one of her people up without real cause."

"It's just a simple question: Is this our Jackson? Yes or no?"

"*Our* Jackson? He's not a possession."

"You know what I mean. This trip shouldn't have been a waste."

They approached Bruiser and got in. Rab pulled out into the street and drove back to headquarters. No one said a word.

BACK AT HEADQUARTERS, Harriet was again studying the crime scene photographs of Archambeau's trunk, mainly to avoid Rab and ignore the Ghost of Warren G. Harding's annoying pleas for peace. She focused on the etchings, this time intently. Beaumont Hart's observation kept running in her thoughts. She wanted to figure out if the etchings were Scandinavian runes.

Harriet went through some online searches, but they were all dead ends. However, these deep dives pointed her toward Professor Benedict Saint-Phineas from Chapel Hill, North Carolina. According to his biography, he was the foremost scholar in ancient Nordic magic, particularly emphasizing Scandinavian logourgy and literomancy. She saw his picture. He was a wizened older man, completely bald on top, with long, wild white and silver hair on the sides of his head and matching mutton chops. He had anisocoria, and one eye was physically more prominent than the other. He grimaced as he stared at the camera. "Handsome guy," Harriet whispered to herself.

She opened his bibliography and found that he only published one book: *The Law of the Fiskikarlar: Explorations of, and Meditations on, the Viking runic magic tradition, from 640 AD to 1020 AD*. The book had been out of print for over a decade, making it difficult to find a copy. Harriet became frustrated when her searches and library inquiries turned up nothing. She decided to give up when her cell phone buzzed in her pocket. The caller ID on the screen was blank, and the number had a 510 area code. "This is Harriet," she answered.

"Hi, Detective June." The voice on the other end was a young woman. "This is Lucy from the Morrison Library, UC Berkeley, following up on your request."

"My request?" Harriet thought quickly but had no memory of sending anything to Cal.

"Yes, ma'am. For *Law of the Fiskikarlar*, Saint-Phineas, Benedict? I just wanted to let you know that we found a copy and can offer it today if you're still interested."

"Ah, yeah. I want to pick it up."

"Super! I'll leave it for you at the check-out desk. Just swing by when you're ready."

Harriet got a ride into East Bay, getting off 580 and into Berkeley. She entered the university grounds and headed to the Morrison Library. It was a large building with Edwardian décor and tall, voluminous bookshelves. She went to the check-out desk. No one was around, so she instinctively knocked on its top, but not too loudly.

"Can I help you?" asked a voice behind her. She flinched and quickly shot around.

He was a young man, fit and gorgeous, with striking feminine and masculine features, shimmering green eyes, and long, soft, curly golden-brown hair. His pleasant floral scent wasn't too overwhelming. Unlike any library staff she had met before, he was stylishly dressed in a two-piece, slim-cut black suit paired with a white button-up shirt opened at the collar.

"Hi there," Harriet said, "I've come to pick up a book?"

He smiled, and it was theophanic. "*Law of the Fiskikarlar,* is that right?" he asked.

"Yes. How did you know?"

"I was told that Detective Harriet June was coming over to check it out before my shift started."

"Oh, right."

He went behind the check-out desk, pulled the book out, and sat it before her. It was a giant book, close to two thousand pages, and when she opened it, she saw that it was written in dense academic language. She flipped through it, reviewing the different traditions and variations of runic magic.

"You were lucky," the young man said. "That's the last copy in the library, probably the last one in the whole Bay."

"Do you know it?" Harriet asked.

"Only by reputation, you can say. Hopefully, it's helpful to you."

Harriet gave the clerk her information and was given the book.

Returning to headquarters, she ran into Rab and the Ghost of Warren G. Harding in the lobby elevator. "Hey," Rab said.

"Hi," Harriet said.

They rode in silence for a few seconds. "Hey, listen, I'm sorry I was snippy earlier," Rab said.

"It's alright."

"But it's not. I was unprofessional. I should've understood where you were coming from. It was an ignorant hump move on my part."

Harriet smiled gently. "Don't worry about it, Rab. It's all good."

Rab saw the book under Harriet's arm. "What's that?" she asked.

"Something to help me understand Nordic runes."

"You're thinking Beaumont Hart is on to something?"

"Maybe. It's at least something to follow up on. I'm sure not having any luck with Holly Hemlock."

They got off the elevator and headed to their desks, passing by a briefing room where Lawrence Matt met with a group of officers and detectives. "There was another attempted murder, this time in Lower Pac Heights," he announced.

An undercurrent of murmuring came from the assembly. "What're the details?" someone asked.

"She was nearly torn to shreds but managed to get away when the perp was distracted by a passing car," Lawrence Matt answered. "The perp was a goddamn animal."

"Any description?" another asked.

"The vic didn't see his face," Matt said. "But he was described as big, tall, muscular, and laughing hysterically." He placed his hands on his waist and sighed. "She was lucky to have survived."

"The mayor's not going to like this," a detective said.

"No, she's not. Tell your people that we're increasing patrols. We already have enough maniacs running around in the city; can't have another one loose."

7

A SAVAGE TIP

Harriet began leafing through Saint-Phineas' book when she reached her desk. She was surprised to see its single blurb was from Selene Archambeau herself, testifying to Professor Saint-Phineas' immaculate knowledge and expertise on the subject of runic magic. It was strange to her that a Hellenic initiate would vouch for a Scandinavian magic scholar until a quick online search revealed that they were family. Cousins, specifically. Harriet thought about coincidence and how coincidence meant something in the universal sense before turning the page to chapter one.

The reading was laborious. She made it to chapter three: *"Language has a tremendous weight in our practices; it is understood. The use of language in all its permutations has allowed mankind to harness the universal, to channel it into his hands, and to manipulate nature and substance as he so finds fit. And there is nothing greater, cleaner, logical, and more elegant than the written word to control magic's raw, awesome power. The man will die, his accomplishments relegated to the oral tradition, passed down imperfectly from generation to generation. But*

it is his written word, and the power they convey, that will
live on."

The thesis led into a rambling history of Nordic
logourgy, its similar practices east and west of the Baltic, and
its effects on Scandinavian events. One section interested
Harriet: *"Some commentators, chroniclers, and I believe that a
certain magician named Pfluegr, under the employ of Hrolfr (835-
933 AD), also known as Rollo, the first duke of Normandy,
ancestor to the illustrious William I of England, found that by
compounding complimentary runes together, the magic produced
wonderous results.*

*"For example, an ill-inspired artist seeking to rekindle their
flaccid imagination can do so by just compounding the runes
Kaunan (translated in our modern lingua franca as Torch – fire,
burning, but as understood by our ancient Scandinavian brethren
as creativity, revelation, illumination) and Dagaz (here translated as Day – dawn or awakening, but again, using my former
example as a lodestar to the point, understood to mean awareness
or, most importantly, breakthrough), the resulting magic would
be inspiration eternal, so long as the artist paid the proper toll.*

*"Pfluegr also observed that compounded runes produced even
greater magical yields during cross-celestial vectors. If planetary
bodies and constellations aligned at a crucial point, the
compounded runes achieved results beyond the magician's original intentions..."*

Harriet was distracted when her cell phone started to
buzz. She didn't recognize the number on the screen, so she
answered cautiously, "Hello?"

"Hi, Harriet!" Beaumont Hart nearly shouted. Someone
was screaming obscenities in the background.

"Beaumont? How did you get my number?"

"You're easy to find, Ms. June!"

"Are you okay?"

"Oh, *mas o menos*. I was following up on a really hot lead before I was attacked."

"You were attacked? Where are you?"

"I'm in Lower Haight," he told her, giving her the address. "I could use some police assistance!"

"Sure, we're on our way. Take cover if you can!"

She ended the call and went to find Rab. She was in the breakroom making a cup of tea while the Ghost of Warren G. Harding was talking, "So, as I was saying to Colonel Calhoun during the convention in '20, it *was* a mighty fine thing that Governor Morrow honored you so excellently, no argument there. But a 'Kentucky Colonel' isn't exactly a real military officer's commission, you know? Now that I think about it, that might've been why he nominated Lowden so adamantly."

Rab looked relieved when Harriet approached. "What's up, Harriet?" she asked.

"Beaumont's asking for us. He needs help."

"Is he alright?"

"Sounds like he's having a hard time. But he says he's on a lead. That might help us."

"Let's head then!"

Bruiser roared to Haight Street, then looped around on Webster Street and parked beside a car where Beaumont Hart was waiting. He looked unharmed, greeting the detectives and the ghost as they exited the vehicle.

"Thanks for coming down," Beaumont said.

"Are you okay? Are you injured?" Harriet asked.

"Yeah, I'm fine. I'm not injured. If anything, my pride is the only thing hurt. I'm usually perfect in these familial situations."

"Who were you here to see?" Rab asked.

Beaumont pulled out a notepad and opened it, "Waverly

Todd, age twenty-eight. He's a Ronan witch with a sizable rap sheet."

"What's his connection to the Dionysus heist?"

"You two might appreciate this. His long-time prison buddy was Javier Baruch."

"Oh my god," Harriet said. "Of course!"

"You were able to connect this Waverly Todd and Baruch?" Rab asked.

"Sure did. After I learned about the maintenance men from you, I did a little digging on them and found that Baruch served time in the same prison as Todd."

"That doesn't establish a relationship," Harriet said.

"It doesn't. But I had some friends in Sacto who located witnesses from that prison. Apparently, Baruch clung onto Todd for protection from the crank hexers and filth casters he pissed off."

"So much for not associating with witches," she commented.

"Does Todd have any specialties we should be worried about?" Rab asked.

"Nothing definite. He's self-taught, from what I was able to learn."

"Was he the one attacking you?"

"No. It was his brother. He was preventing me from seeing him."

"Alright, then. Let's go talk to him."

The group made their way to Waverly Todd's house. It was a duplex near the intersection of Webster and Haight. Dirty and needing a fresh coat of paint, its small front yard was closed off by a steel-bar fence. Children's toys were strewn about, and a rusted charcoal grill stood in a corner. Beaumont pushed open the gate.

The group walked up the stoop. Harriet rang the doorbell. Someone shouted from inside, "What the fuck do you want now?" A man threw open the door. He was squat, with mussy black hair and a thick, dark five o'clock shadow. He was wearing a wifebeater and black jeans. Hot, ugly anger emanated from him. His eyes darted between Harriet and Rab. "Who the hell are you?" he asked.

Harriet and Rab showed their badges. The man grimaced, "Oh Christ, seriously?"

"Are you Waverly Todd?" Harriet asked.

"I'm his half-brother, Warwick." He pointed at Beaumont. "This motherfucker called you?"

"I'm investigating a possible lead..." Beaumont started to say.

"Bullshit! You was trespassing! I'll file a complaint, swear to God!"

"Is your brother in?" Rab asked sternly.

He glared impotently at her. "Why?"

"We would like to ask him a few questions. Is he in?"

He appeared to be thinking fast but ran out of space in his decision tree. "I can't say no to the police, can I?"

Warwick led the group inside. The house was sparsely furnished and decorated, and a TV blared in the living room. He went there, sat in an old cloth recliner, grumbling to himself, and turned off the TV. "Waves!" he screamed. "You gotta come down right now. The cops are here, and they want to talk to you!"

A high, excited voice came from upstairs, "The cops? But I just had my PO visit. Everything's good!"

"I don't think it's about that!"

After a moment, a lean, shivering man with a gaunt, acne-scarred face glistening with sweat appeared in the hallway. He wore a faded black hoodie, matching beanie, a Megadeth sweatshirt, and sagging jeans. A palpable aura of junk sickness lingered around him. His large black eyes focused on the detectives and the ghost.

"You have credentials?" Waverly Todd asked.

They showed their badges. "I'm Detective Rabinowski, badge number four-five-seven. This is my partner, Detective June. We're following up on a call from Mr. Beaumont Hart of the Coronado Detective Agency."

Todd pointed a trembling, dirty finger at Beaumont. "He ain't no detective," he accused. "Can't you feel it?"

"I can assure you, I am, Mr. Todd," Beaumont said. He was about to pull out his wallet when Todd shouted, "Keep your hands where I can see 'em!"

Harriet placed her hand on Beaumont's shoulder, nodding her head gently. Rab looked at Todd. "How long since you last used?" she asked.

"Huh?" he answered.

"You're shaking all over, and your pupils are needle points. You look bad sick."

He rubbed his hand along the back of his neck.

Rab continued, "You just saw your PO, is that right? Did you pass your report with flying colors? Didn't need a drug test?"

Todd didn't answer.

"What if I order one right now? What are the odds of you pissing dirty?"

He swallowed drily, "What do you want?"

Beaumont stepped forward, "Are you acquainted with Javier Baruch?"

"Javi? Yeah, I know him."

"When was the last time you spoke with him?"

"God, maybe when he made parole. About five years ago or something. What's this about?"

"Did you hear about the theft at the Palace Hotel a couple of days ago?"

"Yeah, some cup or whatever was stolen, right? So much fuss over a stupid fucking cup."

"I hear you have a thing for magnificent magical items, Waverly."

"Huh?"

Beaumont crossed his arms. "You did time for the *Svyatoy* Katarina heist, right?" he asked.

Harriet gasped, "That was you?"

"What was that?" Rab asked.

"There's a coven in Outer Richmond dedicated to *Svyatoy* Katarina the Cursed, a great and influential Russian witch from the sixteenth century," Harriet said. "Her followers settled in San Francisco during the Russian Civil War after securing her famed hornbeam staff from the Bolsheviks, which was stolen almost a decade ago..."

"Despite the *Lunnyy svet* ward on it," Beaumont said.

"A Russian's most powerful protective ward," she muttered. "And you cracked it, Todd?"

Waverly Todd grinned, showing gaps of missing teeth. "Not bad for an eighteen-year-old kid, huh?"

"So, we can say you have skills," Beaumont continued. "It's in the record. Were you ever near the Palace Hotel on the night of the Twelfth?"

"On Market? Nope, I wasn't there." Todd thought quickly. "Wait, you think it was me?"

"That's what I'm trying to figure out before your brother jumped down my throat. You and Javier Baruch had a friendship in prison. He works for the hotel. And you're a crackerjack thief. You can see why I'm thinking that way, right?"

Waverly Todd's eyes went from each detective to his

brother, his mouth working erratically. "That's impossible," he said. "I can't!"

"But you have before," Harriet said.

"No, for reals! It's impossible. See?" Todd pulled up the sleeves of his hoodie and sweatshirt; an odious energy cascaded out from the cloth like a gruesome deluge. Dark, blood-like scarring, pulsing with malevolence, snaked down his arms, connecting to terrifying rings of eldritch script around his wrists. Harriet and Beaumont backed away, horrified and disgusted.

"What happened to you?" Harriet asked breathlessly.

"I've never seen a curse of that... *nature* before!" Beaumont said.

Rab stepped closer to inspect his arms. "I don't know," she said, "I kind of like them. They're like if Hieronymus Bosch designed a Cannibal Corpse album cover."

Harriet shook her head. "Todd's destroyed!"

Rab was confused, "What do you mean?"

"Todd has a binding curse on," Beaumont interrupted. "And just from the look and feel of it, it's a really nasty one, too. I can't imagine what would happen if he trips it. Man! I feel it in my guts from here!"

"*Who* did that to you?" Harriet asked Waverly.

He didn't exude any emotion as he slid the sleeves back down, much to the relief of Harriet and Beaumont. "The Ruskies," he said.

"The *Svyatoy* Katarina coven?"

Todd nodded. "It came one day after my parole. It was a simple letter—just a plain paper letter in a plain paper envelope. There was no return address, nothing except my name. It had some Russian words written on it. I didn't know what it said, and I still don't. Then, it happened.

"It started with a little nick on my arm. I thought I

scratched it on something. The nick grew and kept on growing. Before I knew it, something was cutting the scars into my arms, inch by inch, day by day, for two weeks. I was in constant pain, and I couldn't stop it. Then, it did.

"After it stopped, a woman came to the house when Warwick was at work. She looked wild, with monstrous hair and yellow and haunting eyes. She told me she was the one who placed the curse on me. And if I knew what was good for me, I would never practice magic again. If I did, my death would not be the end of my hell."

"Jesus," Beaumont whispered. "You pissed off the wrong people."

"Why didn't you report this?" Harriet asked.

Todd shook his head. "What good would that do? The Ruskies have friends in city hall. They wouldn't do anything. It'll probably put another target on my back!"

Warwick got up from the recliner, walked over to his half-brother, and touched his shoulder. His face betrayed his fear and concern. "You never told me this, Waves," he said. "Why didn't you want me to know?"

"Because you don't need to get involved with them, Wick."

The detectives and the ghost left the house and returned to their cars. "Sorry for dragging y'all down here," Beaumont said, opening his driver-side door.

"It was worth a look," Harriet said. "But Todd's curse is going to give me nightmares tonight."

"Yeah, no kidding. I'll see you two later, hopefully with something better."

Beaumont entered his car and drove off. Harriet, Rab, and the Ghost of Warren G. Harding got into Bruiser. "Well, there we go," Rab said. "We can scratch Baruch off the suspect list."

"I mean, it's possible that he and Jackson could've partnered up," Harriet said.

"But there's no definitive proof that Jackson practices any magic."

Harriet slumped in the passenger seat, "No, we don't have that."

"I feel that you two are in a Haynes coupe stuck in a sandy dune," said the Ghost of Warren G. Harding. Rab and Harriet slowly turned to him. He continued, "The case is becoming a morass, what I'm saying."

Rab sighed, "Yeah, we're getting bogged down." Her cell phone buzzed. She glanced at the screen and answered, "What can I do for you, Mr. Gregarian?" Her face morphed in horror. "What? Okay, hang tight. We're on our way!"

Bruiser's engine roared thunderously. "What happened?" Harriet asked.

"Jackson's in trouble!" Rab answered.

The car peeled down Market Street, the flashers spinning. Rab turned to Mission Street and slammed the brakes near the back of the Palace Hotel, where a crowd had gathered. Harriet was the first out of the car, breaking through the circle of people.

Jeremiah Lucian Jackson was writhing and convulsing on the sidewalk, a dull glow coming off his skin, his jaw locked, the muscles in his neck straining, looking like he wanted to scream. Sweat and blood beaded and mingled on his skin; sickly yellow steam vaporized off him.

"Did anyone call an ambulance?" Harriet demanded. She placed a hand on his chest, its skin sizzling. She pulled back, screaming obscenities.

"They're coming!" someone from the crowd answered.

Rab pulled out her badge and commanded the crowd to

disburse. "Go about your business! Go back now! This is a police matter!"

8

WHAT HEX? WHAT CURSE?

The hospital's lobby was still, only disturbed by the sudden hiss of HVAC. Rab slumped in her chair, arms crossed, a leg trembling. Harriet ran her hands down the length of her hair over her shoulder. The Ghost of Warren G. Harding sat straight in his chair, trying to articulate words mutilated by the confluence of his loquaciousness. Rab slowly shook her head, asking, "You recognize what hit Jackson, Harriet?"

"I have no idea," she said. "I couldn't get a feel for it. My guess is it was a hex."

"How certain are you?"

"Not very. But the simplest explanation is usually true."

"It's just... I've been around, right? I thought I'd seen all kinds of curses, hexes, whatever. But Jackson getting annihilated like that? Not that."

"He wasn't annihilated."

"Sure looked like it to me."

They sat quietly for a moment. The soft steps of a nurse echoed behind them. "I was thinking about this case my first partner worked some years ago," Rab said. "When we were following the ambulance here. I don't know why."

"Yeah?"

"Yeah. When he moved to the detective pool, his first partner was a forensic witch. One day, they were working on a big robbery at the Palace of Fine Arts. A moving exhibition on the history of Moorish Alchemy had numerous precious antiques going back to the thirteenth century plundered, despite all the hardcore wards Ibn al-Suhr, the curator, put down. Many gold, silver, and jewel stuff were just gone."

Harriet interrupted, "I heard of al-Suhr. He's major, major league. He's a master. Who had that kind of power?"

"The same guy who pulled off that major heist at the Mint not long after."

"I remember that story! Several tons of gold bullion vanished instantly, but the department and the FBI had no suspects."

"Oh, but they did. The problem was they couldn't touch him."

"What? Why?"

Rab was serious; her features darkened. "Because he was Rufio Serengeti."

Harriet stared at Rab in complete disbelief. Her brows were furled, and her mouth hung open slightly. "That's not a real name," she said.

"Oh, but it is."

"That *can't* be his real name! It's so ridiculous!"

"My old partner used to talk about him in hushed, shaky tones. Serengeti is a criminal mastermind."

"Here's what I don't get it. Why couldn't Serengeti get pinched?"

"Because the man is a damn ghost. He doesn't appear in

any record, no pictures, no video. His crimes are the only thing that speaks of his cunning and ruthlessness."

"So, how does anyone know he exists?"

"From the only survivor of Serengeti's raid in Martinez. He was the only person from Serengeti's gang who lived to talk about it. When the raid went south, Serengeti executed every member of his crew before disappearing."

"Did the survivor mention how he managed to escape?"

"I don't know. I wasn't privy to the interrogation." Rab sighed.

From the shadows of a nearby hallway, an abnormally tall figure in a billowing white gossamer robe materialized and glided into the waiting room. A long, baggy hood covered the head, and shadow hid the face. Rab's eyes grew large. "What the hell is that?" she whispered.

Harriet turned to the figure, then back to her. "Ah, you've never seen our doctors before. Don't worry. That's what they look like."

The figure approached the three. "Detective Rabinowski, Detective June." The figure's voice was feminine, airy, and almost musical. "My name is Doctor Kincaid."

"How's he doing, doctor?" Harriet asked.

"Mr. Jackson is stable. He was fortunate that others were close by during his attack."

"What happened?"

"My mortal colleagues and I examined Mr. Jackson and found no evidence of any physical infliction. I found no curse or hex on his person."

"But that doesn't make sense. We were there, doctor. He was attacked by something. Someone tried to kill him."

"I don't doubt your account. It's very unusual."

"Is Mr. Jackson going to be okay?"

"He has passed through the worst of it. I will keep monitoring his progress. But I'm unsure if he'll ever be the same again."

They thanked Dr. Kincaid, who then vanished back into the shadows. Rab, Harriet, and the Ghost of Warren G. Harding left the hospital and drove back into the city. It was midnight, and the fog glided across the large, bright moon.

"What a goddamn day, huh?" Rab said.

"Yeah. All that work and all we have is an assault victim and no leads."

"I'll send the report on Jackson's attack to the assault and battery division. They can take care of it. We'll start fresh tomorrow."

Harriet shook her head. "As if anything's going to happen. What are they going to find out that we couldn't?"

Rab shrugged. "It's not our case. We have our own. Let's focus on that."

"Alright."

RAB DROPPED off Harriet at her home. When she stepped through the front door, Ditzy ran to her, jumping against her legs and whining. "Oh, I'm sorry, baby! I was out later than I should have!" She went to the kitchen and poured Ditzy's food into her bowl.

After a shower, Harriet dressed in her pajamas and sat in the living room. Jackson's attack haunted her; the images of his torturous position seared into her mind. She needed a distraction and pulled out *Phantasmagoria of the Shou-Earth* from her messenger bag:

Louie heard the whispers not long into his journey through the land of the baleful volcanic domes. He searched around but couldn't find their source. The whispers weren't unnerving to him at first, as he thought himself a brave lad who was looked up to by his younger siblings, cousins, and peers for his ability to stare down the unknown and laugh. But as the journey continued and the whispers grew in intensity, he felt the pang of that unmentionable, ineradicable sensation that was still a part of his nature.

"Come on, come on!" shouted the agelast Fenz. "We haven't got all day!"

A roundish, breviloquent, noisome fellow with short legs and a long torso, Fenz found Louie wandering the Somnambulist Plain after Im'vu brought him to the Shou-Earth. Though usually a charming young man, prone to make friends even among the most disagreeable, Louie grew an immediate distaste for the rapscallion. And if Fenz hadn't needed Louie, he wouldn't have thought twice about cracking open the boy's skull and gulping his brains.

After rounding the third magma cone, the erinynic whispering became disturbing. Distraught by the audible madness, Louie ran off, his hands held firm against his ears, yelping like a wounded pup.

"Get back here, you!" Fenz yelled furiously, then begged pathetically as the boy's silhouette blurred away from his vision. Fenz stood in the middle of the desolate wastes, himself whimpering, feeling – but failing to understand why – that he had committed a grave sin.

Louie ran through the wastes, his arms flailing, past multitudes of ghostly sentinels of eruptive piles, fleeing bubbling, miasmic calderas, until he stopped before an ancient castle. Though weatherworn, with faceless gargoyles and warped crenelations, it was a magnificent structure. He looked around. The omnipresent whispering had stopped as if prevented from their pursuit by the stately edifice. Louie made his way to its vast portal and knocked. Hearing no one, Louie pushed open the massive door and entered.

The interwoven corridors stretched eternally toward a blind horizon. The walls glowed from an illuminating fungus, and a pleasant perfume wafted in the air, wafted by ghostly censers. Louie continued into the castle. A great hall opened before him. Inside were tapestries of exquisite beauty displaying delicate figures dancing and playing across fruitful fields in the light of nearby flambeaux. A sudden philocalia came over him, morphing into joy for the figures in the tapestries.

Louie studied them closely. It was then that he noticed they were all nude. He was ashamed. But then, gentle whisperings, insouciant and euphoric, filled the hall. Louie tensed up, fearful of their intentions. They were soothing and mellifluous, encouraging him to look once more upon the figures of the tapestries. The heavenly scent of the perfume engulfed the hall, making Louie's head spin. The figures were moving sensuously now, coming together into a hedonistic orgy. Louie wanted to join them in their lustful escapades, to fling himself into the enthusiastic clash. And he cursed his physical nature, becoming angry and desperate that he couldn't transcend worlds.

But then, he relaxed. The tapestries were a medium, not a destination, he thought. He, too, can translate the joys of the figures here in the Shou-Earth. And, as he lowered his hand down, stroking intimately, the pleasure of that revelation filled his heart with...

Behind Harriet, there was a slight sizzle, followed by a pop. Ditzy stared from her bed in the corner of the living room toward the altar. Harriet turned back and saw the faded photograph blacken further, its corner turning ash and crumbling to the floor.

9

WITCHES ON CALL

Early morning, Harriet returned to the hospital carrying a large jar filled with earth, minerals, and dried flora. She checked in with the desk nurse, who pointed toward Jackson's room. Harriet heard soft, harmonious singing coming through the door when she arrived. She pushed it open. Chanteuse Kind was leaning over the unconscious Jackson, one hand over his chest, the other shaking a percussive instrument. Incense smoked aromatically. Though her singing was gentle, the melody seemed to fill the room. Harriet felt the *Manbo's* maternal energy course through the air powerfully and into the unconscious man. *Manbo* Kind finished her ritual. "You can stop hiding now," she said. "Come on in, Detective June."

"I'm sorry for bothering you."

Manbo Kind turned to her, "No bother at all."

Harriet entered the room. She inched closer to Jackson's bed, seeing a small clay figurine resting on his chest. There was something clutched in his hand.

"What's that there?" *Manbo* Kind asked, pointing to the jar.

She held it up. "*Raiz de Oaxaca.* It's good for healing."

"Where'd you get that?"

"I made it. It's from my grandma's book."

"*Tu abuela era una bruja?*"

Harriet nodded. "She was."

"*Y tu mama?*"

"She didn't want to learn the craft."

"Well, that's a shame."

"What were you doing, *Manbo* Kind?"

"You can call me Chanteuse, darling." She held out her hand over Jackson. "Brother Jeremiah needed me. When we heard what happened to him, our *hounfo* came together and offered everything we had in sacrifice for his recovery. I came here to complete the job."

"Will he be alright, Chanteuse?"

"He will. The spirits have heard us. Mawu will keep him safe." She looked at Harriet earnestly. "And now They want answers."

"I wish I could offer them," Harriet said sadly.

"The doctor told me you and your partner were there when Jeremiah was attacked."

"We were. But I didn't see or feel anything that could've been responsible for Mr. Jackson's attack."

Chanteuse went to a nearby chair and sat down, facing Jackson. "Something about that hotel is wicked," she said. "There's a dark pall hanging over it."

"Totally. Nothing's right about it."

"What do you need?"

"What do you mean?"

"What do you need to find out who did this to him?"

"I don't know where to start, *Manbo.*"

"I think you do, young witch. You're not lost in the forest like so many."

Harriet thought for a moment. An idea came to her. "Mr. Jackson was attacked because he knew something."

"That's a good start, darling."

"What he went through was so violent. It only means that he was supposed to die. But maybe it wasn't enough?" Harriet's eyes grew large. She looked to the *Manbo*. "It was because we were there?"

"I can't answer that. You have to find the guilty person."

"I need the names of Mr. Jackson's friends in Tranquil Mawu so I can talk to them. I'm sorry, *Manbo*, but this is important."

Chanteuse nodded slowly, not breaking from Jackson. "Jeremiah has a good friend in the *hounfo*. I've seen them hanging around all the time. He's called No-No."

"Is that his actual name?"

"It's what he likes to be called."

"Can I talk to No-No?"

"He can be... a little cagey around the police. Understandably so. You're not allowed to be Black and free in America."

Harriet sighed deeply.

"I'll talk to him," Chanteuse said. "He, more than anyone, sacrificed to Mawu for Jeremiah's recovery. No-No will want justice."

"Thank you, *Manbo*."

They walked out of Jackson's room, side by side, down the hallway towards the lobby. The golden morning sun burst through the windows. "What made you want to be a cop?" Chanteuse asked Harriet.

"I wanted to make a difference, to help people."

"Is that really it?"

"I don't understand."

"With your skills, you can help people in innumerable different ways. But you chose to become a cop. Why?"

Myriad shadowy answers came together in Harriet's mind, but none satisfied her.

"Was it for justice? For truth?" Chanteuse mused.

"Maybe a part of them both. I do like puzzles to solve. And I'm a Libra. I despise injustice."

The *Manbo* smiled serenely at the young witch. "I can sense that," she said. "Beware of the system then, Detective June. Its shade is merciless and corruptible."

"Will you let me know when No-No wants to talk?"

"I will be in touch."

HARRIET MADE it to headquarters and headed to her desk. Rab and the Ghost of Warren G. Harding were already there. She leaned back in her chair as Harriet put down her messenger bag and the jar of *Raiz de Oaxaca*. "A new spell?" she asked, pointing to the jar.

"It was something for Jackson. I was hoping it'd help him recover."

"And did it?"

"*Manbo* Kind beat me to the punch. When I got there, she was performing a healing ritual."

"Will it help get Jackson out of the woods?"

"She assured me it would."

"Ah, that's good."

Harriet sat down and started her desktop. She opened the tabs that contained the facts of the Dionysus case. But as she stared at them, she saw more pitfalls and dead ends.

"Are you alright, Ms. June?" asked the Ghost of Warren G. Harding.

"Yeah. Why?"

"You look disturbed."

"I should after everything."

She looked at Rab, who was on her desk phone. "Okay. Send him to an available room. We'll meet him in five. Thanks."

"What's up?" Harriet asked.

"Our old friend Javier Baruch is in the building and wants to talk."

"Interesting. Talk about what?"

"I'm not sure. He didn't tell the desk sarge but says he has something important for our case."

Harriet, Rab, and the Ghost of Warren G. Harding walked down a wing of headquarters that was more formal than the rest of the building. It looked like a resort hotel with warmer lighting, softer carpeting, and lighter wall paint. Rab led them to a room, knocking on the door before opening it. Javier Baruch was sitting at a table, slumped in his chair. He was in a dark blue maintenance uniform. "Heading to work?" Rab asked as they sat across from him.

"The hotel has no one else," he answered. "By the way, thanks for the wall. I love doing drywall work." His sarcasm was dripping.

"Who's taking care of Freddy?" Harriet asked.

"Mrs. Sabedra. She's a neighbor who takes care of kids from time to time."

"And your wife?"

"She's doing a little better. Still on the ventilator, but she's more conscious."

"You have something for us, Mr. Baruch?" Rab said.

Baruch sat up straight. "I do. But you must understand I can't be named if anything goes down. Can you do that?"

"It depends on the quality of your information."

He sighed deeply, running a hand over his hair. "The hotel... has secrets. You saw the secret tunnel and shit. There's more of them everywhere. But it's not just the building. It's the people who run it."

"The management?" Harriet asked.

"Yeah," Baruch said. "Look, they're willing to keep things under wraps if shit looks bad for them, like a robbery, and especially an assault."

"No different than anyone else."

"But this could seriously get them in deep fucking shit if it comes out."

Rab and Harriet leaned closer. "Like what?" Rab asked.

"We have secret witches on staff."

"Secret?" Harriet said.

"Yeah. Did you know it's still illegal for a hotelier to hire a known piff?"

A flash of annoyance crossed her face. She crossed her arms over her chest, "Plenty of professions are still closed off to us, yeah."

"But that's it about the Palace. It's some tradition that goes back to the thirties or something. With your stay, you can get room and piff services, all on the same tab. It's just not advertised, is all."

"Why are you telling us this?" Rab asked.

"'Cause I heard about the staff piffs from Jeremiah. They sound like a bunch of motherfuckers. One of them has some major beef with him."

"You think this staff witch was responsible for Mr. Jackson's assault?"

"Yeah. Jeremiah told me that he thought something was happening in the hotel and that one of the piffs was responsible. It would make sense if they tried to shut him up."

"Did he tell you who or what it was?"

"Nah, he kept that to himself. He kept a lot of things to himself. Maybe he was trying to protect me. I don't know."

Rab and Harriet looked at each other. "Okay," Rab said, "why didn't you tell us about them earlier?"

Baruch licked his lips, "I just... I don't know. I didn't think to until Jeremiah was sent to the hospital. He's a really good guy, and I owe it to him to make things right."

"Sure. Alright, we'll look into them."

"You'll keep me out of this, right? I don't want them coming after my family or me next."

"We promise, Mr. Baruch," Harriet said. "I'll be sure of it."

10

THE WINOOSKI PROTOCOL

Rab parked Bruiser near the lobby entrance on New Montgomery Street, showing her badge to the valets as a warning not to cause any trouble. They strolled into the ornate lobby, which was bright and lively with guests. Having not seen the Palace Hotel's interior in over a century, the Ghost of Warren G. Harding stared around, gobsmacked by its modern opulence and the different peoples of the world congregating within.

Rab and Harriet approached the front desk. A small, thin, tired-looking woman with dyed light brown hair was on duty. Her dark, almost black, eyes focused on the detectives as they approached. *Monica* was printed on her name tag. "How may I help you?" she asked, a hint of irritation.

They showed their badges. "Is Mr. Gregarian in?" Rab asked.

"Yes, he's in." Monica leaned closer, asking earnestly, "Is this about the robbery?"

"Can you please call him?"

She called Mr. Gregarian. In a moment, he walked up to

the front desk. He smiled widely as if Jackson's assault was nothing more than a transient dream. "Good seeing you again, detectives. How may I help you?" he said.

"We have a few things we'd like to discuss with you," Rab said. "Do you have time?"

"Of course. Please follow me. We can talk in my office."

They were led into a large, bare office. The desk was plain, with a laptop and a couple of picture frames displaying photographs of Mr. Gregarian and his Pekingese decorating it. Mr. Gregarian stepped around the desk and sat down. "What would you like to talk about?" he asked.

Harriet said, "We were informed that you have witches on your staff."

The blood drained from Mr. Gregarian's face, giving him an ashen look. "I don't know what you're talking about, detective. That's illegal!"

"It came from a very reliable source."

"We can do this in one of two ways," Rab said. "You can voluntarily tell us everything about your staff witches, or we can dig and turn them up. How will your employers react when we publicly announce that this hotel has witches working for them?"

"And that two crimes were committed on their hotel's grounds using magic?" Harriet said.

Mr. Gregarian swallowed audibly. "Alright," he said. "Yes. We do have witches on call."

Harriet glared at Mr. Gregarian. He hesitated, sinking his head low and cracking his neck before continuing. "We... Well. Look, we have guests from all over the nation and the world. Some folks come from places where sorcery is banned, violently banned in some cases. And they may come here with needs in the paratemporal. That's what we offer: discrete, world-class conjuring services—to a degree. Requests must be reasonable."

"Just like the bootleggers' tunnel," Harriet said. "The Palace Hotel always has ways around legality."

"Do you just offer these services straight up?" Rab asked. "Or does someone need to know someone?"

"There are networks that inform our guests beforehand. If they have a passcode, our witches will work with them."

"Were these witches on duty on the night of the robbery?" Harriet asked.

Mr. Gregarian shook his head. "No. Our witches have nights off. To prevent any potential mischief our guests might want to get into."

"What about yesterday?"

He held his breath before answering, "They were, but I believe they were assisting guests at the time of Mr. Jackson's assault."

"Are they available now? May we talk with them?"

"I don't have a choice, do I?"

Rab made a show of shaking her head. Mr. Gregarian stood up and left the office.

Three uniformed staff members entered the office sometime later, two women and a man. One woman was raven-haired, with alert gray eyes and a sharp chin. Her colleague had long, thick, curly red hair and soft golden eyes peering through a pair of delicate glasses. The man was so unremarkable that one could lose him in a crowd. He was pale, with thin brown hair, dull brown eyes, and unusually shaky hands. He closed the office door after Rab and Harriet showed their badges. "Loving your hat!" the redheaded woman said to Harriet as if to add fun to the situation.

"Thanks," she answered.

The man pointed to the Ghost of Warren G. Harding, "Is he a cop, too?"

"Nah, just some phantom we picked up," Rab said.

"I'm not *just* some phantom!" he bellowed. "I was the president of these United States!"

"Really?" the raven-haired woman said skeptically.

"Maybe he's one of those nineteenth-century presidents," the redheaded woman said to her.

"But that's not..." The Ghost of Warren G. Harding said before Rab raised a hand to silence him.

"Doesn't matter," she said, taking a notebook and pen from her hoodie pocket. "You wanna take over, Harriet?"

Harriet sat on the edge of Mr. Gregarian's desk and cleared her throat. "First thing's first. Maybe some introductions?"

"Sure," the raven-haired woman said, "I'm Molly. Molly Alay."

The redheaded woman raised a hand, "Elyria True. But you can call me El."

"Tad Collinson," said the man.

Rab looked up from her notebook, glancing at him.

Harriet continued. "I'm sure you've heard about the robbery, yes?"

"For sure," Elyria True said. "Ms. Archambeau had raised all kinds of hell before she left."

"What about the assault on Jeremiah Lucian Jackson yesterday?"

The staffers shifted uncomfortably. "We did hear about that," Molly Alay said. "Mr. Gregarian told us about it."

"Is he alright?" Elyria True asked.

"To a degree," Harriet answered.

"What happened?"

"Mr. Gregarian didn't mention anything?" The three staff witches answered negatively.

"He was possibly attacked with a hex. We're not entirely sure."

"A hex?" Molly Alay exclaimed innocently. "You think a witch was involved?"

"I did wonder if Jackson had connections in that world," Elyria said. "Maybe someone had it out for him?"

"I think we can drop the act," Harriet said. "We know what you three are."

The room's energy changed darkly, and the staff witches became grim and suspicious. "Did someone from the hotel talk to you about us?" Molly asked.

"We're asking the questions," Rab said.

"Did any of you have a disagreement with Mr. Jackson?" Harriet asked.

"Why do you ask?" Molly cut in.

"Did you?"

Molly Alay inhaled sharply through her nose. "It's not like Jackson was the most agreeable person to work with," she said. "He can be confrontational sometimes."

"With you?"

"With anyone. Talk to everyone who works here. He always walked around here with a chip on his shoulder."

"Mr. Gregarian said that you three were assisting guests at the time of the assault. Could you provide names and times?"

Molly Alay turned hostile. "You're suspecting *us*?" she nearly shouted. Elyria True placed a hand on her shoulder, using her thumb to massage the collarbone.

"And while you're at it, give us your locations on the night of the robbery, too," Rab interjected.

Molly's wrathful eyes turned to her. "Why are you on us?

What about Jackson? He's in that voodoo cult! Him and his buddies probably robbed Archambeau, and he got shafted by them after the fact!"

"Molly!" Elyria whispered.

"When Mr. Jackson can talk, we'll get a statement from him," Harriet said. "But y'all are variables we were not aware of. So, that's why we're talking to you."

"Means, motive, and opportunity," Rab said. "*Cui bono*, you know?"

"Well, detectives, if we had something to do with these crimes, why would we talk to you?" Molly said hotly. "Besides, there's no way we could've been involved. It's impossible!"

"Nothing's impossible, Ms. Alay."

"It really is. For us, anyway." She was quiet for a beat, her eye twitching. "Management placed a curse on us."

Harriet stood up from the desk, and Rab straightened. "Curse?" Harriet asked. "What kind of curse?"

"The Winooski Protocol," Tad Collinson said.

Harriet squinted at him, "I'm sorry, what?"

"What's the Winooski Protocol?" Rab asked.

"Is that from Vermont?" asked the Ghost of Warren G. Harding.

"It's an extremely painful, terrifying curse that I wouldn't use on the worst of my worst enemies," Tad Collinson said. "It activates if we break any of the hotel's compacts."

"Yeah, it's... not great," Elyria said.

"Understatement of the millennium." His tone was petulant. She shot him a look, but he didn't notice.

"What does it do?" Harriet asked.

"Words can't even describe the horror of the Winooski Protocol," Tad said, haughtily philosophical. "Our language is too limiting."

"It attacks you physically, mentally, and spiritually, all at once," Molly said, her voice faltering. "You feel all three aspects of yourself get rend apart inch by inch, slowly, methodically, by the invisible hands of hellions while the words of your infractions are craved into your flesh."

"It's something out of Kafka's most demented nightmares," Tad interrupted.

"Then, once you think you've reached the curse's limits, that the pain can't get any worse, the fragments of what's left of your being gets compacted into a star of excruciating pain. And you remain like that... forever."

"Not forever," Tad said, annoyed. "Until the heat death of the universe. That's our only saving grace."

Harriet, Rab, and the Ghost of Warren G. Harding stared wide-eyed at the three staff witches. "Golly," he muttered.

Rab cleared her throat roughly. "Um. Huh," she stammered. "Okay. So then, I guess I want to know, for my own curiosity's sake, why take this job if that curse is a part of the gig?"

"Job security," Elyria said. "The bennies are good. And the tips."

"Well, then," Harriet said. "That's a lot to process. Thank you all for being so forthright with us."

"Sure thing," Tad said, almost hurriedly. "Is that all? We should get back to work."

"Yeah, I think that's it. Thank you for your time."

The detectives and the ghost left the office, going through the lobby. Rab pulled a cigarette out and clamped it in her teeth. "It takes a lot of imagination to fashion a curse like that," she said, pulling out a Bic lighter.

"Some witches are just inherently cruel," Harriet said. "Especially if the money's good."

"Don't I know it. I ran into one who was no better than a fascist."

"If they have that curse hovering over them, they couldn't have pulled the robbery and the assault."

"That's if they're lying. How do those three know how that curse works if they hadn't experienced it?"

"That's one way to look at it."

"But wouldn't lying to the police cause that Vermonter curse to activate?" asked the Ghost of Warren G. Harding.

"It depends on the structure of the curse," Harriet said. She thought for a moment. "I feel like there's more to the staff witches than they're letting on."

"For sure, I got the same vibe. But how are we going to find out?"

"By asking more questions, Rab."

She scoffed. "That's if they're willing to talk to us anymore. That Alay girl was ready to bite our heads off. And Collinson? He seems like a dud."

"Yeah, there's something off about him. And Alay is too angry. But Elyria True barely squeaked out a word the whole time. I think she's my best bet for a talk."

"You think?"

"She seems capable. If I'm wrong, I have other ways to get her talking."

"How?"

"An old tradition that forces a witch like her to talk."

"Do you need my help, Harriet?"

"I think this has to be a witch-to-witch job."

IT WAS six in the evening, and Elyria True was putting away her materials at her workstation when she heard a knock on the door behind her. She opened it. Harriet stood there, severe and determined, her alewife hat firmly on her head. "Can I help you, detective?" Elyria asked.

"I need to ask you a few questions," Harriet said. "It won't take long."

"I'm sorry, but I'm just closing shop here. I need to get home."

"Are you refusing?"

Elyria stood up straighter, her chin out. "I have my rights, don't I?"

Harriet held up not her badge but a bronze medallion of a woman with three faces. "*Ostende pretium tuum*," she said.

Elyria stared at the medallion, her lips parted, then up at Harriet. "Is this about the robbery? Jackson?" she asked.

"Do I have to repeat myself?"

"No, you don't. Please."

"I need to come in, El."

"Yes, of course."

Elyria moved out of the way so Harriet could enter. She looked over the room where the staff witches worked. It was a gloomy, cramped room, with three heavy workbenches set up side-by-side against the far-end wall under bare light-bulbs. Various Mason jars filled with substances were stored haphazardly on the shelves above the workbenches. Harriet looked around. "This is where they placed you?" It was more of a statement than a question.

Elyria crossed her arms and stood worriedly. "Can't have us out in the open, you know?"

"But with your talents, I'd expect a much more comfortable place. Maybe less dingy."

"It is what it is." Elyria bit her lower lip. "How did you know what I am?"

"I didn't," Harriet answered. "I was hoping you were an old Mayflower witch. That's all."

She grinned slightly. "Isn't that stereotyping?"

"I guess you can say that." Harriet studied Elyria. "You and Molly Alay seem close," she said.

"We are."

"She was pretty upset with me and my partner earlier."

"Molly doesn't like the cops much. ACAB and all."

"Right. But that's not just it, is it?"

"What do you mean?"

Harriet leaned against a workbench. "We looked up Molly Alay. She has a juvie record from way back, sealed, of course. It won't take long for us to get it unsealed. I'm trying to figure out if she didn't like us or was afraid of us discovering her past. That's never a good look."

Elyria's face conveyed unease.

"I also tried looking up that Winooski Protocol," Harriet continued, "even cracked open the old New England index. I can't seem to find it anywhere."

Elyria sighed. "It's not from there. Not originally. It's a French curse from Quebec if I remember correctly."

"That makes sense. So, it does exist is what you're telling me."

"Did you think we were lying?"

"My partner thought so. And I'm not going to lie; I also leaned toward it. It seems like an over-the-top thing to place on someone for a job."

Elyria shrugged, "It's a fail-safe. Something to keep us quiet and honest. Besides, why not hang a curse over us while exploiting our labor? Isn't that what owners do?"

"I hear you." Harriet hummed tunelessly. "Honest, huh? So, you and the others can't steal anything, great or small. Is that right?"

"No, nothing. Not a guest's pocket change, or..." Elyria looked at Harriet, a corner of her lips perked up, "A priceless Grecian artifact."

"Otherwise, the body horror nightmare would get you."

"You know it."

"Okay. Then, maybe you can help me out, El. Was it you, Molly, or Tad who had the beef with Jeremiah Lucian Jackson?"

"Even knowing that the Protocol's over us, you think we were responsible for his assault?"

"I'm trying to see everything in front of me."

Elyria hesitated. "I had nothing against him. I barely run into him because he's just a maintenance guy. Molly... she doesn't like anyone. Kind of a misanthrope."

"She likes you."

"We have history. Molly trusts me."

"What about Tad Collinson?"

Elyria clenched her teeth before answering. "Molly and I don't hang out with him, so I can't say. And even if Tad had something against Jackson, I don't think he can get him with a hex."

"Yeah? How so?"

Harriet saw the earnestness in Elyria's eyes; her face finally relaxed. "He's not a good witch," she said. "Not even a mediocre one. He's legit terrible."

"Really?"

"Yeah. I can't tell you how often Molly or I had to bail him out of a badly done spell. It's gotten to the point that the secret networks stopped recommending the Palace."

"Why hasn't he been fired?"

"He's about to be. Mr. Gregarian took me and Molly aside about a couple of weeks ago to tell us that management is planning on shitcanning him."

"They haven't yet."

"I think they're trying to find the right way to let him go. No witch has ever been fired from the hotel."

Harriet tapped a ringed finger rhythmically against the edge of the workbench. "I think that's all you can give me, El," she said.

"It's all I know. I'm sorry, detective."

She pulled the medallion from her dress pocket and held it in her hand. "For sure. Thank you."

11

NO-NO AND EL SATAN

"Oh, shit," Harriet uttered hotly under her breath. She was reading from her desktop monitor, scrolling the mouse wheel aggressively. Rab looked at her; the Ghost of Warren G. Harding's right eyebrow arched. "Anything interesting over there?" Rab asked.

"I'm on the Codex of Jeanne d'Malcoeur," Harriet said.

"Fascinating. Why?"

"Elyria True told me more about the Winooski Protocol last night. Just enough to lead me to the right place about it."

"It's real then?"

"Very real. A follower of Catherine Monvoisin created it for a French aristocrat before he sent her to the *Place de Greve* for a date with the stake. It was called *le malediction de l'enfer* then. It went over to the New World in the late seventeenth century and was used extensively against the *Filles du Roi* in Quebec. A version reached Vermont by the eighteenth century, mutated, and bastardized, and became the Winooski Protocol." She looked away from her monitor and to Rab. "It practically has the same afflictions, down to the 'star of pain' finale."

"And this Winooski Protocol is triggered by any infraction?"

"You name it. Any act against your employer, however small, is enough to trigger it."

"What about lying to the police?"

"If it's against the employer's best interest, then yeah, you get tortured and transformed into eternal pain."

"Dude," Rab muttered. "That curse sucks major ass."

"Yeah." Harriet sighed. "That's capitalism for you. Whatever goes against every human right imaginable is acceptable. The only consolation is that Louis XIV brutally executed that aristocrat for employing witches."

Rab stood up from her desk and paced a bit. "What if one of the staff witches had someone, some friends maybe, commit the robbery and hex on Jackson?" she said. "It would be perfect. They provide intel, and their hands are clean."

Harriet shook her head. "The Winooski Protocol is activated by intention. If they intend to rob, injure, or commit them, then the protocol starts up."

"What if they intend to do those crimes but don't? Does Winooski start up?"

"I don't know. The codex doesn't record that. It focuses on the protocols' victims."

Rab growled frustratedly. "God damn it! Why can't anything about this fucking case go smoothly?"

"There's always something blocking us." Harriet picked up her mug, wanting coffee, but saw a uniform approaching her desk. "Detective June?" he asked when he was close.

"What's up?"

"There's someone waiting outside. She wants to talk to you."

"Who is it?" Rab asked.

"Not sure. She was asking for Detective Harriet June specifically."

The uniform left. Harriet put her mug down and locked her computer. "Are you heading out there?" Rab asked.

"It might be important."

"Do you need backup?" Rab's voice had a tinge of concern.

Harriet thought for a moment before shaking her head. "I think I'll be alright. I doubt the people responsible for these crimes believe we're any danger to them."

Harriet went outside. The receptionist of the Tranquil Mawu Society was leaning against the wall near the entrance, cold hostility emitting from her. She stood up straight when she saw Harriet. "Detective June?"

"How can I help you, miss?"

"*Manbo* Kind asked me to see you."

"What is this about?"

"She said you wanted to talk to Brother Jeremiah's friend, No-No."

Harriet's heart raced. "Is everything alright?"

"Yeah, he's ready to talk to you, but it has to be on his terms."

"I completely understand. What are his conditions?"

"He wants to meet in a public place." The receptionist pulled a folded piece of paper from her sweater pocket and gave it to Harriet. The jade necklace around the receptionist's neck glistened brightly. "He'll be there tonight at seven," she continued. "Your partner is invited, too. But no recording devices or any of that. He doesn't want his voice with the police."

"I promise. Nothing sneaky."

The receptionist scoffed loudly. Harriet clutched the paper in both hands, "Look, I know it's tough..."

"You don't know nothing, detective."

"What's your name?"

"Yolanda."

"I'm sorry, Yolanda. I understand you don't exactly trust us..."

"*Exactly*?" Yolanda interrupted. She rested a hand on her hip. "Detective June, did you know that one of our practitioners was shot dead by the police three years ago?"

Harriet shook her head sadly.

"He was setting up a protection offering for someone's house when a neighbor called to complain, some big money motherfucker. It took *less* than five minutes when the police arrived to unload their guns on him. He didn't have a chance. And you know what happened next?"

"No."

"Nothing. Not a single investigation, trial, anything. As far as we know, those cops are still on the force. Probably here in this building!"

Harriet stood still, unable to say a word. Yolanda held the jade necklace gently between her thumb and index finger. "And this is what's left of my brother," she said, swallowing hard. "A piece of his soul I managed to save after the New Orleans police were done with him. It's all I have of him, detective! So, no, I don't have a single fucking reason to trust the police. None of us have a good goddamn reason to trust any of you. We couldn't believe that *Manbo* Kind would even help you!"

"It's for Mr. Jackson."

"Jeremiah was put in danger because of you! You put the target on his back!"

A group of uniforms started coming out of headquarters, standing and staring at them. Harriet held out her hand. "It's alright," she said. "We're having a discussion."

They didn't disperse. A couple crossed their arms over their chests.

Harriet held the paper up. "Thank you, Yolanda. Please give *Manbo* Kind my thanks."

Yolanda rolled her eyes, saying, "Whatever," as she walked away.

The uniforms disappeared into headquarters. Harriet followed suit, then stopped in the middle of the lobby. She opened the paper and read the address. "I know this place…"

THAT NIGHT, Rab, Harriet, and the Ghost of Warren G. Harding headed down to Polk Gulch, parking near a bar on the corner of Van Ness and Lombard Street. "How do you know this place?" Rab asked as they got out.

"My friends and I were regulars. I have friends who work here."

"A woman who drinks?" said the Ghost of Warren G. Harding. "How disgraceful!"

"And you're a filthy degenerate who can't keep his dick in his pants, Warren," Rab answered.

The bar was dimly lighted and lightly packed with men. Donna Summer played from a pair of speakers hung above the bar top. Two bartenders worked quickly, making cocktails or pouring beer. One was a handsome young man in a flannel shirt with his sleeves rolled up. He had curly, dark brown hair and dazzling blue eyes. The other was tall, shirtless, and stunning. Light stubble covered his sharp jaw;

gothic letter tattoos ran across his muscular chest. His dark, wavy hair concealed small, curling horns. Rab had a smirk on her face. Harriet was joyfully happy. The Ghost of Warren G. Harding didn't know what to make of the place. It seemed at once familiar and foreign. "Hey, girl!" said someone with an excited voice. "Long time no see!"

Harriet turned towards the voice and beamed. "Oh my god! Hi!"

Rab and the Ghost of Warren G. Harding followed Harriet as she bounded to a nearby table. Its occupant was an exquisitely dressed older man. He had thin, carefully brushed silver hair and a pencil mustache above his upper lip. A gin martini stood near his well-manicured hands. Harriet swung around him and embraced his shoulders from behind. He kissed her cheek. "How are you, darling?" he asked.

"Oh, better after seeing you!"

"And you're doing good as a police officer?"

"It's good, a bit stressful. You understand."

The man examined Rab and the Ghost of Warren G. Harding. "Friends of yours?"

"Right! I'm sorry! This is my partner Rab and Warren. Guys, this is El Satan."

"Whoa, *the* Satan?" Rab asked. The Ghost of Warren G. Harding looked ill at ease.

El Satan shrugged playfully, grinning. "Well, make whatever you want of it, young lady. I'm here for it."

"Wait, why are you called 'El' Satan?"

He sighed joyfully. "I took it up after my time in Spain. Those were the best times of my life! Have you ever been?"

"No."

"You should go! Seville is beautiful this time of year."

"Are you the actual Fallen One?" the Ghost of Warren G.

Harding asked without much trembling. Rab shot a scornful look at him.

El Satan smacked his lips, took a sip of his martini, then looked straight at the ghost. "You seem like you were a good citizen when you were alive. A god-fearing man? Right?"

The Ghost of Warren G. Harding nodded slowly.

"Okay. So, you believed in your god and all of his goodness and righteousness, whatever. Did you also believe in his omniscience?"

"Of course."

"And in that regard, you believed in his foreknowledge?"

"His what?"

El Satan grinned. "Knowing something will happen before it happens, or something will exist before it exists."

"It is evident, Fallen One. Nothing had happened, is happening, or will happen without God's knowledge."

"Okay then. Answer me this: god's revelation was written down in what language?"

The Ghost of Warren G. Harding thought for a moment. "Greek?"

"Sure, let's go with that. The New Testament books were written in Greek. Attic Greek, Ionic Greek, Doric, and Arcadocypriot Greek. Whatever. Then, those books were rewritten in other languages. Phrygian, Coptic, ancient Armenian. Latin came around pretty late. Thanks, Jerome. Now, how common are any of these languages nowadays?"

The Ghost of Warren G. Harding was confused. "As in, spoken?"

"Exactly!"

"Well... I. That is, I mean. Latin is still used. Ancient Greek..."

El Satan laughed uproariously. "Only in court cases or as

party tricks! Come on, man! How many fluent speakers of these languages are there today?"

"I've never even heard of some of these languages," Rab said.

"I'm acquainted a bit," Harriet said. "There are whole schools of magic dependent on Coptic or Phrygian."

"Are those witches fluent speakers, though?" El Satan asked.

"Well... fluent enough to get the magic right."

"Conversationally fluent?"

"Probably not."

"Where is this going?" demanded the Ghost of Warren G. Harding.

El Satan leaned towards him. "All these languages are either dead, replaced, or evolved, friend. Phrygian and Coptic are now Arabic. The varieties of ancient Greek are now dulled under modern Greek. Latin has become Europe's Romance languages, and they underwent a constant fluid change. And I'm not including the Scandinavian, Germanic, Slavic languages, nor the great, nearsighted, red-headed bastard child English. New rules are taught. Grammar changed. Definitions that worked in one generation are entirely different things in another. Everything dies, and everything changes. That's the one constant in life.

"What I'm asking you is this: different ways to communicate and convey ideas. For every generation. Is that one way to preserve timeless revelation? Especially revelation as important as god's? Trusting that revelation will survive pristine, without change, mistranslation, or misinterpretation? How could god have thought that would work? How can god not have known that his revelations, his message, would go through the wringer of linguistic evolution, coming out scathed and corrupted, and did not come up with a backup plan? Is it that he lacks foreknowledge and, therefore, isn't omniscient and, hence, not all-powerful? Well, there goes the entire operation of god, wouldn't it?"

The Ghost of Warren G. Harding was determined not to let El Satan get the better of him. A challenge came thundering across his mind. "What about Hebrew?" he asked.

El Satan cocked an eyebrow. "Hebrew?"

"I now remember reading something when I was a young man. Hebrew was being revived by the Jews of Europe. And it's one of the oldest continuous languages in the world!"

"Yes, indeed. The *L'shon Hakodesh* is among the oldest continuous languages of the world," El Satan grinned knowingly. "Now that we've established that, explain how that's relevant here."

"Why, the Jews were the first to write about you! They named you, Fallen One!"

El Satan leveled his hand up, angled it lazily, and smirked. "They sure did, on both accounts. Now, since you're such an expert on Judaism, Mr. Warren Harding, Esquire, what *is* the rabbinic tradition concerning me?"

The Ghost of Warren G. Harding stood still; his eyes widened. His courage drained, and he decided that the best course of action was not to reply.

"I thought so," El Satan said.

"I think he got you good there, Warren," Rab said.

"God, that was embarrassing," Harriet whispered. "I'm so sorry, El Satan."

"It's okay, girl!" he said. "More than okay. These trials invigorate me! It reminds me why I love being humanity's prosecutor. Now, come and have a seat with me!"

She sat down on his right side. He patted her hand. "What are you doing here?" he asked.

"We're investigating the Cup of Dionysus heist."

"Ah, yes! I read about it in one of the Hearst pubs." He glanced at her skeptically. "Why *here*?"

"We're meeting up with someone who might have some useful information. He wanted to meet here."

El Satan nodded. "How exciting! A stakeout! And in our own bar, no less! You *must* let me know how this shapes up!"

"I will!" Harriet stood up from her chair. "Sorry, El Satan. Duty calls."

"Oh, don't mind me. I don't want to get in the way of duty. Happy hunting, Harriet! It's terrific meeting you, Rab!" He gave the Ghost of Warren G. Harding a twisted, sinister look, growling, "And I'll see you *very* soon, Warren."

The Ghost of Warren G. Harding yelped and staggered back, falling to the floor. Harriet stood above him, "He's screwing with you, Warren. Come on, we've work to do."

The three strolled to the bar. "Who are we looking for?" Rab asked. Harriet pulled out No-No's note and read through it quickly. "He says he'll be in a dark blue sweatshirt with a crane logo on the breast."

"Okay. That's not much to go on."

"Hey! Look who it is, the fuzz!" someone called from behind.

Harriet saw the bartender with the dazzling blue eyes waving at her. "How's it going, Max?" she asked, grinning.

"Ah, just livin' the dream. You know how it is."

The tall bartender with the horns sat a pint of beer before a customer, turned to Harriet and Max, and smiled brightly. "Hey girl!" he said, his voice rich and baritone. He strode over and threw his arms around her. "You look good! Still beautiful!"

"You too, Justinian! How are things?"

"Staying out of trouble mostly."

"I bet."

"At least I have you if I ever get into trouble, right?"

"It depends on the trouble."

Max stood next to Justinian, resting his arm on his shoulder. "You want anything? It's on the house," he said.

"I wish, but we're on duty."

Justinian was serious when he asked, "What's going on?"

"You heard about the Cup of Dionysus theft?"

"How can't I? The maenads are tearing themselves apart, screaming, vowing to get revenge."

Harriet pointed to Rab, "We're investigating it."

"No shit!" Max said. "A witch was involved?"

"Maybe. We're looking into it," Rab said.

"Do you need anything from us?"

"No, not right now," Harriet said. "We're looking for someone who might have some information. He agreed to meet with us here."

Justinian's brows furled. "Here? Why here? Is this gonna cause us trouble?"

"No, it's a simple interview. Nothing more."

"Who are you looking for?" Max asked.

"A man in a blue sweatshirt with a crane logo."

He snapped his fingers. "I just served him! Vodka soda. He's at a table in the back."

"Ah! Point him out, Max."

Max showed the detectives where to go and then returned to the bar. Harriet, Rab, and the Ghost of Warren G. Harding reached the table. The man in the dark blue sweatshirt was bald but had a luxurious black and silver beard. His eyes followed the detectives as they approached. He didn't look nervous but wasn't pleased. He stood up to greet them. He was tall and fit. "Are you Detective June?" he asked.

"I am. No-No?"

"That's right. You can call me Antonio. That's my given name." He pointed to Rab. "Is she your partner?"

"Yeah. This is Detective Rabinowski."

"Hey, man," Rab said.

"Alright. Let's get to business."

They sat down. Antonio opened his backpack and pulled out a thick binder, placing it on the table. "This is what I think got Jeremiah in trouble," he said. He opened the binder and spun it towards Harriet. She studied the contents. It was photocopied pages of strange writing and diagrams, marginalia of esoteric symbols, crude illustrations of people in unidentifiable costumes, unknown fauna and flora, and bizarre constellations that didn't fit usual astronomical conventions.

"What is this?" Harriet asked.

"I'm not sure," Antonio said. "Jeremiah said it was a book with many bad portents."

"Where did he find it?"

"In his hotel. Some weeks ago, he told me he felt this funky, dangerous energy there. That's when he found this book but couldn't understand it. He thought I could help."

"Why is that?"

"I'm a top practitioner in Tranquil Mawu, and I dabble with all kinds of disciplines in our world."

"You sound like a Virgo," Harriet joked.

"It's my moon-rising, so it tracks."

Harriet leafed through the pages. The penmanship became more erratic, as if the author was undergoing a frenzy.

"He photocopied these?" she asked.

Antonio nodded. "He did. He copied the whole book, from page to page."

"Did he say where exactly he found this book in the hotel?"

He looked serious, then lowered himself towards the table. He motioned with his hand for the detectives to come closer. "Don't let this get out," he said. "It might cause more trouble than it's worth."

"Your friend was severely injured on our watch," Harriet said. "Whatever it is, let trouble come."

Antonio hesitated, clicking his tongue. "Alright. He found the book in one of the staff witches' workstations."

Harriet and Rab turned to each other. "Was Jackson sure it was their workstation?" Rab asked.

"Positive. He knew where they worked."

"So, he found the book. But he couldn't take it without rousing them," Harriet said.

"Exactly. But he wanted to learn what that book was. He was sure it was dangerous, especially in the hands of the staff witches."

"Really? Why?"

"He told me that one of them is a lunatic with a hair-trigger temper."

"That's good to know. So, he copied the book and gave it to you."

"Yeah. I just needed to see the book's contents to see what it was capable of," Antonio said.

"What did you find out?"

He leaned back in his chair, shaking his head. "Nothing. I couldn't even figure out *what* language it was written in. I searched every possible known and secret writing system and compared it to those pages. I got nowhere."

Harriet studied a page in the binder. "But it can be used," she said. "If Mr. Jackson felt that dark energy, it must've come from the book. The writing isn't a hindrance."

"It's not. But I can't make heads or tails of it." Antonio clutched his hands together on the table. "And with what happened to Jeremiah, I don't know if I want to continue working on it."

Harriet closed the binder and tapped on it. "This is a major clue. It could link everything at the Palace Hotel."

"You just need to figure out how to read it, buddy," Rab said.

"Do you mind if I take this with me, Antonio?"

He shrugged. "You can have it. I don't want to get involved any more than I already did. I have a husband and a family. I probably endangered them all by helping Jeremiah out."

"You probably helped us bust a criminal organization," Rab said. "That's some major karmic reward right there."

He smiled at her. "I hope you do bust them. I want to know what they did to Jeremiah, and I want them to pay for it."

"We'll do our best, Antonio," Harriet said. "Thank you. And please thank *Manbo* Kind for me. I won't let you all down."

"We'll see, young witch. We'll see."

Harriet picked up the binder. And she, Rab, and the Ghost of Warren G. Harding got up to leave the bar. But before that, Harriet went up to say goodnight to Max and Justinian. "Are we gonna see you again, girl?" Justinian asked.

"Maybe when I finish up this case, I'll come around. I'm going to need some forget juice after."

He strolled around the bar and gave her a big hug. Max reached over, tapped on her shoulder, and wished her luck. She returned to Rab and the Ghost of Warren G. Harding, and they left.

12

A VERY GRIM GRIMOIRE

Rab's eyes were two angry, glassy, illuminated points dashing over her monitor's screen. She held her cigarette lighter, tapping it absentmindedly on the top of her desk. The Ghost of Warrant G. Harding stared at her. "Penny for your thoughts?" he asked.

"Where to even start," she answered.

"What's going on, Victoria?"

She leaned back in her chair, toying with the lighter. She used it to point to the monitor. "Molly Alay's juvenile record. The court finally got it to us."

"That's good, yes?"

"Yeah. She was a little hothead when she was a kid, hexing and cursing people left and right by the time she was twelve. It wasn't terrible, from the sound of it—very Dennis-the-Menace. That was until she turned thirteen and flew off the handle one day. A hex of hers left her math teacher with a permanent disability."

"Good lord! I would never have guessed in a thousand years that young lady was capable of any violence."

"She's trouble for sure, Warren. Alay was put in juvie

after that. It says here that the facility started hampering her skills then."

"She still has them."

"That she does. Whatever they tried didn't take." Rab turned to the Ghost of Warren G. Harding. "What if Alay was the one who stole the cup and attacked Jackson? He was on someone's shit list and had the initiative to discover secrets."

"How do you figure your theory?"

"Here's how I see it. Alay had that book. She was using it to do who-knows-what. She found out that Jackson was snooping around. And she decided to plug him before he could do something that might get us involved."

The Ghost of Warren G. Harding thought for a moment. "But those staff witches are under that Vermonter curse," he said.

"The Winooski Protocol. Yeah."

"If Ms. Alay was using that book to commit nefarious deeds before Mr. Jackson's assault, wouldn't she have been subject to its effect?"

"That's the hitch."

"Perhaps Ms. June could provide that piece of the puzzle."

"Speaking of, have you seen Harriet? Is she around?"

The phone rang on Rab's desk. She answered, "Yo! Hey Harriet, we were talking about you. Huh? Now? Alright, be up soon."

When she hung up, Rab stood from her desk. "What's happening?" the Ghost of Warren G. Harding asked.

"We gotta head, Warren. Harriet's found something. Something worthwhile."

They went upstairs to a conference room and entered. The binder with the strange writing sat open on the long table. One of the whiteboards hanging from a nearby wall was covered with esoteric writing. Harriet was jotting something down on another opposite from it. She turned to them. Rab noticed the exhaustion on her face. "Have you slept at all, buddy?" she asked.

"I couldn't," Harriet whispered. "Not with what I was finding out."

"So, what you got?"

Harriet pointed to the binder. "I've discovered what this book is!"

"Hell yeah! What is it?"

"It's an *earrach* coven's grimoire."

"Wait, what?"

"They were a secretive Scottish coven from the Highlands, around a few centuries ago. They mostly practiced during the spring and summer seasons before the English hunted them down or scattered them worldwide. Some form of the *earrach* coven still exists, but not at the numbers like before."

"What kind of grimoire is it?"

Harriet leaned over the conference table and gripped its edge. "Something that should never have been written at all."

Rab's eyes grew large. "Why?"

"It's called the *Leabhar Cogaidh*. It's a witch's war book."

"How did you figure that out? Antonio had trouble with it."

"Through metisophsey."

"Huh?"

She straightened up. "It's an old Levantine writing style, extremely rare in the wild." Harriet picked up the binder and held it high. "It's a psychic language machine, using pneuma-geometry and the mind's eye to decipher the book's code. The real hard work is setting up the manuscript for metisophsey, like numbering the letters, words, sentences, and paragraphs. That, and translating old Scottish Gaelic into English." Harriet grinned. "Ironic, huh?"

"How far along are you in translating this Laid-bear Cog-Weight?"

"Not very, unfortunately. It's time-consuming. I spent all night finishing just three pages, and there are over seven hundred in the manuscript."

Rab thought quickly. "Would a computer help?" she asked.

"I think so. But I don't know how to set it up."

"Don't worry, Harriet. We have people. Take that binder and follow me."

Rab, Harriet, and the Ghost of Warren G. Harding went to a floor above the underground garage. Rab led them into a room humming with electrical equipment. It was freezing and bright. Stacks of processors stood on every inch of floor space. "Yo, Vinny!" Rab called. "You here?"

"That you, Rab?"

A man appeared from behind a stack, holding up a clipboard. He was tall, with a warm, pleasant face and thick glasses. His black hair was long and combed to the side. He smiled when he saw Rab. "God, when I heard you transferred back, I couldn't believe it!"

"Why didn't you look me up, Vinny?"

Vinny waved a hand around the processors. "Someone has to keep the brains of the operation running!"

He approached Rab, and they hugged. "Your new partner?" he nodded to Harriet.

"Yeah. Harriet, this is Vinny Chang, head of IT. Vinny, this is Harriet June, our new forensic witch."

"Pleased to meet ya," Vinny said, offering a hand.

"Likewise," Harriet said.

He motioned towards the Ghost of Warren G. Harding, seemingly unbothered by the apparition, "You two are being haunted? What's up with this?"

"He's a complication," Rab said. "Don't worry about it."

"I'm not a 'complication'!" roared the Ghost of Warren G. Harding.

"Get used to it, Warren!" she roared back.

"Well..." Vinny said, taken aback. "Now I know this isn't a social call. What brings you all here to my humble abode?"

"We have an issue with a potential clue," Rab said. "You heard about the Cup of Dionysus thief?"

"Briefly. But not the full details."

"We're working on it. A person of interest was savagely attacked earlier, and this book might be a connection."

Harriet held up the binder.

"What do you need?" Vinny asked.

"The book's contents are hidden by a linguistic system called metisophsey," Harriet said. "I've figured it out, but it'll take weeks or months to break this manuscript down by hand fully."

Vinny scratched his neck. "And I take it you need some awesome computing power to ease the burden."

"That's the plan," Rab said. "Can you help?"

"Does the pope shit in the woods? Follow me."

Vinny led the group into a dark office, where the only illumination came from multiple monitors. Two men sat at desks pushed together, working diligently over keyboards. "Danny! Oscar!" Vinny shouted. "Are you guys up for a little challenge?"

The two men twisted around. One was young, with big, intelligent eyes and a messy mop of dark brown hair. The other was broad-shouldered, with a stern face, steely eyes, and a crooked nose. Vinny pointed to the young man, "Danny Lopez, our software engineer. He can jury-rig code like no one else. His partner here is Oscar Shevchenko, the best data analyst in the biz. Boys, this is Rab and Harriet. They're working a case and could use our help."

"We're not forensics," Oscar said. "Our skills are only computers."

"This is going to be a computer challenge. Take it away, you two."

Harriet placed the binder on Danny's desk and opened it. Oscar came around to look. She explained metisophsey: the numbering system, the hidden keys in the marginalia, how to use them to identify base and suffix words, and the rules to make everything grammatically correct. Danny listened carefully, nodding along. "It's an algorithm," he said. "It should be easy to build something to organize and analyze the data, maybe use AI to round everything out. What do you think, Oscar?"

"Sure, real easy. But how are you going to read it once it's done? No software exists to interpret that stuff, even with AI."

"Trust, it'll be easy for me," Harriet said. "I just need something to help speed up the work of bringing out the words."

Danny grinned. "I should have something ready in a day, two tops. I'll have this thing readable before you know it."

"That fast?"

"You'll see. And you'll understand why I'm not getting paid enough around here."

Harriet, Rab, and the Ghost of Warren G. Harding exited the headquarters building and walked towards Bruiser in the dark parking lot. "You need a ride?" Rab asked.

"Please. I'm so tired, I don't think I can do the streetcar."

"Sure thing, Harriet. I'll get you home."

A shadowy silhouette of a person was standing beside Bruiser. Rab stopped, followed by the others. "You've been ignoring my calls, Detective Rabinowski," the person said merrily. It was a woman's voice.

Rab snorted. "You're chasing me down now?"

"I wouldn't have if you'd answer your phone."

"I have nothing to say, which is the problem."

"Oh, now, come on, Rab! You always have something to say. That's why you're my favorite inside source."

The woman walked into a street lamp's light. She was blond and medium-height. She wore a blue button-up shirt, black blazer, and jeans. A large purse hung on her shoulder. "Is she your new partner?"

Rab smirked. "Yeah. Harriet June, meet Marion Nix of the Chronicle."

13

APOKALYPSIS

The sushi restaurant was on Laguna Street and Linden, a short walk from Harriet's house. The group sat at a table near the entrance and ordered various sashimi and nigiri and a round of beers. Marion studied Harriet and Rab and smirked at the Ghost of Warren G. Harding. She shook her head gently, "The ghost of a former president? Life never gets dull for you, doesn't it, Rab?"

"It shouldn't with this job," she answered.

Marion turned back to Harriet, looking at her alewife hat. "Is the hat standard kit, Detective June?"

"I wanted to accessorize my look. Make myself unique."

"I bet. I've met a lot of forensic witches. Some were eclectic, others deranged, and most were very business casual. You straddle all worlds. I like that."

The sashimi arrived and was carefully placed on the table. "Domo," Marion said to the server. Everyone picked up their chopsticks and started eating. The Ghost of Warren G. Harding made a face. "Is that fish?" he asked.

"Yup," Rab answered.

"It looks raw."

"That's where the flavor comes from."

After finishing her Hamachi, Marion took her phone out of her purse and opened its recording app. "So, now that I've bought you dinner, what do you have for me?" she asked.

"A little presumptuous of you, isn't it?" Rab said.

"Oh, come on! You have to give me something about the Dionysus case. Our readers are dying to know."

"How did you know we were on the case?"

"You think you're my only source in SFPD?"

"If you have so many of them, why are you chasing me around?"

"We have a fabulous working relationship. That's why."

Rab waved her chopstick hand amusingly. "Sure. We do. But like I said before, I don't have anything to say."

"Is it because of the nature of the case?"

"It's more like we don't have anything to tie onto. There are barely any clues, a very shallow suspect pool, and more questions than answers."

"The only thing we have is a hypothesis that witches committed the crime," Harriet said.

"Yeah," Marion said, dipping a piece of sashimi into soy sauce. "Reginald Yee wrote about that. Selene Archambeau could only describe the thieves as shadowy individuals who vanished before her eyes."

"Other than that, we have nothing more."

"You didn't find any clues at the scene?"

"Not even. I tried to find any remnants of dirty magic in Archambeau's suite, but it led nowhere."

"That's how we ended up with this guy," Rab said, pointing to the Ghost of Warren G. Harding. He smirked embarrassingly.

Marion shook her head while chewing. "What about astral projection?" she asked. "It might be plausible."

Harriet sipped her beer, saying, "I thought about that. But it isn't possible. To transport a physical object through the plane, you must transmute it to its ephemeral properties. But then you would lose your astral self in the process. You can transmute something or project but can't do both."

"So, you have no evidence and only guesses," Marion said. "You mentioned a shallow suspect pool, Rab. What's that about? You don't have any suspects?"

Rab looked hesitant. "We investigated two maintenance workers who were supposed to be on duty the night of the heist but weren't. One had a record, but he had an alibi. The other was connected to the Tranquil Mawu Society. He was the closest to a person of interest we had. But before we could dig further, someone attacked him."

"Physically?"

"Magically. We were there for the attack. He could've died."

"Well, that's interesting."

"What's more interesting," Harriet said, "is that our POI has a practicing friend in Tranquil Mawu. They were collaborating on something he found in the Palace Hotel—a grimoire."

Marion crooked an eyebrow. "A grimoire?"

"Have you heard of the *Leabhar Cogaidh*?"

"Can't say that I have, detective."

"It's a seventeenth-century Scottish war book. Very rare. And from what I can tell, it's very powerful."

"How did you verify its potency?"

Harriet shrunk a little from embarrassment. "It's a guess. I only managed to go through three pages."

"That's not a lot."

"No. The text is obscured by metisophsey."

"Hm. That's a challenge."

"We have people helping us with its translation," Rab said. "Once they're done, we'll have a fuller picture."

"What does the grimoire have to do with any of this?"

"The POI found it in a staff member's workstation," Harriet said.

Marion's attention was firmly on her, "A *hotel* staff member had a grimoire?"

Harriet realized what she had let out and turned to Rab. She nodded slightly, "You better tell her."

"The Palace Hotel employs witches—three of them—and our POI found this grimoire in their workstation."

Marion leaned closer to the detectives, showing amazement. "Who knows about this?" she asked.

"About the grimoire? Or the staff witches?"

"The witches!"

"Management, the owners, everyone," Harriet said. "Everyone within the organization."

"That's... trouble. That's a whole lot of trouble! Not just fines, but jail! How could the Palace Hotel be so reckless?"

"That's for a future investigation," Rab said. "Right now, we're focusing on the stuff on our plate."

Marion sat up in her chair. "Okay. So, a witch illegally working for the hotel had a dangerous grimoire in their possession when the robbery and the assault were committed. That's what you're saying?"

"You can say that."

"Pardon me, Rab, but I feel connections are all over. A staff witch has that grimoire. The Cup of Dionysus is stolen. And the maintenance worker who knew about the book is attacked nearly to death."

"It's tenuous, Marion."

"How is that tenuous?" Marion nearly shouted.

"We don't know who owned the grimoire. Our only witness who can connect it to our witch is in a coma. On top of that, what we have isn't the original but a copy. So, we're not able to connect it to anything. And other than being a war book, as Harriet described it, we don't know what it can do."

"And if we question the staff witches again with what we know," Harriet said, "they'll deny everything. If we bring up the *Leabhar Cogaidh*, they'll deny that even harder. I know my people. And we can't get a warrant to go snooping because we don't have any probable cause."

"It'll be thrown out of court quick," Rab said.

Marion finished her beer and stopped the recording app. "Alright, my friends, this is a tremendous story. I wondered what you guys were doing all this time, but it sounds like you've uncovered more than you would admit to yourselves."

"We might've. But until we run into more evidence, we're stuck."

"I'm sure something will happen once my story runs, Rab. And when it does, I get first dibs on the scoop, you hear?"

THE STORY RAN in the *Chronicle* the next day. Harriet read through it quickly on her phone. "Jesus Christ," she whispered. "So many heads are going to roll after this."

Rab leaned back in her chair after finishing the story on her computer. "Yup. I thought about feeling bad about Gregarian but can't even muster that. What do you think the staff witches are going to do?"

Harriet shrugged. "Panic, rage. What more can they do?"

"What if they're laid off because of Marion's story? Will they be freed from that Winooski thing?"

"Probably. But I'm not worried."

"Why not?"

"They don't know it was us who talked to Marion Nix. And if Molly Alay or the others decide to go on a spree, that gives us cause to look into them further. Their best bet is to stay put and keep quiet."

Danny Lopez appeared from a hallway, the binder under his arm, and headed towards Harriet and Rab. "Detective June?" he called out.

Harriet twisted around in her chair, "How are you, Danny?"

He held up a USB drive. "I've done it!"

She stood up. "Oh, thank god! Bring it here!"

Danny sat at her desk and plugged the drive into her desktop. Rab went around and joined Harriet. He opened a file and allowed it to load. "It didn't take half as long as I thought it would," Danny said. "Even Vinny and Oscar were impressed. They said I should patent my software."

"It followed all the perimeters of metisophsey?" Harriet asked.

Danny nodded, "To the letter, like you told me. Metisophsey is just like every other line of code. But when it was done, I couldn't make any sense of the manuscript."

"It's a psychic art. You can read it through the sixth sense."

"And that's something you can do?"

Harriet nodded.

The monitor was filled with characters, each stranger than the next. Danny spread his hands out. "There you go, pages and pages of it. All broken down from this." He tapped the binder.

"This is perfect, Danny," Harriet whispered as she read line after line, the outline of each letter glowing in her eyes. "Ah, you're a lifesaver!"

"You can make any of that out?" Rab asked.

"Perfectly."

It was early morning. An occasional car drove up Fell Street, but traffic was otherwise dead. Harriet's apartment was dark except for the living room—a single lamp burned in the corner, casting a dull glow.

Harriet was asleep in her leather chair, her stockinged feet propped up on the coffee table, a laptop balanced precariously on her lap. Ditzy snored away in her cushioned bed near the television. A sharp chime sounded repeatedly, waking Harriet. She yawned and stretched, then patted herself. She pulled out her work cell phone from her dress pocket. "Hello?" she answered.

"Is this Detective Harriet June?" The voice was male and strict. Harriet imagined his buzzcut hairstyle.

"Yes."

"This is Sergeant Bill Will, San Francisco County Jail. How are you this evening?"

She looked up at the clock on the wall before her: 1:45 a.m. "Fine," she answered, stifling another yawn. "Just fine. How can I help you, Sergeant?"

"I have a man in custody claiming he knows you. He keeps demanding to talk to you."

"A man? Who's he?"

She heard pages rustle in the background. Sergeant Will

whistled a rhythmless tune. "Here. Todd, Waverly. Sound familiar?"

Harriet straightened in her chair. "Waverly Todd? He was arrested?"

"Affirmative, Detective. Possession of a controlled substance. A serious violation of his parole." He sounded like he was commenting to himself.

"Why does he want to talk to me?"

"Not sure, ma'am. But he's making one hell of a racket. I thought I'd give you a heads-up in case he starts pestering HQ."

"Is he there with you right now?"

"No, he's in holding."

Harriet thought for a moment, tapping the edge of her laptop. "Is it possible for me to come around?"

"If you're on duty, you can."

"I'm always on duty, Sergeant. I'll be there in a minute."

She took her coat and alewife hat from their racks and laced up her boots. Ditzy followed her every step, whining and gearing up for anxious barking. Harriet went to the kitchen and removed a jerky treat from a pouch. "I'm sorry, baby," she said, holding the treat. "I have work." Ditzy bit down on the jerky and bolted back to her bed.

Harriet called a taxi and was taken to the county jail building on Seventh Street. She met Sergeant Bill Will at intake. He was tall, thick around the middle, with muscular arms and chest. His head was close to a square shape, tiny dark eyes set close together, and a nose set after a fight too many times. He did have a buzzcut. "Sorry for the late call," he said, offering a hand.

"It's okay, Sergeant. This is better. Get Todd out of the way so I can focus on other things in the morning."

Sergeant Will led Harriet into an interview room before

disappearing. A few minutes later, he returned, his head turned away as far back as possible, pushing a haggard, sweating Waverly Todd at arm's length. Todd looked terrible, maybe worse than their last meeting at the Webster Street house. Harriet stared at the darkly mottled sleeves of his jail-issued light grey sweatshirt, cringing at the memory of the awful Russian curse etched bloodily on his arms.

Then, the door was closed. The room was filled with a putrid odor, like wet, raw animal fat and garbage water left under a blazing sun for many days. She quickly found that the smell was coming from Todd, recoiling from him as he approached. Todd smirked sadly, "Yeah, I know."

"What the hell is that, Todd?" Harriet asked, covering her nose and mouth with both hands.

He shrugged. "The smell came outta nowhere. I'm assuming it's the Ruskie curse."

"Are you rotting?"

"I think I am. And yet, I ain't dead."

"What the fuck? Is this the next level of the curse?"

"I have no fuckin' clue. I can't go anywhere near the Ruskies to ask. All I know is I'm stinkin' something fierce."

Harriet coughed. "Alright. Sergeant, can you open the door? Get some air in here?"

Sergeant Will shook his head. "No amount of air circ helps with that smell. Trust, we've tried."

"Fuck, okay. Okay, so you wanted to talk to me, Todd. I'm here."

Waverly Todd cleared his throat. "I'm in a bad way, detective. You know, trying to keep on the up-and-up? I tried, I really tried."

"Sure, you tried."

"Well, it's hard. It's hard to get a job with my record, hard to find a place of my own that I can afford, hard to stay clean, and all that. Hell, man, I'm dependent on my older bro for everything. I wanna be my own man."

"Can you get to the point? You're rambling."

"Look, Detective, I can't go back to prison. I just can't. That last stint fuckin' killed me. I just can't!"

She asked Sergeant Will, "What was he holding when he was busted?"

"H," he answered through a pinched nose.

"Felony narcotics, Todd. Your parole is done. I can't help you."

Todd moved closer to her, his hands held out, eyes bulging. Harriet rushed backward, keeping her distance. "What if I have information that can help you?" he begged.

"Help? Help with what?"

"That heist you're investigating! The cup of something or whatever."

"It depends."

His head trembled. "That book, that book..."

"What book, Todd?"

"*Leabhar Cogaidh!*"

Harriet stared at him intently, her mouth slightly parted. "You know about it?"

"I read that news story and knew you and your partner were involved. Am I wrong?"

She hesitated, then sighed. "You're right. It was us."

He smiled briefly. "See? I still got my brains. I can still pick up on shit."

"What do you know of the *Leabhar Cogaidh*?"

"I've run into it. There're so many copies floatin' around, it's insane!"

"Do you have one?"

"No, no. It's too hot and unpredictable if you don't know what you're doing. I don't want anything to do with it. But I have buddies who know the hook-up. They laid it down on me."

"Where's the hook-up?"

Waverly Todd looked like he finally had an opportunity. He grinned, "Now, detective. I can't just give something up for free, can't I? This is America, not a charity."

Harriet felt her patience drain immediately. She wanted nothing more than to break away from this conversation, go home, and go to bed. But a potential lead stood in front of her. Various schemes flew lazily across her mind, each playing on the current power dynamic more and more. "You're right, Todd," she said. "This isn't a charity. Everyone should get paid for their efforts. But that's contingent on the buyer. And I'm not buying."

"What?" Todd's eyes grew wide.

"I don't have to negotiate. I don't have to agree to anything. I'm tired, very tired, Todd. I can count on one hand the number of hours I've slept since I started working on this case. If you won't tell me anything about the grimoire hook-up, I don't have to be here."

"What about your partner? The redhead?"

She shrugged. "You can reach out to her if you want. But if you think she'll work with you, you're dreaming. Rab's a Valkyrie. She won't stoop to being pushed around by someone like you."

Waverly Todd's desperation began to crack his façade. "That PI guy! I can go to him!"

"Sure, you can. But Beaumont's working for his clients. What pull does he have in the system? The best thing he can do for you is load up your commissary card."

He stepped back from her, realizing he was losing territory in this game of Go. "Can't you do anything for me?" he begged.

"Maybe. I can talk to the ADA in charge of your case and say you greatly assisted our investigation. But it'll depend on how they respond and how good your lawyer is. Do you have one?"

"A public defender."

Harriet sucked air through her teeth. "And they're all overworked. What do you think your chances are, Todd?"

"Come on, detective! Work with me here!"

"Tell me who the hook-up is, and we can go from there."

Todd swallowed hard, staring at the floor. He trembled in place. "His name is Tiny. He owns a liquor store. That's where he peddles the books."

"Where's the store?"

"It's on San Pablo and Market in Oakland."

"God, serious?"

He nodded. "It's easy to do business there."

Harriet thanked Waverly Todd and promised to lay the groundwork for a possible deal. "Can't I get off?" he asked.

"With your record, you'll be lucky to get a ten-year stint. I can hopefully get parole considered after five, especially if your tip is good."

"It's good, detective, trust. My buddies know the score."

"Let me look into it, then. And we can work from there."

Sergeant Will led Todd back to his cell and escorted Harriet to her taxi, waiting outside the county jail. "Do you think Todd's information is any good?" he asked her.

"For his sake, I hope so. It could be our biggest lead yet."

He shook his head. "Oakland, huh? I should've figured the town had something to do with this."

"I'm just not looking forward to calling OPD for help. I heard they're difficult."

"Difficult doesn't even begin to describe them, detective. You'll be lucky to get a call back from them."

Harriet sighed deeply. "Great. Fantastic. And it's not like we can go barging over there, busting people, and demanding answers."

"Negative." Sergeant Will shrugged. "Maybe you can reach out to Clytemnestra Rose. She'd help you."

"Who's she?"

"OPD's forensic witch. She's a legend out there. Busted some pretty gnarly perps in her day."

"Do you think she knows something about this grimoire ring?"

"I wouldn't put it past her. She knows everything that goes on in her city. And if she doesn't, she'll figure out how to know about it." He made a pantomime of surrender. "But... that's if she'll work with you."

"Why wouldn't she?"

"From what I hear, she doesn't work with anyone. Not in her department, and especially not other witches."

She stood in a thoughtful stance, hand to her chin. "That's unfortunate."

"All I can say is good luck, detective. Nothing's ever easy in Oakland."

A LOW AND lonesome train whistle rang from a distance near the water line of the Oakland estuary. The alley off 98th Street was dark, briefly illuminated by a passing car heading towards Bancroft Avenue. A shadowy figure shuffled slowly, his left foot skidding against the pavement in a dance-like imitation. Low giggles broke the stillness of the alley. The figure emerged onto the street, made visible by the brightness of a nearby street lamp.

He was small, frail-looking, with black wooly hair

covered by a green knit cap and wearing a dirty Warriors jersey covered by three oversized, heavily stained jackets. His pair of jeans was close to tatters. His eyes darted around wildly. A deep grin cracked across his patchily stubbled face. The man shuffled and danced on torn, filthy sneakers towards Verdese Carter Park, giggling. Drivers slowed slightly to observe him and his strange gait, sizing him up. He waved madly at them with both hands, his giggles morphing into cackles. The cars sped away.

The man reached Bancroft and looked around. Crossing the lanes, his step began to quicken. His walking became determined and disciplined. His face was stern, his eyes hard. He looked around again when he was near the corner of Springfield Street, then continued up 98th Street to a motel where a pristine, black-as-a-moonless-night '69 Cadillac De Ville stood parked in the lot.

"*Friends, don't be in awe of these creatures of Satan,*" drawled the voice from the radio. "*They'll show you tricks, call themselves revelators and messengers, and proclaim themselves miracle workers. But it's all lies, my brothers and sisters! They'll tell you that you don't need God almighty, that they can perform the miraculous works he cain't, that they themselves can offer you salvation!*" the voice roared.

The audience reacted uproariously in the background.

"*That's the hubris of the witch, brothers and sisters. But we have the means to shatta that hubris. Bring them back down to earth! Looky at Leviticus 19:26 and tell me what it says.*" The audience responded ecstatically.

"*Looky at Exodus 22:18! And tell me what it says!*"

"*Amen, Reverend!*" a voice wafted up towards the stage.

"*And looky at Leviticus 20:27,*" the voice said menacingly, "*and tell me what it commands!*"

"Turn it off," said the woman in the driver's seat,

scrolling on her phone while drawing from a vape pen. "I can't listen to Tommy Marlow."

A billowy cloud of smoke filled the cabin. The man in the passenger seat leaned toward the radio, turned off the program, and found a story about the Athletics.

"Sorry about that," he said.

"It's alright. Nothing's ever good at this hour."

He listened to the story for a moment. "Why the fuck are the A's movin' outta Oakland?" he asked angrily.

"They've been threatening to for a while."

The man scoffed. "These team owners, man. Always tryin' to use our love to extort us for the privilege of stayin'."

"There's no loyalty among millionaires and billionaires, Harris. It's always extract, extract, extract."

"No joke."

The woman clicked her tongue, turned off her phone, and slipped it into her jacket pocket.

"Anything special?" Harris asked.

"You heard about that massacre up in the hills?"

"Yeah. A whole family was jumped in their own home. A robbery gone wrong, yeah?"

"That's what the brass wants everyone to think. They're keeping a tight lid on the whole thing, not letting one thing slip. They're even keeping it from the mayor." She took another drag on her vape pen. "It wasn't a botched robbery, Harris. Something mauled that family."

"Jesus. *Mauled*?"

"Yeah. Father, mother, children, grandma. Just drained."

"*Drained?*"

"I hadn't seen anything like it before, man. 'Drained' is the only operative word I can use to describe it."

"You were there, Metra?"

"Who else was the brass going to call?"

"What hit them?"

She shook her head. "Not sure."

"You're thinkin' creature?"

"That's one angle. Or it could've been a witch."

Harris looked incredulously at her. "A witch?"

"Yeah. The mother was a higher-up in the Coven Cannontin. And she had her fair share of enemies in the community."

"No shit?"

"Nope."

"How could a witch go and massacre a whole family like that?"

The woman sighed deeply. "I heard there was a spate of Desanguis attacks in SF, so I was looking into that."

"Desanguis? The hell is that?"

"It's a nasty blood curse. Drains blood slowly and painfully from the victim, through every pore and opening, until the vic is just a withered sack."

"Fuckin' hell. Seriously?"

"As serious as I'll ever be."

"What happens to the blood?"

"No one's sure. Desanguis is one of the oldest curses and has a lot of mystery behind it. Folks say an immortal entity consumes the blood with a certain ravenous appetite. But that's just one interpretation."

Harris crossed his arms, his face hardened by intense concentration. "Like a vampire?" he muttered to himself.

The woman's eyes darkened as she lifted the vape pen to her mouth. "Biters are a different animal." A cloud of smoke came from her mouth. "What I saw up in the hills was very different."

"Hm. So you think this Desanguis curse was responsible?"

She gripped the steering wheel with both hands, the vape pen held between them. "I don't know. What's going on in the city and here seems similar, but there are differences in attack. I was hoping my contact in SFPD would've given me some insight. But there are more questions than answers now."

Harris saw a shadow approaching the parking lot and peered through the windshield. "There's Alvin."

"I see him." She flashed the Cadillac's headlights. The man in the dirty Warriors jersey quickly approached the car and leaned against the driver-side door. She lowered the window.

"Good god, Al!" Harris said. "You smell, son!"

"What do you expect? This is undercover," Alvin said.

"Did you have to go *that* deep undercover?"

"It's FBI 101, Detective Harris. Next time, you do the work if you have complaints about the bureau's processes."

"Don't mind him, agent," the woman said. "He's just grumpy the A's are moving out of town."

"Sure, sure."

"Did the lead get us anywhere?"

Alvin shifted his weight on his legs. He lowered his head. "Yeah, it did. But they pulled up stakes by the time I started scouting around."

Her arched eyebrows were visible in the light of a passing car. "They're gone?"

"The whole operation. I've never seen such a clean scene before."

Harris groaned in the passenger seat. "All that work, all that searchin'. For nothin'?"

"They must've had help. Moving all those books isn't easy for three dudes."

"I don't doubt it," the woman said.

"You're thinkin' witches?" Harris asked.

Alvin nodded. "No way humps could leave a crime scene that pristine."

Harris turned to the woman, smirking, "You witches can work with humps?"

"Witches won't work with humps unless there's something in it for them," she said, drawing from the vape pen and blowing a stream of smoke against the windshield. "And I can think of a lot of advantages in this case. Monetarily, magically."

"So, what now?" Harris asked the group. "We're back to square one?"

She sighed deeply and leaned back in her seat, gripping the steering wheel again. "I think we are. God, that was our best bet!"

"I'm sorry, Detective Rose," Alvin said.

"No, you're good, Agent Grey." Clytemnestra Rose took another puff of the vape pen and placed it into the car's ashtray. "If only another lead would just fall into my lap."

14

THE OAKLAND CONNECTION

Harriet entered headquarters and walked tiredly to her floor. It was seven a.m., and the bustle had ramped up inside. The cacophony of activity assailed her. She winced and settled her messenger bag on her desk before sitting down, her shoulders slumped. Closing her eyes, she settled herself back against her chair, seeking the solace of her dream sanctuary. As the sound of a soft trickling creek and a gentle piney breeze going through a dark forest shrouded in moonlight formed in her mind, it was quickly disturbed by a simple question: "You okay, buddy?" She opened her eyes and saw Rab standing near her, a cup of coffee in her hand. The Ghost of Warren G. Harding stared at her worryingly.

"Hey guys," Harriet said.

"Are you alright, Ms. June," asked the Ghost of Warren G. Harding. "You seem ill."

"I'm tired, so very tired. I went to sleep around five in the morning, and before I knew it, my alarm went off."

"Late night?" Rab asked.

Harriet recounted her trip to the county jail and the

meeting with Waverly Todd. "Now, my brain's buzzing with this information, but I feel like I'm thinking through sludge," she said.

Rab nodded her head gently, then went to her chair. "You think his information is good?" she asked, sitting down.

"Why wouldn't it be?"

"I don't know. He could be making it up."

"I told him that if what he told me didn't help us, I would not help him. What did he have to lose?"

Rab chewed on a thumbnail. "It's something. Stoolies rarely survive long in jail, especially guys like Waverly Todd. So, he's making a big sacrifice to talk to you." She rocked in her chair, "If that's the case, we should look into this Oakland connection. It might shake some names loose."

"We only need one name," Harriet said.

"I know." Rab thought for a minute. "How far along are you in that Legume Goldthwaite?

"The *Leabhar Cogaidh*? Not very far, unfortunately. There are so many esoteric incantations, formulas, and commentary. Parsing it all out is taking a lot of time and effort."

"You haven't found anything that can lead us to what caused the robbery and Jackson's assault?"

Harriet shrugged. "Considering the nature of the book, I wouldn't be surprised if there's something like that."

"Hm. Well, first thing and stuff, I guess. We should learn more about this grimoire hook-up in Oakland before we ask more questions."

"You have any ideas on where to start, Rab? Alameda County isn't our jurisdiction."

"Oh, I have an ace. Have you heard of Clytemnestra Rose?"

Harriet perked up a little. "Back at the jail," she said.

"Sergeant Will told me about her. But he said she doesn't work with others."

Rab snorted. "She loves cultivating that image, but that's not true."

"It's not?"

"Nope! I've worked with her plenty of times."

"You have?"

"Yup. Here, let's see if she's available."

Rab picked up her desk phone, turned on the speaker, and dialed a number. It rang audibly three times before someone answered, *"Is that you, Rab?"* The voice was feminine, strong, and friendly.

"How you doing, Metra?" Rab said.

"It's been a long time! How's it going, baby?"

"Nothing much. Living and stuff."

"How's XNC16 treating you?"

"I'm back in robbery-homicide."

"Really? They couldn't handle your heat, eh?"

Rab hummed tunelessly, "You can say that. Hey, listen. I'm working on a case that might have some connections in Oakland. My partner and I are wondering if you might know some things."

"Lay it on me. What do you have?"

"Tell her about the book, Harriet."

"Harriet? What happened to Johannes?"

Harriet looked up to Rab. Though it was slightly imperceptible, she was grimacing. "Things have changed, buddy," Rab said. "Harriet June's my new partner."

"Harriet June. What a lovely name. Well, okay, Harriet June. What do you have?"

Harriet cleared her throat and moved closer to the phone. "Hi, Detective Rose. Like Rab said, we're working on a case—a robbery and an assault. During our investigation, we found a copy of a grimoire that might be attached to the crimes. An informant told me about a hook-up in Oakland last night."

"*Okay, sure. What type of grimoire are we talking about?*"

"The *Leabhar Cogaidh*."

Clytemnestra was silent for a while. Rab, Harriet, and the Ghost of Warren G. Harding leaned closer to the phone. Finally, Rab said, "Are you there, Metra?"

"*Yeah, yeah. I'm here. The Leabhar Cogaidh, huh? Are you sure? This is the earrach coven's grimoire, yeah?*"

"Yeah," Harriet said. "I've been studying this copy for a minute."

Rab interrupted, "It sounds like you've heard of this book, Metra."

"*I have. Copies of that particular grimoire have been found at many crime scenes around East Bay. Especially here in Oakland. I keep getting a line on the distributors, but they disappear before I have a chance to catch them.*"

"Are they getting help?" Harriet asked.

"*Most likely. It's the only explanation I have until I start cracking skulls. Who is this hook-up? You have a name?*"

"Some guy named Tiny. I don't have a last name. But he has a shop on San Pablo."

Clytemnestra chuckled sarcastically. "*Oh, Tiny. Of course, he's involved. I should've known.*"

"You know him?" Rab asked.

"*Yeah. Tiny McDaniel. He's a two-bit hump who likes getting himself in trouble with magic. I've had my run-ins with him.*"

"How cooperative will he be?"

"*Depends. He will clam up quickly if pushed a little. But with a little help, I think he'll talk.*"

"Mind if we're that help?"

"You know I can't deny you, Rab. Meet me at headquarters, and we'll roll on out."

They ended the call. Rab shoved her cell phone in her pocket and grabbed her car keys. "Come on, Harriet," she said. "We're going to Oakland."

Harriet tried to stifle a yawn. "Let's do it…"

Rab peeled out of the headquarters parking lot and drove Bruiser towards an on-ramp to the Bay Bridge. She lighted a cigarette and lowered the window. "What's XNC16?" Harriet asked as she stared out the passenger side window.

Rab blew out smoke, "It's nothing. Nothing worth talking about."

"Nothing? Is that the reason you transferred back to robbery-homicide?"

"You can say that."

"Who's Johannes?"

Rab gripped the steering wheel tightly with her free hand. "He was a friend," she said.

"Was?"

"Yeah. Was." She turned to Harriet, seeing her asleep through the window's reflection. "You falling asleep on me?"

"Just resting my eyes," Harriet said.

"Come on, June!" Rab started the car's CD player and cranked the volume knob to its maximum. "No sleep 'til Oakland!"

Pantera's *Cowboys From Hell* blasted through the speakers. Rab headbanged to the god-like thunderous drums and the sublime, wailing guitar. Harriet shot up straight in her seat. The Ghost of Warren G. Harding slammed his hands to his ears instinctively, the mimic of a twisted, pained expression on his face.

"What is this hellacious noise?" he screamed.

But Rab ignored him as they raced down the bridge to Oakland.

ON THE CORNER of Seventh Street, near Broadway, Clytemnestra Rose sat on the trunk lid of her Cadillac De Ville, drawing from her vape pen, then billowed smoke from her mouth and nose. She was gorgeous, with luminous Black skin and large almond-shaped brown eyes. Her long, braided hair was exquisitely tied at the back of her head. She was tall, nearly six feet, and wore all-black clothes, finishing the look with a black leather trench coat. She wore a leather harness over her torso. It held several objects and medallions, capsules, and small silver accouterments. The most prized object on her person was a long, elegantly etched silver spearhead with an ivory handle holstered to her waist, close to the seven-pointed badge of the Oakland Police Department.

Clytemnestra was drawing on her vape pen as Bruiser pulled around the corner from Clay Street, driving down Seventh, and parked behind her. Rab stepped out of the car, followed by Harriet. "You don't like *Cowboys*?" she asked.

"I prefer *Peach Kelli Pop*," Harriet drawled.

Clytemnestra hopped onto the street and stepped towards Rab, smiling, "Well, well. San Francisco's finest!" She pocketed the vape pen and embraced Rab. "Looking good, babe!"

Rab had a big grin on her face. "You too, Metra!"

Clytemnestra saw Harriet. She nodded towards her. "The new partner?"

"Yup. Harriet, this is Clytemnestra Rose. Metra, this is Harriet June."

Clytemnestra stepped towards Harriet, offering her hand. "Good meeting you, Harriet."

She took her hand and shook it. "You too, Ms. Rose."

The Ghost of Warren G. Harding was now on the sideway, shaking, a piercing din in his ears. He kept gasping as if he was losing breath. Clytemnestra arched an eyebrow. "Who's the pasty poltergeist?" she asked.

"Oh, that's Warren," Harriet said.

"Yeah, he's cool. Kinda awkward, but you get used to him," Rab said.

Clytemnestra sat back on the lid of the Cadillac's trunk, crossing her arms. "So, what's the scoop?" she asked. "How did you two run into the *Leabhar Cogaidh*?"

Rab and Harriet went through the Cup of Dionysus heist and Jeremiah Lucian Jackson's assault. Clytemnestra listened carefully. When Harriet spoke about Waverly Todd's tip, Clytemnestra nodded quickly. "A lot of crank hexers have been getting their hands on copies of that damn grimoire," she said. "No surprise that there's word about it on the streets."

Rab lighted a cigarette. "You think this Tiny McDaniel guy is the only hook-up?"

"There's only one way to find out. Let's roll."

The three detectives and the Ghost of Warren G. Harding got into their respective cars and drove off, with Rab following Clytemnestra.

They parked outside a small convenience store on the corner of San Pablo Avenue and West Street. They got out. In the distance, cars and big rigs roared down the 980 freeway. Above the store's entrance, an ancient sign advertising Seven-Up was lighted up.

Clytemnestra walked into the store with Rab, Harriet, and the Ghost of Warren G. Harding following her. The proprietor stood behind the counter. He was a tall, very rotund man, wearing an Athletics tee shirt and a backward baseball cap. A scraggily blondish-coppery goatee grew on his face. He kept a wary eye on the group as they approached him. "Mornin' Metra," he said. His voice was deep, with a lilt of an indistinguishable accent.

"How've you been, Tiny?" Clytemnestra asked. "You've been keeping out of trouble?"

"As much as I can. Who're your friends?"

"This is Detective Rabinowski and Detective June from the San Francisco Police Department. Don't mind about the honky ghoul, he's along for the ride."

The Ghost of Warren G. Harding moved to say something, but Rab's look backed him down.

"Huh. Kinda far from your jurisdiction, ain't you?" Tiny McDaniel asked Rab and Harriet.

"They're with me on this one," Clytemnestra interjected.

"Sure, okay. So why am I so lucky to be paid a visit by the finest?"

Clytemnestra leaned an elbow on the counter between them. "Oh, nothing, Tiny. I just wanted to chat."

"Chat about what? The weather?"

She grinned. "I've been hearing some things, man. Some interesting things."

"What interesting things?"

"Ever heard of the *Leabhar Cogaidh*, Tiny?"

Tiny McDaniel didn't look disturbed. "Can't say that I have, detective. What is it? Can I use it?"

Clytemnestra stood up and crossed her arms, her face neutral. "Detective Rabinowski and Detective June are working a case, a big robbery in the city. They'd found a copy of the *Leabhar Cogaidh* that might've been used in the crime."

"Really? Huh."

"And possibly in the attempted murder of a man."

He did not break. But sweat beads started to form on his forehead.

"Come on, Tiny," Clytemnestra drawled slowly and seriously. "Is this how you're gonna play me?"

"I don't know what you're talking about, Detective Rose."

"Look, how many times have I given you a break? That time I busted you with that Salvadorian curse doll up at the lake? What about when I had you for possession of that bottle of *exitiale* elixir?"

"I still did time for that one."

"Yeah, the minimum mandatory sentence. I gave you that one because you didn't know what the *exitiale* did."

"Sure, okay."

Clytemnestra gave Tiny McDaniel a tired expression. "Don't make me go to work in your shop, Tiny," she said. "I might not be charitable afterward."

Tiny McDaniel's face twitched slightly. His eyes narrowed. But he didn't voice any opposition or confirmation. Clytemnestra nodded, then stepped away from the counter.

She removed a silver capsule from her harness and twisted the top until it opened. Inside was a frosty pink and gold powder that sparkled in the store's lights. Harriet, Rab, and the Ghost of Warren G. Harding stepped back as Clytemnestra chanted over the powder, waving her hand above the capsule, and stared intently at Tiny McDaniel. He looked worried as Clytemnestra crouched close to the floor, spreading the powder into a circle around her. Her chanting became rhythmic when she completed the circle, becoming more intense as she stood up and stretched out her hands.

She never broke eye contact with Tiny McDaniel. Sweat trickled down from his forehead.

Clytemnestra clapped her hands three times, shouting, "Obeah!" at every beat. The powder flared, becoming an inferno, engulfing Clytemnestra, while the phantom screams of a hundred thousand mouths filled the store. The inferno extinguished as quickly as it appeared. Clytemnestra stood unharmed in the middle of the burnt-up powder. She turned her head towards a door near the counter. "Rab, mind keeping an eye on Tiny for me?" she asked.

"For sure, buddy," Rab said, pulling her forty-five from its holster.

Clytemnestra walked towards the door, trying its knob. It was locked. She pulled out her silver spearhead and placed its tip between the door and jamb. With one quick push on its ivory handle, the door was opened.

"Don't you... um... need a warrant?" Tiny McDaniel sputtered.

"Probable cause, Tiny. Obeah never lies," Clytemnestra said.

She pushed the door open further. Behind it was a small office filled with warped, bulbous, overloaded cardboard boxes. Clytemnestra flipped a nearby light switch. A bulb above flickered before the current equalized, casting a harsh light. She approached one of the boxes and tore open its top panels. Inside were large paperback books with blank brown covers. Picking one up, Clytemnestra leafed through the pages. "Ms. June, can you come here a minute?" she said.

Harriet entered the office, studying the boxes before approaching Clytemnestra. She held the open book close to Harriet. "Is this your grimoire?"

"It is," Harriet said sternly.

"And it's mine too." Clytemnestra snapped the book closed. "Alright, Tiny, we're going for a ride."

There was a commotion in the store—shouts followed by things crashing on the floor. Harriet and Clytemnestra ran back to the counter, where they saw Tiny McDaniel flat near the entrance, groaning. Rab, who sat on top of him, was twisting his arms behind his back. She applied handcuffs to his wrists and stood up. She pointed at him and said, "He tried to run."

"You okay, Rab?" Harriet asked.

"Yeah. He didn't know about my right hook."

Clytemnestra walked up to Rab and tapped her on the shoulder. "I owe you one, friend," she said. Rab just nodded her head.

Clytemnestra pulled out her phone and dialed a number. "Harris, we got a big lead on the *Leabhar Cogaidh* case. I need a squad car at 2207 San Pablo now, please, and thank you." She hung up and glared at Tiny. "You just had to make things difficult, didn't you?"

15

DISTRIBUTION BOYS

A t OPD headquarters, the three detectives and the Ghost of Warren G. Harding stood in an office near the interrogation room. Clytemnestra twirled her spearhead in her hand. Rab and Harriet watched Tiny McDaniel fidget in the next room from a monitor. "Other than the books, was there anything else in the store?" Rab asked.

"A secret camera he had set up above the counter," Clytemnestra said. "That's it."

"What about the video?" Harriet said.

Clytemnestra gently shook her head. "It's encrypted. Tiny might not look it, but he's smart. He probably had a feeling I was closing in on him and wanted to protect his customers."

"Is there any way to decrypt it?"

"My tech boys are working on it. It'll take some time, but they'll get there."

"How do you want to handle him?" Rab asked.

"Fast and easy. I don't want him to see it coming."

They walked into the interrogation room. It was well-lighted, with greyish-white walls and industrial carpeting. Tiny McDaniel sat despondently at a small table, his wrists cuffed. He looked up and gave the group a small, broken smile. "I thought you'd forgotten about me," he said.

"Oh, Tiny, how could I forget about you?" Clytemnestra said, sitting down near him. "With the haul from your store, I'm looking at a serious promotion."

He nodded slowly. "What's gonna happen to me?"

"How many chances have I given you in the past again?"

"I don't know."

"Too many, but you're all out of chances. Those grimoires are dangerous—more dangerous than the stuff you used to peddle. That's several enhancements. And with your record? You might be looking at a couple of decades."

Tiny McDaniel choked back a sob, then braced his face in his hands. The detectives and the ghost didn't break the silence in the interrogation room, letting him feel the trouble he was in. Finally, he straightened up in his chair, "Isn't there *anything* you can do for me, Metra?"

Clytemnestra crossed her legs, dangling one over a knee. "I can see what I can do, Tiny. I am buddies with the DA. What do you have to trade?"

"How about the whole operation?"

Her face softened a little, "The peddlers? All of them?"

He nodded. "There are only three of them. College kids. They're practically babies playing with a gun. They're the ones pushing the books."

"Are they witches?"

"No, man. Just a bunch of slack-ass humps."

Clytemnestra smirked at him, "Sounds familiar." Tiny McDaniel didn't respond. "Where are they, Tiny?"

"If I tell you, can I get a deal?"

"Listen, man, so that you don't accuse me of shit. I can't

promise you won't do time. Selling and distribution of grimoires is a major felony in the State of California—especially war-book-style grimoires. You had a pretty sizable business, Tiny. How many copies of the *Leabhar Cogaidh* did you manage to move out of your store?"

He sat still, not saying anything.

She continued, "Tens? Hundreds? Thousands?"

He stared at Clytemnestra with watery, puffy eyes. He stammered, "I... don't..."

"You don't know?"

"Yeah."

"People knew where to find you. This means the word had gotten around wide and far, right? Word of mouth, that's some advertisement you had, Tiny."

"Metra..."

"You had a security camera on while you made the sales, Tiny. The footage is encrypted. But it'll take our team no time to unlock it. And when they do, I'll have the numbers. That's not going to help you."

"Metra, please..."

"And you don't just have Alameda County to worry about. Remember my friends here? From SF? Remember, one of your books was used to commit a crime in the city? I think their ordinances on grimoires are stricter than here." She leaned closer to him, "That's probably another decade tacked on when all the DAs are done with you."

Tiny McDaniel started weeping, covering his eyes with his left hand. Clytemnestra returned to her usual sitting position.

"They're in Jingletown!" Tiny McDaniel cried out.

"Jingletown?"

"Yeah, near the Park Street Bridge. That's where I picked up my last shipment of the books."

"Where exactly, Tiny?"

"I don't have the address. But it was in a vacant Mexican restaurant, I swear!"

Clytemnestra pulled out her cell phone and opened the maps app. "Is this the place?" she asked, holding the phone to him.

Tiny McDaniel studied the screen, seeing an image of a storefront on Google Maps, "Yeah, yeah! That's the place! Metra, you gotta believe me. I'm saying that's it; that's where I got the books last!"

She turned the phone's screen to Harriet and Rab, "Glascock and Twenty-ninth. Not far from us."

"What's the plan now?" Rab asked.

"Oh, we're going in." Clytemnestra speed-dialed a number. "Harris. We got a tip-off on the grimoire gang. They're in a vacant restaurant on Glascock and Twenty-ninth. How soon can you get a team together? Promise them hazard pay and overtime; come on, man! We have to move now! Okay, get on it. Let me know when you're done. Huh? Sure, I'll let Alvin Grey know. Just get the team together."

She ended the call and sighed, "The number of times I have to bribe people to do their jobs…"

"Who's Alvin Grey?" Harriet asked.

"FBI. He's working with us to locate the grimoire cabal."

"The books crossed state lines?" Rab said.

"A shipment was stopped in Nevada. And they were connected to us."

"Man, those guys are going to be in a world of hurt when this is all over."

"That's their problem."

The detectives and the ghost turned to leave. Clytemnestra was dialing another number when Tiny McDaniel whimpered, "Hey, what about me, Metra?"

She slowed and said over her shoulder, "I'll throw you a ticker tape parade in Santa Rita, Tiny. Don't you worry."

Within an hour, Harris called back to inform Clytemnestra that a strike team had been assembled and was in position. Agent Alvin Grey reported that he and his colleagues were en route. Her, Harriet, Rab, and the Ghost of Warren G. Harding were in a breakroom, waiting. Clytemnestra set down her coffee cup, nervously tapping the counter. "We'll give 'em thirty minutes, wait for the signal, then head in," she said.

"Sounds good," Rab said coolly. Harriet stood in nervous anticipation. It was her first raid. The Ghost of Warren G. Harding scowled. He never enjoyed violence. After thirty minutes, Clytemnestra got a text. She pulled out her car keys, "Alright, y'all. Let's hit it."

Everyone piled into the Cadillac. Clytemnestra roared down the 880, easing the big car onto Twenty-ninth Avenue. She parked across the street from a building with boarded-up windows, and a large "For Lease" sign hung prominently above the entrance. Police cruisers and unmarked cars were parked in front of it with their flashers on. A uniform directed traffic off the Park Street Bridge, causing a pile-on.

Clytemnestra led the group to the building. A husky man in a loose-fitting black suit, a large bushy mustache, and a helmet of gray and white hair greeted her near the entrance. "We had good timin' Metra," he said. "We got 'em with their pants down."

"Good. Any trouble, Harris?

"I was worried about trips. But the place's clean. You can tell it was a hump operation."

Harris led Clytemnestra and her guests into the building. Numerous cardboard boxes were stacked chest-high on the main floor. Sorcery paraphernalia and other cursed items were on a long service counter near the back. Police in tactical gear surrounded three young men near the counter. They were on their knees, with their hands behind their heads. They were gangly, shaggy-haired, in tee shirts and jeans stained with printer's ink. One was pimply, red-headed, worn in an attempt of an afro, and wearing a large, thick pair of glasses. He looked like he was about to cry.

Harriet broke off from the group and started rummaging through a few boxes. Rab and the Ghost of Warren G. Harding continued with Clytemnestra as she approached the young men. She crouched in front of them, grinning. "I've been looking for y'all a long time," she growled.

The one in the glasses choked back a sob.

"Detective Rose," someone called from the entrance. Clytemnestra stood up and turned to the voice, "Over here, Alvin."

Alvin Grey, followed by two agents in aviator sunglasses, approached her. He was dressed in a white Oxford shirt, gray slacks, and the ubiquitous dark blue vinyl jacket of the FBI. He whistled as he surveyed the boxes. "This will make your career, Clytemnestra," he said.

"This is government intrusion... and harassment," one of the young men said loudly and shakily. He was pale, with twitching green eyes and uncombed brown hair. He was wearing a vintage Goofy Movie tee shirt marred with streaks of black ink.

Clytemnestra sneered at him, then focused on the one with the glasses. "You know what the penalties for distributing forbidden grimoires are, don't you?" she said.

"Especially across state lines?" Alvin Grey said.

"The state has no right to control what we consume," Goofy Movie continued. "We have a right to read them, study them. This is freedom of information, freedom of the press!"

Clytemnestra looked down at Goofy Movie. "You're right, boy. The state has no right to control what we read. We should read what we want without fear of intrusion." She stepped closer to him, placing her hands on her hips. "But we also bear responsibility for what we do with what we read."

Harriet returned to the group, carrying a brown, blank-faced paperback book. She showed it to Rab and the Ghost of Warren G. Harding. "Check it out," she said, opening it. It was a new copy of the *Leabhar Cogaidh*. "The ink is still wet."

Rab took the book from Harriet and went to Clytemnestra to give it to her. She opened it, flipped through the pages, and then snapped it shut. The three boys on the floor flinched. "Do you think the people who have copies of this book are using it for good?" she asked.

Goofy Movie pinched his lips together. His colleagues trembled.

She continued, "A war book, a particularly dangerous war book. Do you think people should have this on their shelves?"

"It's... it's not up to us how people use them," Goofy Movie said. "That's their choice. Their... their freedom..."

Clytemnestra hummed. "Freedom, yeah. You would say that, huh, ofay." She held up the book, "The witch who wields this is making a choice, sure. But what about the victim of the witch? You would sacrifice one's freedom for another's?"

The three boys did not respond.

"I didn't think so. I guarantee you, boys, there are victims aplenty around here and beyond. And I'm going to connect every one of them to you. Oh, the enhancements are going to be spectacular."

"Please, don't!" Glasses sniveled. "I can't!"

"Shut the hell up, Bobby!" Goofy Movie ordered.

"Go to hell, Ricky! I'm too fragile for jail!"

Clytemnestra stepped closer to Bobby. "Are you willing to cooperate?" she asked.

He whimpered, then nodded his head vigorously.

"God damn it, Bobby!"

Clytemnestra asked Harris to close the scene. He gave the command. His officers started loading the boxes and paraphernalia onto trucks. The three young men were cuffed and hauled away. Clytemnestra turned to Rab, Harriet, and the Ghost of Warren G. Harding. "I'll send them to holding to scare them a little," she said. "Maybe a couple of hours. Is that it for you, Rab? It might be the end of the line as far as your case is concerned."

Rab shrugged, "Maybe we'll stick around, if you don't mind, Metra. That Bobby kid might pass along something we can use later."

16

RAB'S PAST CATCHES UP

Bobby fidgeted in the interrogation room chair, tucking his arms into his tee shirt. An empty soda can sat on the table next to him. Rab, Harriet, and the Ghost of Warren G. Harding stood with Clytemnestra as she observed Bobby from the monitor in the next room. "Less than twenty minutes," she said. "That's how long he lasted before begging to see me."

"Did his buddies try to talk him out of it?" Rab asked.

Clytemnestra nodded. "It's a good thing I kept them in separate cells. They kept screaming, 'Get a lawyer, get a lawyer!' when the boys got Bobby out for the long walk."

"How certain are you that he'll gab about everything?" Harriet asked.

"Very certain. These dweebs might not believe in the state, but they sure don't want trouble from it." She grinned, "And I have a feeling our Bobby here doesn't want to see the inside of a prison cell for as long as he has to."

"For sure."

"Y'all stay here. I'm gonna handle this one Han Solo."

Clytemnestra entered the interrogation room. Bobby's

head shot up as soon as the door closed. His expression was fearful. She took a chair in front of him. "How was your stay?" she asked.

Bobby mumbled incoherently.

"Listen, Bobby, I won't waste your time or mine. You know the charges against you and your friends are airtight. And considering the trouble y'all gave me with your constant moving around in *my* city, I'm recommending to the DA to go full maximum."

Bobby whimpered, lowering his head. Clytemnestra leaned back in her chair, crossed her legs, and rested her hands on her lap. She looked serious and grim. "And that's just the charges in Alameda County. You also have San Francisco County and the Feds gunning for you."

He started sobbing. "Please!" he begged. "I don't want to go to jail!"

"Yeah, none of you good little white boys ever do. I looked you up, Bobby Johannessen. Mom's the top neural surgeon out of UCSF. Dad's a VC down the Peninsula, a way. Saint Alban's Prep, all-expenses paid to Stanford, just like your Daddy, before dropping out. What was it for? Taking a year off? Going to find yourself?"

"Please, stop!"

"And on top of all of that, all that money and prep, you were still an abysmal student—barely cracking above a gentleman's C. And I have to wonder whose spot you took. What hardworking, truly deserving high school student— probably from here, Bobby—did you steal that roster spot from?"

Tears streamed down his cheeks. His face flushed with shame.

"But I'm sure Daddy would've found you a position in

his firm," Clytemnestra continued. "Or a friend's firm. Isn't that right?"

He sobbed into his tee shirt.

"Look, Bobby. Don't you cry. I'm sure Mommy and Daddy will get you the best lawyer money can buy. Call it a feeling. The lawyer will recommend things and try to downplay your role. Maybe they'll politely ask the judge for a light sentence. But in the end, with what I have on you, the judge isn't going to listen because the judge will be required by law to give you a hard time.

"However, I can be amicable about downplaying your role in the group. Give the DA something she can use to knock a few years off your sentence. Hell, maybe you'll get probation. But only if you cooperate with me. Help me help you. What do you say?"

Bobby rocked back and forth in his chair. He looked up at Clytemnestra. "I'll tell you everything, I swear!"

"Good. How about from the beginning?"

Bobby spoke of how the group formed. Ricky and the other boy, Olly, were long-time friends, and he was a mutual acquaintance of the two at Stanford. Somehow, over a summer break, Olly got his hands on an old manuscript copy of the *Leabhar Cogaidh*. But it was useless to him, as he wasn't magically inclined, and neither were Ricky or Bobby.

When Olly learned how collectible it was, he thought about selling it. Plans changed when a witch from his economics class practically salivated when he mentioned his manuscript, begging to let them go through it. It turned out to be a fruitful lesson. Here, he had a commodity that could easily be replicated, and there was a demand for it.

Olly proposed to Ricky and Bobby that they make copies of the manuscript and sell them to the Bay Area's witch community. The trio wasn't deterred when they learned that doing so was illegal due to the book's dangerous nature. They hid their greed under the guise of academic inquiry and freedom.

Ricky collected the tools and machinery, and Olly found a local seller for the proper cut. Success came to them instantly, allowing them to grow their interests into other areas of the forbidden magic industry.

"I swear I was just a small part of this thing!" Bobby said adamantly.

"Oh, of course you are," Clytemnestra sighed. "How knowledgeable are you of the sales?"

"Huh?"

"The customers, Bobby! Are you acquainted with any of the purchasers?"

He shook his head violently, "No! We didn't face any of them. It was the seller, I swear!"

"Do you even know the seller's name?"

"No, no! That was Olly!"

"So, you put up a front to hock the books. Probably hoping he'd be the only one busted once we caught wise, is that it?"

Bobby stammered, his mouth chewing on missing words. Clytemnestra clicked her tongue, "You didn't think about that man, didn't you?"

He lowered his eyes.

"You had a pretty sizable operation, Bobby. My guys are still inventorying the shop." She glared at him. "Don't you think for a minute I wasn't on your trail the whole time. But every time I was close to busting you, y'all up and vanished. That's very impressive for a bunch of humps. In fact, it's so impressive that I truly don't think you could've moved out on your own. Tell me this, Bobby, did you have help?"

Bobby nodded slightly.

"I need a verbal answer, boy."

"We did. A witch."

"I gathered that. Where'd you meet them?"

"I didn't. Olly brought her in. She said she'd help us out for a cut of the profits. She was tipping us off about the cops and moving the operation when you're getting close."

"How did she figure out we were getting close?"

"I don't know. When we worked making copies in one spot, she'd burst out of the blue, screaming the cops were close. Then, she'd move the stuff to a new place."

"Did you all choose the spot or her?"

"She did. It was all her idea."

Clytemnestra sat in quiet contemplation as the various points of her case came together in her mind. She smiled gently and said, "She set you three up."

Bobby shot up from his chair, shouting, "What?"

"Think about it. I first connected your operation to the grimoire networks near the Coliseum. A lot of cover there, kept me bogged down for a spell. It probably could've kept me busy for a year or more.

"Then, *out of the blue*, she moved you to Sobrante Park? Plenty of industrial resources exist, including connections to highways and railroads. But wide open, kid, very wide open. You and your friends might as well have put out a billboard for me and my crew to find you. And I did, in no time.

"But then she moved you to Jingletown? Not just Jingletown, but right on the bridge to Alameda? There's nothing in that area to move out the books or get supplies. And she trapped you in a little triangle of traffic where we boxed you in easily. Did she even warn you we were coming?"

His eyes shook in their sockets, and he swallowed dryly. He slowly collapsed onto his chair.

"This witch used you three, then hung you out to dry,"

she said. "Now, was it just for the profits the grimoire brought in or the cultivation of a coven? I will have to answer those questions. First, I need her name. What is it, Bobby?"

He closed his eyes, rocked back and forth slightly, and whispered to himself before speaking. "Kull, I think," he said. "Yeah, because it sounded like 'skull.' She had this name…. It sounded foreign. Are-sin-no-way?"

Suddenly, the door to the interrogation room burst open. Clytemnestra and Bobby looked at it. Rab entered with a twisted grimace of rage. Harriet and the Ghost of Warren G. Harding followed close behind. With both hands, Rab grabbed Bobby by the collar of his tee shirt, pulling him up. "Arsinoe Kull?" she screamed. "Where is she? Where is she, goddamn it!"

Harriet took Rab by the arm, trying to pull her away, "Shit, Rab! What the fuck?"

Clytemnestra held Rab's shoulder, "Rab, look at me," she ordered. She looked up, becoming calm. "Go get some fresh air."

Rab nodded her head, letting go of Bobby. She turned and walked out of the interrogation room. Everyone watched her. Clytemnestra sighed, "Okay, I think that's all. I have enough to work with."

Bobby trembled in his chair, wanting to ask if he earned Clytemnestra's amnesty, but was too petrified to speak.

Harriet, Clytemnestra, and the Ghost of Warren G. Harding stepped onto Seventh Street. The sun was beginning to descend onto the horizon. Rab was standing near Bruiser, a smoldering cigarette between her lips. She saw the trio approach her. "Sorry back there, guys," she said.

"You okay?" Harriet asked.

"I'm gonna need a minute before I'm okay."

"You know this Arsinoe Kull?" Clytemnestra asked.

Rab drew on her cigarette, the ash tip burning longer. She held it over the street curb and tapped the ash free. "I don't, that's the problem."

SAN FRANCISCO TWINKLED BELOW, and cars and buses slowly driving up and down Nob Hill roared all around. Their headlights appeared and disappeared behind buildings and trees before mingling with the rest of the city's nebulous illuminations.

Rab rested her arms on the balustrade of her apartment building's rooftop, her last cigarette burning close to the filter. She looked up to the night sky. Though the stars resisted valiantly against the city's electrical haze, they were barely perceptible. But the crescent moon was bright. The Ghost of Warren G. Harding sat near the rooftop's entrance, his legs up and his arms resting on the knees. "We've been out here a while," he said. "I missed my program."

"I'm sorry," Rab said over her shoulder.

He was taken aback. He thought of all the times Rab had ever apologized to him and was astonished when he realized this was the first time. "Is everything alright, Victoria?"

"Just thinking, Warren."

"You've been awfully withdrawn since we returned from Oakland. You had Ms. June and me concerned. You still do, might I add."

"I know. I really am sorry."

"Do you want to talk about it?"

"I have nothing to say until I put some things together. Trust, Warren, you'll be the first to know, I promise."

The coal of the cigarette burned down to the filter. Rab

mashed it onto the balustrade. She looked at the smeared black ash. The scene came to her again, more vividly than before: Running down the dark, twisting hallway, the screaming everywhere and nowhere – was it real or in her mind? – exiting into the eldritch chamber of some abominable underground structure. The sickening scroll of some extinct cursed language glowed on every inch of the wall. Were they glowing? Johannes Cato had finally reached her; the thickness of the air muted his shouts of warning. Then, a brightness she had never experienced before filled the chamber. Johannes shielded her before being blown off her feet. The brightness dimmed slightly. She was on her back, her gun in her hand, though she doesn't remember pulling it out. Johannes was nowhere to be seen. More screaming. In the center of the chamber was the shadowy visage of a woman. She held something in her hand as she approached closer. Rab drew a bead and pulled the trigger. When she woke up, backup had finally arrived. They were helping her onto a stretcher. An EMT was slipping on an oxygen mask, but she was refusing it. She was screaming. What was she screaming? She thought it was for Johannes, but her memory couldn't support that conclusion. Consciousness evaded her as they wheeled her out of the chamber. Her last thought before succumbing to the veil was of Arsinoe Kull.

Rab breathed in and out to control her racing heart. She turned around and said, "Alright, Warren, let's head in."

"Yes, ma'am."

They were walking down the stairway to Rab's floor when her cell phone rang. It was Lawrence Matt's number. She answered, "What's up, Cap?" Her eyes widened. "What?"

17

A NIGHTMARE ON JONES STREET

A uniform stood in the middle of the Palace Hotel's lobby, the visor of his black baseball cap close to his eyes. When Rab and the Ghost of Warren G. Harding walked through the entrance, he approached them. She noticed his lips were pressed tight, and he looked very pale. He swallowed hard as they were near. "Detective Rabinowski," he croaked out.

"Yeah."

He pointed towards an open utility door near the front desk before swallowing again. "They're waiting for you down there," he managed to say before dry heaving.

"Okay, I need you to get some air," Rab said. "You're no good to us if you're going to be sick all over the place."

He nearly ran to the entrance, forcing open the large bronze doors. Rab sighed deeply. She was losing her patience with this hotel. She and the Ghost of Warren G. Harding went to the utility door and descended the stairs.

They reached a floor landing, where another officer stood near an opened utility door. Her eyes were the two hard beads of a defeated stoic. When Rab showed her badge, she nodded slightly and pointed to where she needed to go, but she said nothing.

Rab didn't recognize this part of the hotel as she walked down the barren cinderblock hallway. A group of officers greeted her and guided her inside of a room. It was dimly lighted, large, and industrial, its walls lined with steel lockers and heavy tables opposite each other. Muted screaming echoed all around. She looked around to locate its source but didn't find it.

Lawrence Matt was huddled with others in the open space between the lockers and tables. "Hey, Cap," Rab said. He turned around quickly. He attempted to smile, but his fear and disgust tempered it. "Glad you made it, Rab," he said.

"Everything alright?"

"No. Not at all. Nothing's alright. We're in a pretty big clusterfuck."

Matt waved her closer, and he and the group parted for her. Rab glanced down. On the floor was a withered thing, almost like a caterpillar's discarded cocoon. She crouched closer to it and nearly jumped away.

It was a human body. Its skin was a brittle, cracking white and gray membrane stretched tightly over delicate bones. The jaw hung open in the obscene parody of a scream. The eyeballs were shriveled gelatinous sacks sunken in gaping eye sockets. A mop of tangled raven black hair was oozing off the skull with the scalp.

"Good lord..." the Ghost of Warren G. Harding gasped.

Rab gathered her courage and returned to the corpse. The clothes were the only part of the cadaver undisturbed. She saw a name tag above the blazer's left breast pocket: *Molly*.

"Shit..." Rab breathed out.

"I've never seen anything like it," Matt said. "In all my years on the force."

"Any witnesses?" Rab asked.

"Can you count her?"

He pointed to a ghostly form standing a short distance from the corpse. It hunched forward, its arms angled and trembling, before bursting into a shuttering scream. Rab went closer and realized that the ghost was Molly.

"We tried talking to her," Matt said. "But all she does is scream."

"Anyone else?"

"A room service lady discovered her. She's in the other room, practically catatonic."

"I bet. Was Molly the only one on duty tonight?"

"Yeah. Slow week for the hotel. She was supposed to have clocked out at seven."

"Did you call Harriet?"

"I sent a whole squad to pick her up."

"Good. Yeah, good. She's gotta look this over." Rab held something back in her mouth. "Oh god..."

"At least there's no smell," Matt said. "Something like this, you'd expect some putrefaction."

"Sure. I guess. It's still something I never want to see ever again."

Someone from the group turned to the utility door. "There she is," he said.

Rab looked over and saw Harriet approach. Her alewife hat tipped back on her head, and her messenger bag was slung over her shoulder. She approached her quickly. "Have you ever seen a body?" Rab asked.

"And good night to you, too," Harriet said.

"Have you?"

"A couple of times in the academy. Why?"

"Just preparing you for what you're about to see."

Harriet approached Molly's corpse and nearly doubled back, her mouth hung open. "What the fuck?" she screamed.

"And that's not just it," Rab said, gesturing to the Ghost of Molly Alay.

Harriet stared at the ghost in complete disbelief. "Is that all she does?" she asked.

"Since we first arrived," Lawrence Matt said.

"Can you get her to talk?" Rab asked her.

"I'm not a necrokinesis expert. I don't know the first thing to do." She turned to the Ghost of Warren G. Harding, "How about you?"

"Me?" he said.

"You two are the same now, Warren. Maybe she'll respond to you."

The Ghost of Warren G. Harding held his head high as if understanding his importance. "Give me a moment with Ms. Alay," he said, then moved to her.

While the Ghost of Warren G. Harding attempted to talk to the Ghost of Molly Alay, Harriet pulled out her silver tuning fork from her messenger bag and held it over the corpse. She concentrated on it, chanting quietly to herself. Her eyes were wide, and sweat beads grew on her forehead. The chanting stopped. She stared at the fork with a mesmerizing intensity. Her lips moved slowly as if enunciating each syllable of a word. Rab was astonished by the quick evolution of her demeanor. Harriet broke from her trance. "I can feel it," she said slowly.

"The magic?" Rab said.

"Yeah. It's very dark, very ancient."

"How can you tell?"

"It feels like the thirst of dying gods."

"Oh. That it?"

"I can follow it. I can lead us back to where it started!"

She turned and ran out of the room. Rab yelled at the Ghost of Warren G. Harding, "Anything from her?"

"She won't talk to me!" he answered. "All she does is this caterwauling!"

"Never mind then, come on!"

Rab drove Bruiser slowly down Market Street, looking to Harriet occasionally in the passenger seat as she held the silver tuning fork out of the open window. She brushed it through the air like a painter on a canvas. Then, she shouted enthusiastically and pointed to a direction for Rab to go. She turned on the car's flashers and roared down the street.

They parked in front of an apartment building on Jones Street near Lombard. It was a three-story Italianate structure, with exterior stairways leading to the two wings of apartments, wrapped with floral iron railings and white Corinthian columns. Its darkened bay windows stared out toward the street.

Harriet stepped out of Bruiser, stood in the middle of the sidewalk, and held up her fork. "It's here," she said. "This is where the root of that magic is planted."

Rab stood beside her, looking at the building, "Is it dangerous?"

"I don't think so. Not anymore. It's growing weaker every second."

Rab pulled out her gun, "Alright then, let's hit it."

They ran up the stairs, with Harriet leading the way. She stopped Rab and the Ghost of Warren G. Harding on the third-floor landing, pointing to a door on her right. She held the silver tuning fork at an angle like she was casting a fishing line. They approached the door of apartment 3.

Harriet stood close to it, touching the tines of the fork against the wood. "Here," she said.

Rab went up to the door and slammed it four times. "SFPD," she shouted. "Is anyone inside?"

Silence.

She tried the doorknob. It turned with ease, and the door opened slightly. She peered through the crack. There was darkness and nothing more. "SFPD!"

Rab holstered her gun and pushed the door open further. "Hold on, Rab!" Harriet said. "Don't we need a warrant?"

"Not if we have probable cause to go inside."

"Do we?"

Rab pointed to the silver tuning fork in Harriet's hand. "Isn't that cause enough?"

"The law is very vague when it comes to magic, especially when it comes to the Fourth Amendment."

"Well, if we get in trouble, I'll take the fall."

They entered the tenebrous apartment. A faint, unnerving odor permeated the air. Rab found a switch on the nearby wall and turned on a light.

It was a small, crowded one-bedroom. Two scuffed and worn faux leather Pottery Barn chairs, gray and tan, and a large coffee table dominated the living room. A crowded bookshelf stood flushed to a corner. Past the living room was a tiny ill-lighted kitchen. Harriet approached the archway separating the two rooms and stopped. "Rab," she called. "You better take a look at this."

She and the Ghost of Warren G. Harding went to her. She whispered, "Oh... fuck."

A body was crumbled on the floor, the arms and legs crooked at different angles. It was surrounded by a pool of dark, congealed blood, a large, jagged, oozing stab wound on the side of the neck. The kitchen knife was still clutched in its hand. Thick, curly red hair obscured the face. Harriet flipped on the overhead light as Rab crouched down and turned the body over. Elyria True's lifeless golden eyes peered toward oblivion. "Well," Rab muttered, then looked up at Harriet, "our night keeps getting fucking better, doesn't it?"

18

LOVERS' SPAT?

The scene was quickly secured after Rab's call. Harriet scoured the apartment with other officers, documenting anything of interest. The Ghost of Warren G. Harding sat near the edge of the pool of blood, staring at it hungrily. Rab stood with Lawrence Matt in the kitchen as EMTs carried Elyria's corpse out. He looked on silently as the body bag disappeared past the front door. "What are the odds?" he said. "Two witches on the same night?"

"You're being sarcastic, right?" Rab said.

Matt looked at her sternly before sighing. "The hotel's management is flipping out," he said.

"I bet. It's just worse news on top of bad news. How could they recover from all of this?"

"They will. Everyone forgets that a murder happened after a while. Hell, ghouls might want to stay in that place because Alay's haunting it."

Rab looked around. "That's weird," she said.

"What?"

"Where's Elyria's ghost?"

Lawrence Matt joined her in looking around. "Yeah. Where is she?"

Rab stopped searching and leaned against the kitchen counter, studying the floor. "I didn't see any defensive wounds on Elyria's arms or hands," she said. "Just that huge gaping one on her neck."

"What are you thinking?" Matt asked.

She mimicked holding up a knife to her neck. "The blade was upside down in her hand like she grabbed it in a hurry."

"To do what?"

"Plunging it in herself."

"Suicide?"

"It's the only thing that makes sense."

The Ghost of Warren G. Harding stood up, "The poor girl. Why would she want to do that? And so violently an act?"

"That's what we need to find out, Warren."

"Hey, Rab, Captain Matt," Harriet called. "Come see this."

They found her standing by the bathroom near the front door. She pointed inside. Blown-out candles surrounded the bathtub. Inside the tub were the remains of a dust-like mixture. It was dark brown, nearly black. "What is it?" Rab asked.

"The root of the magic we ran into at the Palace. It started from there," Harriet said.

She pulled a glass vial from her messenger bag and collected a small amount of the mixture. She then asked the documenting officer to photograph the bathtub.

"That small pile caused that much havoc?" Lawrence Matt said.

"Magic is all about quality, not quantity," Harriet said.

"What kind of magic came from it then?"

"No idea. But it's a real killer."

Rab squinted at the bathtub, "Could Elyria True have created it?"

"It's very possible," Harriet said. "There are no signs of anyone else being here."

"Why would she want to kill Molly Alay, though?" Matt asked. "What was her beef?"

Harriet cleared her throat. "There is something that might provide a motive," she said. "Follow me."

She led Rab and Matt to the bedroom. On the dresser, surrounding an ugly antique porcelain doll with one right glass eye, stood framed intimate photographs of Elyria and Molly. "They were girlfriends?" Rab said.

"It looks that way," Harriet said.

"Lovers' spat?" Matt asked.

"It's possible."

Harriet called in the documenting officer to take pictures of the bedroom, and the two detectives and the ghost left the apartment and went outside.

Police and other emergency vehicles were parked haphazardly, their flashers bathing the neighborhood in vibrant hues. A crowd of civilians stood behind the police barricade, hoping to catch a glimpse of a clue as to what happened in the apartment building on Jones Street. Rab was exhausted. Harriet sat on the street curb, removing her alewife hat, and set it next to her. She supported her chin on the palms of her hands.

"So, Elyria killed Molly. That much can be said," Rab said.

"Yeah," Harriet said, "but something doesn't make sense."

"What?"

"If Elyria is our murderer, why didn't the Winooski Protocol activate? That would've stopped her before she cast her magic. It might've saved Molly."

"Hm."

"And there's the why? Why would Elyria kill Molly? There didn't seem to be any hostility between them when we spoke to those three. And Elyria didn't mention anything to me."

"We should talk to Collinson," Rab said firmly. "Maybe he has the scuttlebutt."

"That's if he's still alive."

"Hope springs eternal, buddy." Rab dialed a number on her cell phone. "Yeah, I need Tad Collinson's address, pronto. Yeah, it's about the murder." She waited.

"Who did you call?" Harriet asked.

"The night desk. Gregarian told them to assist us in any way." Rab spun around, "Yeah, I'm here. Where? Okay, thanks." She hung up and pulled out her car keys, "Alright, Harriet, Warren, load up. We're heading to the Avenues."

THEY DROVE down Geary Boulevard to the Richmond District, pulling onto Tenth Avenue. Rab parked Bruiser in front of an old dingbat, stretching out to see the building number. "That's it," she said.

"What apartment?" Harriet asked.

"Two. Very simple."

"Should you have permission to speak with Mr. Collinson?" the Ghost of Warren G. Harding asked from the backseat. "Perhaps he has an attorney. My friends from Ohio always lectured about the importance of an attorney's permission to speak with a client."

"We're working a murder investigation, Warren," Rab said. "He has to talk to us."

"Especially since the victims were his colleagues," Harriet said.

They stepped out of the car and headed to the apartment. Harriet knocked on the door. Someone called out, "In a minute!" The door flung open, and a young man in a faded Santa Cruz tee shirt and yellow shorts with palm tree silhouettes running down the legs stood before them. His eyelids drooped, and he had a stupefied smirk on his face. The smell of bad, skunky weed wafted behind him. He leaned against the door frame, "Well, hello, ladies," he drawled in a parody of seduction, "to what do I owe *this* pleasure?"

Rab and Harriet held up their badges. The young man's smirk vanished instantly, and his red-tinged eyes widened as best they could. He backed away slightly, holding up his hands, "Hey, now! Wow! Are those real?"

"Back up, boy. Now," Rab commanded. When he did, she motioned for Harriet and the Ghost of Warren G. Harding to follow her inside.

The living room was nothing more than a gathering of decrepit, mismatched furniture vying for space. However, the entertainment center, taking over nearly the length of a wall, was state of the art: a large, gleaming, black aluminum console with a ninety-eight-inch Samsung plasma flatscreen and four different video game systems, each expertly installed in their racks. It loomed over the space like a technological Baphomet.

Rab and Harriet examined the scene. There were four sloven men, each no older than their middle twenties. They stared at the detectives with wide, trembling eyes. Harriet saw two glass bongs surrounded by numerous PBR empties on the coffee table. She looked up at the man in the Santa Cruz tee shirt. He pointed to them, "Hey, that's legal, man!"

"No one's gonna hassle you for that," Rab said.

"Then, what do you want?"

"Tad Collinson," Harriet said. "He lives here, yes?"

"Tad? Yeah, yeah! He does!"

"Where?"

Santa Cruz guided the detectives and the ghost down a small hall to a bedroom at the end. He pushed open the door. The room was dark. "Is he in trouble?" he asked.

"Is there any reason to believe he would be?" Rab asked.

He quickly answered, "No, not at all. He mostly keeps to himself, you know?"

Harriet turned on a light. The room was clean but sparse: a single queen-size bed, a small desk with a laptop, and a simple particleboard dresser. She walked around and inspected everything. Rab asked Santa Cruz, "How do you know Tad Collinson?"

"He's my roommate."

"And your name?"

"Don't I need a lawyer?"

"I don't know. Were you involved in tonight's deaths?"

Santa Cruz's mouth hung open, panic washing over his face. Rab could see his heart pounding through his shirt. "Deaths?" he croaked out.

"His co-workers were found dead not long ago. So, name?"

"Dennis! Dennis Mulcavany!"

"Are you a witch, Dennis Mulcavany?"

"What? Oh, god, no! I can't stand magic!"

Harriet turned to him with an evil glare.

"I mean, I have nothing against those who do it, you know?"

"Where is Tad?" Rab continued.

"He told me he was going to Oregon to visit family in Portland."

"When was that?"

"Last night."

"Last night? Did he tell you about it earlier?"

"No. It was like all of a sudden. He just said he was going on a trip and left, which was weird. He never goes anywhere, and he hates flying."

Rab saw Harriet standing near the dresser out of the corner of her eye. She picked something up from it and studied it closely. "What do you have there?" Rab asked. Harriet held up the object. It was an old, ugly porcelain doll with a missing left glass eye. "That looks familiar."

"I saw this one's sister," Harriet said. "Back in Elyria's apartment."

Rab leaned against the door frame. "Coincidence?"

"I don't know. Could be." Harriet pulled out her silver tuning fork and held it against the doll's head. "No magic." She stared at the doll in her hand, then whispered to herself, "What are the odds of them having the same doll?"

19

DESANGUIS, THEY CALL IT

Back in her home, Harriet worked on the sample from Elyria's bathtub until three in the morning. But no matter what method she used, the results were the same: inconclusive. The elements were too burnt up. The only thing she had left was a chemical analysis of Elyria's hands. Harriet requested that the medical examiner run tests as soon as possible. With that done, she threw herself into her living room chair and stared out.

The sameness of her place, with its dim lights, plants, and Ditzy snoring away in her bed, plucked annoyingly at her nerves. Nothing had changed except the complications. She felt the twin weights of her exhaustion and frustration. All the pieces of her cases were there, she thought, but how was she going to bring them together? That was eluding her. She looked up at the clock on the wall and decided to get a few hours of rest.

Her phone buzzed nearby. Ditzy whined gently and trembled in her bed, her ears up, staring at her. Harriet gritted her teeth hard and answered.

"Hello?"

"Is this Detective June?" The caller's voice was melodious, almost hypnotic.

"Yes, who's this?"

"Sorry, my name is Crystalina Alba. I'm the forensic witch at the Southeast precinct. I hope I didn't wake you."

"Oh, no. No! I was up already. How can I help you, Detective Alba?"

"Crystalina is fine. I heard there was a murder at the Palace Hotel tonight, and you are working the case."

"That's right."

"I also heard some very strange rumors about your victim. Would you mind terribly describing the state of the body?"

Harriet described Molly Alay's corpse thoroughly, not sparing any detail. When she was done, Crystalina hummed nonchalantly. "That sounds exactly like the victim in my case," she said.

Harriet leaned forward in her chair, "I'm sorry?"

"I'm on a murder case as well. My victim was discovered in a similar state."

"How long were you working the case?"

"About close to a month, I'd say."

"Any progress?"

"Very little, unfortunately. I have some bits here and there but nothing concrete."

"Did you figure out what it was? What magic was used?"

"Yes. It's a curse called Desanguis."

"Desanguis," Harriet whispered. "I've never heard of it."

"I had to scour every reference book I could find to find it. Even when I did, very little was written about it. Either it's a very rare curse or so diabolical that no one wants to touch it."

"'Diabolical' doesn't begin to describe what I saw."

"It is very nasty."

"Who was your victim, Crystalina?"

"Theo De Lyon. A kindly old man, as described by his neighbors."

"And I take it no one could guess why anyone would want to murder him, huh?"

"Not the faintest clue. He was a community leader, a generous donor to his church, and a good Samaritan for the unhoused. No one had a bad thing to say about him."

Harriet thought for a moment. "Do you have time to come to headquarters in the morning?" she asked. "Maybe you can share your notes with me?"

"Absolutely, Ms. June. I'll come around first thing."

RAB and the Ghost of Warren G. Harding entered the headquarters building and went to their floor. They saw Harriet standing at her desk with a strange-looking woman. She was thin, in her mid-to-late forties, and wearing a long, multi-colored dress. A wide leather belt with a pouch wrapped around her hips. A small magnifying glass attached to a silver chain dangled around her neck. Her silvery-blond hair was tied underneath a plain wool scarf. "I didn't know we were expecting visitors," Rab said.

Harriet and the woman turned around. Her dark brown eyes were large and friendly. "Morning, Rab," Harriet said, "this is Sergeant Crystalina Alba from Southeast. Crystalina, this is my partner, Rab Rabinowski."

Crystalina held her hands up to her mouth, "Sergeant Rabinowski, I've heard of you!"

"Hopefully good things," Rab said, giving her a look.

At this, Crystalina didn't say anything, and Rab appreciated it. She noticed large photographs spread out on top of Harriet's desk, "What are these?"

"Crystalina is working a murder case similar to Molly's," Harriet said. "She's catching me up to speed."

"No shit!"

"The victim's name was Theo De Lyon. The state of the corpse was the same."

Rab looked up to Crystalina Alba. "Any idea what got them?"

"Yes," she said. "It's a curse called Desanguis. It's exsanguination magic."

"Molly and De Lyon were bled to death?"

"In the worst possible way. The magic forces blood and every vital fluid out of the victim's body in a very drawn-out process. Some chroniclers call it an execution, others torture. Most use both terms to describe it."

"Jesus Christ," Rab said, sliding a picture closer to her. The corpse of Theo De Lyon was on the floor of an elegant living room. It was pale and withered, just like Molly Alay. His ghost stood hunched in a corner, his eyes glowing fiendishly, and his mouth distorted by a scream. Above the ghost, Rab noticed something. "Wait a minute. Harriet, doesn't this person look familiar?" She held up the photograph, pointing to a large, framed picture. Harriet saw De Lyon dressed in a suit, standing by a young woman in a billowing *Quinceanera* dress. She recognized her.

"She's that front desk girl," Harriet said. "When we first interviewed the staff witches."

Crystalina nodded, "Yes, Monica Benavidez. She's Mr. De Lyon's niece."

Rab, Harriet, and the Ghost of Warren G. Harding stared at her. "His niece?" he said.

"Yes. I interviewed her. She was the one who reported his death."

"What's your take on her?" Harriet asked.

"Forceful. She loves taking charge of a conversation."

"Any magical abilities?"

"Not at all. She's as *homme* as can be."

Rab was confused, "I'm sorry, *homme*?"

"It's where we get 'hump' from," Harriet said. "Non-witches were called *homme* by the covens back in the day to distinguish their mortality."

"Oh. Kind of sexist, isn't it?"

Harriet shrugged. "Everything is sexist when you break it down to its components." She looked to Crystalina, "What about Mr. De Lyon? Any magical abilities?"

"Same with his niece. There is no magic in that family whatsoever."

"Was there anything that tipped you off that something was wrong with Mr. De Lyon?"

Crystalina shook her head. "Everything was in order. There were no major debts, contracts with witches, or broken promises. Other than an anonymous complaint filed with the department."

"What was the complaint about?"

"I'm not sure. Mr. De Lyon was cleared almost immediately, and the case closed with an apology."

"Yet, someone hit him with Desanguis. Why?"

Crystalina shrugged. "After a month's worth of work, I have no answers. That's why I called you when I heard about the Palace murder. I was hoping you two found a clue that might help me."

"Did you tell Crystalina about that substance in Elyria's bathtub, Harriet?" Rab asked.

"I did," she said. "We're both waiting for the chemical analysis of her hands. It might be something."

Rab was thinking, "Monica and Elyria worked together. Did Monica mention any beef with the people she worked with, Crystalina?"

"She didn't mention anything of that sort."

"You're thinking that Elyria killed De Lyon?" Harriet asked Rab.

"It's an idea. You connected her to Molly's death. She and De Lyon died the same way. Why couldn't Elyria have offed De Lyon?"

"Other than they worked together, what connection do Elyria and Monica have? And why kill her uncle? Why go to that extreme when a simple jinx could've done the trick?"

"And there's that Vermonter curse," said the Ghost of Warren G. Harding.

"Yeah. That's still bothering me."

"Vermonter curse?" Crystalina Alba asked.

Harriet explained the Winooski Protocol and how it was placed on the staff witches. Crystalina's brows furled deeper. "What a disgusting thing! And to place that on your employees," she exclaimed.

"Illegally hired employees on top of that," Harriet said. "They have no recourses against management. No protections. They'd be punished no matter what."

"All we have are more questions and not enough answers," Rab said. "We should talk to Mr. Gregarian again. At this point, he has to stop slow-rolling us."

~

MR. GREGARIAN SAT SULLENLY in his office when the two detectives and the ghost entered. He looked up at them, smiled briefly, and turned away. Harriet noticed a glass tumbler with a small amount of amber liquid on his desk. "The owners were all over me since last night," he slurred. "It's been calls on the hour, every hour. Like damned harpies! What are you doing to recover the cup; what are you doing to assure the Bacchae? And now the murder?" He scoffed. "They're closing the hotel until it's solved. We're losing hundreds of thousands in refunds!" He turned in his chair to the detectives, "Please tell me you have something to go on."

Harriet stepped forward, "We're working on something right now. It's a potential clue."

"Good, that's good."

"I have a few questions if you don't mind."

Mr. Gregarian shrugged his shoulders, "Shoot."

"You have a desk clerk, Monica Benavidez. You know her?"

"I do. She is a very capable employee."

"How is she like with other staff members? Any complaints?"

He thought for a moment before answering, "Some complaints. She's too bossy, too assertive. It was mostly from the male side of the staff, mind you."

"How about the women on staff? Did they have complaints about her?"

He shook his head, "Absolutely not. Monica had a lot of girlfriends."

"What about Molly or Elyria? Were they friends?"

"I can't say they were. Cordial, maybe? There was no hostility, though." He furled his brows, "Why?"

"Do you know what killed Molly Alay, Mr. Gregarian?"

"No one's telling me anything. All I was told was she was hit with some curse."

Harriet explained Desanguis and what they discovered at Elyria's apartment. He didn't recoil, but his eyes betrayed his horror. "My god... And you're saying... El used that... *curse*... to butcher Molly?"

"That's what it looks like," Rab said. The Ghost of Warren G. Harding nodded vigorously.

"But... why? They were in love, for crying out loud!"

"So, you knew about their relationship?"

"Everyone did. It was a huge open secret!"

Harriet continued, "The Southeast Precinct informed us of another Desanguis murder in their area. The victim's name was Theo De Lyon. He was Monica's uncle."

Mr. Gregarian sat back in his chair, staring at her in disbelief. "Her *uncle*?"

"She never mentioned it?"

"Monica never said anything about her family. I sometimes wondered if she was an orphan or something. When was this?"

"Over a month ago."

He started shaking his head, "No, she never mentioned a death in the family. And to lose someone... like that! God, if I lost someone I love like that, I'd be destroyed!"

"Could we talk to Monica? Is she on duty?"

Mr. Gregarian slumped over his desk, cradling the glass tumbler. "I wish you could, but she just submitted her resignation and left in a hurry. I've been losing a lot of staff because of what's going on here."

Harriet and Rab looked at each other. "We found out that Tad Collinson left for Portland recently," Rab said. "Do you know when he'll be back?"

He stared up at her, "Collinson put in his notice yesterday morning."

"He quit?"

"Yeah. It was a bitch and a half terminating the Winooski Protocol over him."

Harriet asked Mr. Gregarian, "How familiar are you with the Winooski Protocol?"

He shrugged, "I'm just a normal guy. What do I know?"

"You know enough about how it activates, do you?"

"Just a bit. Mostly to warn people. Why?"

"The protocol should've activated when Elyria was about to murder Molly. But it didn't. Do you have any idea why?"

Mr. Gregarian shook his head slowly. His Adam's apple bobbed before he said, "I can't help you there. I'm sorry."

Rab took Harriet aside, leaning close to whisper, "I think we need to split up to cover ground. You find Monica and get her to talk. I'll start digging for Collinson's trail. Sounds good?"

Harriet nodded. "Can I have Monica Benavidez's home address, Mr. Gregarian?" she asked.

HARRIET TOOK a taxi to the intersection of Leavenworth and Turk, stopping in front of an SRO. It was a haunted-looking early twentieth-century building of brown brick, with weathered Grecian-style window boxes and an ancient neon sign advertising itself as a hotel above a corner liquor store. She exited the car, paid the driver, and headed to the entrance, pressing the buzzer to be let in. In the lobby, she met with the building manager, a grizzled man in his late sixties. He was paunchy, with a pockmark nose and faded obscene tattoos on his forearms. He studied her up and down, scowling in confusion. "Can I help ya?" he asked.

She showed her badge, and he morphed instantly in understanding. "Ah! That figures. Who's it this time?"

"Does Monica Benavidez live here?" Harriet asked.

"Who?"

She described Monica to the building manager, who nodded rhythmically. He snapped his fingers, "Oh yeah, the hot piece. I remember her."

"So, she does live here?"

"Her and her old man. Follow me."

The building manager led Harriet to his back office – a small, claustrophobic, ill-lighted room no bigger than a janitor's closet. He opened a small cabinet and brought out a black ledger book. He opened it and ran his finger down the lines. "Eh, yeah," he muttered. "Room 201, Edward and Monica Cedillo."

"Cedillo?" she whispered to herself. "Not Benavidez?"

He shook his head slowly. "That's how she signed in."

"Okay. Is it alright for me to go up? I want to speak with Monica if she's there."

"Sure, be my guest. Cause some trouble while you're up there. They've been late on rent a lot lately. I'll take any excuse to kick 'em out."

Harriet started her ascent up the stairs to the second floor. She found the door to 201 and knocked on it. There was no answer. Suddenly, she shivered. Memories of last night crawled and oozed through her thoughts. She swallowed and tried the doorknob. It was unlocked. The door opened a little. Harriet pushed it and went inside.

The room was simple: a full-size bed pushed against the farthest wall, a tiny sink and a hot plate underneath a curtained window overlooking Turk Street, and a couple of office chairs surrounding a table with a silver laptop. Nothing was out of the ordinary, the room undisturbed, the humid air languid. Yet Harriet felt a tremendous unease. Her instincts were sensitive, almost hair-triggered. She pulled out her silver tuning fork and concentrated on it, chanting the invocations quietly. The hook reverberated unperceptively; slight palpitations coursed down the tines into her hand, each wave a sensation of knowledge.

Magic was in the room, she knew. Harriet went into the bathroom. Nothing. She searched under the bed. Dust bunnies. She threw open the closet, finding men's shirts and trousers hanging on flimsy wire hangers and little else. Harriet wheeled around; all evidence pointed to the room being clean. But the silver tuning fork was never wrong. She returned to the closet. A large black plastic roll-away suitcase was hidden behind a garbage bag filled with laundry. It was newly purchased; the Ross price tag was still attached to the handle. She moved the garbage bag aside and held the tuning fork above the suitcase. It reacted gently. Harriet took hold of the handle and pulled it out, setting it down on the floor. She pulled open the zippers and threw the lid open. She gasped, falling on the floor, and skittered back. A grey mummy sat inside in the fetal position.

20

THE CHASE'S ON

"I've been workin' the building for years," the building manager said. "Never had no trouble. Maybe a few drug-related issues, some fights. But not out-and-out murder!"

Rab was jotting down relevant information in her notebook. When Harriet reported the mummy, she broke away from locating Tad Collinson and sped to the SRO on Turk Street and Leavenworth. Rab held open the wallet found with the mummy in the suitcase, looking at the driver's license: Edward Cedillo, aged 32.

"How would you describe Edward Cedillo?" she asked.

"He was a good guy overall. Hell, he helped some of our wheelchair-bound folks use the stairs when the elevator went out a while ago, and the owners dragged ass to fix it. Did he have his problems? Yeah." The building manager gestured at the hotel's façade. "But who here doesn't?"

"What about his wife, Monica?"

"Eh, I didn't get to know her much. But she always had this sour puss face every time she walked into the lobby, like she was better than us, ya know?"

"Can you recall any suspicious-looking people paying him or her a visit?"

He shook his head. "None. Look, officer, everyone here is tryin' to live as right as they can. They don't want no trouble-makers around."

"Did they pay for their room with a credit card? Or cash?"

"Cash. What little they had."

"Of course. Okay. Thanks."

Medical examiner technicians were hauling the suit-case out of the hotel and into a van. Uniforms and their squad cars held a perimeter around the block. Rab walked to Bruiser parked across the street. Harriet was in the passenger seat with her laptop open, scrolling furiously, while the Ghost of Warren G. Harding leaned over her shoulder from the backseat, mesmerized. Rab entered the driver seat, lowered the window, and lighted a fresh cigarette. She turned to Harriet. The pupils of her eyes flashed and glimmered as she read through the screen.

"You've been busy since I got here," Rab said.

"Hm," Harriet responded.

"You okay?"

She broke from her laptop, blinking vigorously. "Something came to me when I reported Cedillo's corpse—a few things, actually."

"Like what?"

"Remember what you said when we were with the staff witches: *cui bono*? Who benefits?"

Rab took a slow drag off her cigarette. "Yeah, I remember that."

"Who benefits from all this, Rab? Who's the one person that'll get something from these deaths?"

"Monica Benavidez. Her uncle and her husband are no longer in the picture. For what, we don't know yet."

"For sure. But she's not the only one."

Rab was still looking at Harriet, crossing her arms out of reflex. "Well, don't leave me in suspense, buddy," she said.

"I called the medical examiner's office when you were talking to the building manager. They have a draft chemical analysis report on Elyria True's hands. They were coated with all kinds of herbs and roots. But one thing came up that caught my attention: Ariesian war water."

"What is it?"

"It's a highly potent substance, very volatile, and very dangerous. Especially when used in any kind of offensive magic. Because of that, it's very rarely used. But I remember running into a spell in the *Leabhar Cogaidh* that requires it, a whole lot of it." Harriet tapped the laptop. "It's called *Caraid Sgiath a' Bhais*. The commentary vaguely says it is a curse that can be used on enemies from a long distance. I just never figured out what that meant until now."

"So, it's Desanguis."

"Exactly! It's the Scottish version of it. Much more refined and much more brutal."

Rab thought to herself, flicking the spent cigarette from the window. "Okay, Monica benefits from these deaths. Elyria True pulled the trigger to make them happen. But I don't get why she did it. What does True get out of murdering our victims?"

"Nothing. But that's not the question. I don't think she was conscious of what was happening."

Rab was shocked. "How so?"

"Do you remember what we removed from Elyria's apartment when we found her last night?"

"A few things. Obviously, I don't have the evidence catalog on me."

"What was the one thing that wasn't found?"

Rab grew frustrated, gripping the steering wheel tightly. "Look, Harriet, if we're going to work together for the long run, you can't keep doing this! This... riddle-me-this shit!"

"She used Desanguis on Molly. This very version of it. But where was her copy of the *Leabhar Cogaidh*?"

It took Rab a moment to answer, "There wasn't one..."

"It's such a delicate, complicated spell that no one can remember all the alchemical and ritualistic steps. Even a witch as good as Elyria. One fuck-up can ruin the whole thing. She had help, a lot of it. And I don't believe it was voluntary."

"Involuntary help?"

Harriet opened the laptop and scrolled down the *Leabhar Cogaidh,* stopping at an indecipherable chapter. "There is one thing Elyria had that can connect her to these deaths," she said. "The doll."

"The doll? That ugly-ass doll?"

"Yup!" She pointed to the screen. "The *personae*. Basically, it's a spell that allows a witch to subsume into another person's consciousness, with two talismans acting as the connecting bridge."

Rab's mouth hung open, realization creeping over her face. "The doll's sister! Collinson!"

"Collinson was controlling Elyria! He used her to kill De Lyon, Cedillo, and Molly before having her use a knife on herself."

The Ghost of Warren G. Harding made a sound close to clearing a throat, though ghastly. "One thing stops me from celebrating this conclusion, ladies. It is very intelligently done, Ms. June. But there's still that Vermonter curse. What of that?"

Rab sighed, "Warren's right. For Molly and Elyria, sure, I can buy it. He had the protocol taken off him. But what pins him to De Lyon and Cedillo?"

"Maybe Benavidez and Collinson were working together?" Harriet said.

"That's a big maybe. But we've got enough for a warrant." Rab started Bruiser, then picked up her radio. "Ortiz, I need Captain Matt to put out an APB to all departments for Tad Collinson and Monica Benavidez, nee Cedillo. They are persons of interest in four counts of murder. You got that?"

"*Got it, Sergeant.*"

DENNIS MULCAVANY WAS PLAYING A VISUALLY and auditorily stunning first-person shooter when he heard his doorbell ring. Cursing to himself, he paused the game, got up from the heavily indented loveseat he had picked up for free on Craig's List, and slouched towards the front door and opened it. He stared wide-eyed at Harriet, Rab, and the squad of police officers behind them. "Oh Christ..." he muttered.

Rab shoved a small packet of papers into his hand, then walked into the apartment, followed by Harriet and the Ghost of Warren G. Harding. "Sober enough now?" Rab said.

"Look, man, I don't know what's going on with..." Mulcavany started.

"You know where Tad Collinson is?" Harriet asked.

"Dude! Like I told you last night, he's visiting family in Portland!"

"About that," Rab said, "TSA has no record of him boarding any flights in SFO, Oakland, or any other airport. And there are no ticket purchases on his bank records."

Mulcavany's Adam's apple lolled violently, his eyes stricken with panic. "I... I..." he sputtered.

"You don't know. That's fine. What you have in your hand is a warrant to search your domicile. You can either hang back outside or stay here and observe. But you cannot interfere. Got it?"

"Sure." He leafed through the packet. "What's this about?"

"Your roommate is a potential suspect in a double homicide," Harriet said. "Possibly quadruple."

Mulcavany collapsed onto his loveseat, staring at nothing. "Homicide?"

Rab ordered the uniforms to scour the apartment. They rushed in and started their work. Harriet stood near Mulcavany, "Have you heard of Monica Benavidez?" she asked him.

He blinked. "Monica... Ah, maybe."

"It's important, Dennis. Please concentrate, remember. Has Tad ever mentioned her in the past?"

He smacked his lips absent-mindedly, then shut his eyelids hard. "There was a girl he mentioned. Said they were dating. I didn't take it seriously."

"Why?"

"If you knew Tad like I do, you'd know he was full of shit. Tad is such a true virgin! Nothing about him shouts, 'game with the ladies.' I thought he was making it up because..."

"Because?"

"I mean, look, we have fun here! We make jokes about each other all the time!"

"How often did he reciprocate these jokes?"

He didn't retort back. Instead, he slumped forward and cupped his face in his hands. The uniforms were carrying boxes of things from Collinson's room. Rab and the Ghost of Warren G. Harding followed them. She had two items in her hands, holding them up for Harriet. "Got the doll," she said, "and look what I found." She held up a plain brown book.

"*Leabhar Cogaidh*?" Harriet asked.

"The original Jackson copied from by the looks of it."

She glared at the book, "He abandoned it? Why?"

When they returned to headquarters, Harriet experimented with the dolls from Elyria's and Collinson's apartments using the copy of the *Leabhar Cogaidh* found in the latter. She tested the *personae* ritual. The dolls transformed into talismans, their intact eyes glowing a malevolent purple. Harriet recorded the vibrations of the spell passing through the dolls, indicating they were well-grooved with the magic. She met up with Rab and Lawrence Matt in a conference room afterward, reporting her findings. Matt sighed, "So, that's it, then. Tad Collinson is our guy."

"For Alay and True," Harriet said. "Until we have more evidence, I can't say for certain about De Lyon and Cedillo."

"Did you let Crystalina know?" Rab asked.

"She was the first one I spoke with before coming here. She's digging further."

Rab asked Lawrence Matt, "Any luck on the APB?"

"Got a few things," he said. "A couple of photos of them at a rental lot in San Mateo, driving off in a black BMW. I gave CHP the plate numbers. They're on the lookout."

"They were together?" Harriet asked.

"Yup. The most awkward couple I've ever seen."

"Did she seem distressed?"

"No idea. She was in a baseball cap and sunglasses, constantly looking down."

"I'm assuming they used fake names and everything, yeah?" Rab asked.

"They did," Matt answered. "But used a credit card connected to De Lyon."

"That's gutsy."

"And stupid. But they're not thinking. That card was shut down after they got their car. They're now reliant on whatever cash they're carrying. And those beemers drink up fuel. I don't think they're going far."

There was a knock on the conference room door. Lawrence Matt called on the visitor to enter. An officer poked his head in. "Detectives," he said. "You have a call on line two."

"Connect it here," Rab said.

"Will do."

After a couple of minutes, the conference room phone started to ring. Rab punched in the call. "This is Rabinowski."

"*You sound so official, Rab!*" Clytemnestra Rose's voice sounded light and chipper. Rab smirked. "What's going on, Metra?"

"*My CO just caught me up on the APB y'all issued. Is it true that you're looking for Monica Benavidez?*"

Harriet and Rab looked up at each other. "Yeah," Harriet said. "Do you know her, Miss Rose?"

"*I wouldn't say intimately,*" Clytemnestra said. "*But I know her cousin well—very well.*"

"You do?"

"*Let's say we have history.*"

"Where are they?"

"Same place we left him last. Would you like to come and talk to him? He might have something that'll be interesting."

THE COUNTY JAIL at Santa Rita was a cacophonous maze of cells, hallways, and rooms without a solitary space of peace. Rab, Harriet, and the Ghost of Warren G. Harding were escorted through the atmospheric din by a surly deputy sheriff to an isolated wing of the jail.

They entered a large, windowless, solid gray room with two doors on opposite sides. Clytemnestra Rose sat with a laptop at a circular table underneath two rows of fluorescent lights. When the deputy sheriff closed the door, the room became so silent that the sound of electricity feeding the lights could be heard perfectly. Clytemnestra stood up, smiling. "I hope the drive wasn't too bad," she said.

Rab shook her head, "Not at all."

Clytemnestra pointed to the chairs at the table, and the detectives sat down. The Ghost of Warren G. Harding stood nearby in a corner. "He should be coming soon," she said. "I said we'd meet up at one."

Harriet looked at her watch. "Who are we meeting?" she asked.

Just then, the door opposite of them opened. Tiny McDaniel, clad in an orange jumpsuit and restraints, was escorted inside by two deputy sheriffs. They brought him to the table, pulled out a chair, and sat him down before disappearing to where they came. Tiny kept his gaze down, not meeting anyone's eyes.

"You're Monica's cousin?" Harriet blurted out.

He didn't respond but gestured positively.

"How're you doing, Tiny?" Clytemnestra asked. "Got everything you need?"

Again, he didn't say anything.

"Okay, let's get started," she said, pulling out a recording device and starting it. She began by identifying the detectives present, the date, and the time. "State your name and relation to the Monica Benavidez."

"Arturo Benavidez-McDaniel," he said in a low voice, "I'm cousins with Monnie."

"That's Monica Benavidez?"

He nodded.

"I need you to say it out loud, Tiny."

"Yeah. Monica Benavidez. She's my cousin."

"You agreed to talk to us about her voluntarily?"

"Yeah. What can I say? I don't want to get in any more trouble than I'm already in."

"Monica Benavidez is implicated in several murders," Harriet said. "Did she ever mention any plans she was involved in to you?"

Tiny McDaniel leaned against the table, putting his weight on his outstretched arms. He cleared his throat, "I wasn't aware of nothing. She didn't clue me in on nothing she was doing."

Clytemnestra Rose opened the laptop and started a video. She turned it around and pulled it back so everyone at the table could see. It was an interior shot of Tiny McDaniel's store from above the counter. His head appeared and disappeared from the bottom of the frame frequently. Customers came and went. Elderly men and women purchased lottery tickets. Younger men bought cases of beer. Teenagers picked up snacks and soft drinks. A young woman entered, wearing a long plaid skirt, white tee shirt, and black cardigan sweater.

She was Latina, long, straight black hair that went down to her shoulders, possibly in her early twenties, holding a backpack in one hand. She looked around before approaching Tiny. There was no audio, but they appeared to have talked briefly before he hunched down under the counter, bringing up a copy of the *Leabhar Cogaidh*. The woman slid her money on the counter and then hid the book in her backpack before nearly running out of the store.

"My team was able to decrypt Tiny's security camera footage in no time," Clytemnestra said, looking directly at him as he grimaced. "She's the first customer in the most recent file."

"Do you recognize her?" Rab asked Harriet.

Harriet shook her head. "Just a random witch, from the looks of it."

The video continued. More random customers and a few more witches came in to purchase their copies of the *Leabhar Cogaidh*. Then, Monica Benavidez entered the store with a humanoid figure. The figure was a gray and black shadow, its outline a hazy oscillating wiggle. Tiny McDaniel was visibly uncomfortable as they approached him.

"Holy shit!" Rab burst out, leaning closer to the laptop.

"Monica picked up a copy?" Harriet said disbelievingly.

"Who's the guy she's with?"

"Who knows? But that's not a very good camouflage charm."

"It sure isn't," Clytemnestra agreed. "Piss poor. I mean, look at it. It's falling apart in places."

"And it's not like it takes a lot of strength to maintain it."

Tiny McDaniel and Monica Benavidez talked adamantly while the shadowy figure stood from the side. Monica slapped the counter angrily. Tiny shot his arms out in frustration before slamming a copy of the book in front of her.

She turned to the figure and gestured to the book. The figure took it, and they slowly walked out. Clytemnestra Rose stopped the video and looked up. "So, you just handed a copy of the grimoire to your cousin," she said to Tiny McDaniel, "what did you think she was going to do with it?"

He lowered his head, picking at his fingernails, and mumbled, "I don't know."

"Who was the person with her?" Harriet asked.

"I don't know."

"How did they sound? Did they speak?"

"No. They kept quiet."

"How was this arrangement set up?" Rab asked.

Tiny McDaniel sat back in his chair, his hands on his lap. "Monnie called me out of the blue one day and said I owed her. So, I said what you need? And she told me she needed something that can work magic."

"What did she mean you owed her?"

He clicked his tongue, "Monnie can and does hold on to a grudge if something's done to her. Like, for a long time." Tiny McDaniel shrugged.

"What was done to her?"

He ran his tongue over his lips, hugging his arms together and looking down. "I'm not sure," he mumbled. "Not sure at all."

"Okay. What happened recently that set her off?"

He said sternly, "I don't want to get into that."

"How did she know you were the grimoire hookup, Tiny?" Clytemnestra asked.

"She knew a guy who knew me. He was the reason she knew to call me."

"Who was that guy?"

Tiny McDaniel shook his head solemnly. "I don't know. She didn't tell me. Only that he knew me."

"Okay. Continue."

"Monnie demanded that I give her this magic thing for whatever, or she'll give me hell. I thought of the book and told her about it. She said she'd call me back. About ten minutes later, she said she'd take it and be at my store in an hour. No chance to say otherwise."

"Did she say why she needed the *Leabhar Cogaidh*?" Harriet asked.

He sighed, "She didn't. But I have a theory."

"What's that?"

"Something happened between Monnie and our Tio Theo. No one in the family would say what. But she had major beef with him. I think she wanted to use the book on him."

Rab shared a look with Harriet. "Theo De Lyon?" Harriet asked.

"Yeah."

"Do you know what happened to your uncle Theo De Lyon?"

He didn't budge.

"You know, don't you?"

Tiny McDaniel tried to articulate his thoughts, but hesitation prevented him. Whether it was an attempt to describe the horror of knowing his own role in the murder or to extricate himself from responsibility was the detectives' guess.

"What do you know of her husband, Edward Cedillo?" Harriet continued.

"I knew Eddie from the 'hood," Tiny said softly. "Him and me used to play in the schoolyard during summer vacation, but never together. He was an annoying little shit then. And he grew up to be a hot-headed motherfucker. He was always getting in trouble with the law. Last I heard, he was doing a bit in Pelican Bay."

"What do you know about their marriage?"

"Nothing. Except that, I was surprised they were married. I didn't think Monnie liked him very much."

"Did she ever mention a man named Tad Collinson?"

He shook his head. "She never mentioned that name to me before. Why?"

"Tad Collinson worked with Monica at the Palace Hotel. And he is a suspect in the murder of his coworkers. He used the *Leabhar Cogaidh*. Probably the same copy you gave her."

He rubbed his eyes hard with his index finger and thumb.

"They fled San Francisco. Do you have an idea where they might go?"

"No, I have no idea," Tiny McDaniel said exhaustedly. "Monnie had her whole life here, you know? I can't help you there."

Clytemnestra turned to Harriet and Rab, "Is that it?" she asked.

"Yeah. I think that's all we need," Rab said.

The detectives and the ghost were escorted outside after the interview. Clytemnestra took out her vape pen from her jacket pocket and drew on it. Rab lighted a cigarette and puffed away. "You know, these humps amaze me," Clytemnestra said. "They just think magic is some innocuous thing. That there's no responsibility attached to it."

"No joke," Harriet said.

"Any luck locating Benavidez and Collinson?"

"We're still waiting," Rab said. "It should be a matter of time, though."

Rab and Harriet said goodbye to Clytemnestra Rose, got in Bruiser, and drove out of Dublin on the 580, heading to the Bay Bridge. It was a quiet drive through neighborhoods and towns that lined the way to Oakland. Harriet stared out the window, drowsy, but her head ran with thoughts that organized the details of her case. Then, randomly, she wondered about the Cup of Dionysus. Was it possible that these crimes were connected? She asked herself. One crime could have aided the other. As she was thinking back to the details of the theft, her concentration was broken by the ringing of Rab's phone. She answered, turning on the speaker, "What's going on, Cap?"

"We got a hit on Benavidez and Collinson," Lawrence Matt said.

"Where are they?"

"San Diego. Locals ID'd them and moved in."

"Do they have them?" Harriet asked.

"No. There was some altercation, and they both managed to escape."

"God damn it," Rab muttered.

"Where are they now?" Harriet continued.

"Mexico. Collinson managed to get Benavidez and himself over the border."

Harriet's eyes grew but not from alarm. "Were the authorities contacted?"

"Yeah. Our Mexican partners are looking out for them now. I need you both ready to pick those two up when the time comes."

"It won't be long."

Rab asked her, "How are you so sure?"

Harriet smiled, "No one runs from the Shadow Secretariat for long."

21

LA SECRETARIA SOMBRA

The twins Greta and Gregory ran through the tangles and brambles of the Darkvale Forest, their clothes catching in the excrescent branches of the manyfold flora, holding them back before they gathered enough of their strength to tear themselves free, running towards a large clearing near the edge of a yawning chasm. Greta turned back to the path they came through, holding her brother behind with an outstretched arm. There was no one following them. Still unconvinced of their safety, she tore off a withered branch from a nearby tree, using its dead leaves to sweep away their footprints in the clearing. With the work completed, Greta used her cunning to establish the ruse. "Gregory, come on, help me," she commanded as she stomped around, imprinting her footsteps deep into the dirt. Gregory followed her, twirling his steps into her own, weaving confusing paths and counter paths from glen to glen. Then, Greta held her finger to her lips and showed Gregory how to jump from tree root to boulder and any other outcropping, ensuring their evasion remained intact.

When Greta finally felt the comfort of safety, she guided Gregory to a grotto, obnubilated by a haunting fog, that she caught sight of during their trek. Her brother leaned close to her, "You have to show it," he said. She glanced at him whimsically before producing a gold locket from underneath her shirt. Its center, a smooth, shimmering, oval green emerald, shone brilliantly in an untraceable light. Intersecting circles were delicately cut into the stone, and a single bead of light glowed on the edges of each. Greta studied the object as Gregory stared at it ravenously, recalling their journey to steal the locket.

With Im'vu gone and their cohort scattered in the wind, Greta and Gregory stayed together, as they always have, determined to brave this strange yet compelling world. However, working towards survival was not their strongest virtue. Gregory, an unrepentant epicurean who felt the pang of hunger more sensitively than his twin and usually remedied it with a quick jaunt to his mother's well-stocked pantry between meals, became rudely aware of their privation. And Greta, who depended on the collecting of material things – things to influence friends or build walls to separate others – quickly realized her impoverished condition in the Shou-Earth. And as the days waned, time trickling forth, the twins grew more sallow, gaunt, and filthy. Any citizen who crossed paths with them sneered or bucked away. By looking at them, brigands knew they carried no cash or goods and ignored their presence. Knowing that – knowing that they couldn't muster enough violent avarice from groups of thuggish, unlearned bumpkins – made Greta deeply angry.

That all changed when they met Parnassus in a small stone village on the outskirts of a vast, wasted desert. Parnassus was a strange one, sloven and grotesque, dressed in dirty rags that had been weaved in some immemorial time. But unlike most in similar condition, she had the gift of benignant eutrapely, full of wisdom and mirth, endearing her to the villagers. Greta and Gregory were charmed by old crone Parnassus, and she of them.

However, the day came when Parnassus regretted ever meeting them.

The three of them sat on a large stone overlooking a gorge where a shimmering river ran. Gregory nibbled on a bread roll he had been nursing for three days while Greta stared at the river. The glittering of the gentle, lapping waves reminded her of wealth. Old Parnassus hunched over, humming a tune from her younger years, then snapped from her reverie to look with Greta at the river.

"There was a time when great riches were plentiful on the Shou-Earth," she said. "In the waters, on the hills, in the valleys, and forests, piles of gold and sweet fruits that could be taken by hand as easily as clumps of dirt."

Greta and Gregory turned to her. "Is that so?" Greta asked.

Old Parnassus nodded. "Have you heard of Puce the Great?"

"No, we haven't," Gregory said. "Tell us."

"Puce was greatness incarnate. He was as tall as the highest mountain peak, had the strength of a million men, with mighty seven-fingered hands that could shadow the lands around him, and three eyes that saw into the past, present, and future. Yet, he was as gentle as a lamb, offering whatever he could to the most unfortunate.

"One day, a pestilence gripped the lands of Shou-Earth. Crops failed all at once, and the people starved. They went to Puce in their multitude, begging for his aid. And Puce, in his good judgment, sought out the goddess Saluy, the keeper of the Shou-Earth. She confessed to him that she was punishing the people because of the mortal Emil the Bane, a trickster cleverer and crueler than any before him, who took advantage of Saluy while she was asleep to kidnap her daughter Saluee. And she would not relent until her daughter was returned to her.

"With the people on his mind, Puce then hunted Emil the Bane. From land to sea, he searched for the trickster. But the trickster knew this and, using magic, transformed himself and Saluee into animals to evade him. He and she became deer, wolves, pumas, ravens, and rams, and they stalked, cantered, and flew away.

"But Emil the Bane was only a man and could not sustain himself on magic long. It was only a matter of time before Puce the Mighty found him and cornered him." Parnassus pointed down into the gorge, "In one just like this."

"As you say," Greta said.

"Continue, Old Parnassus," Gregory demanded.

"Well, Emil the Bane was caught in the gaze of Puce's three eyes. He did not know what to do. Exhausted and desperate, the trickster devised a ruse to allow himself time to rest. Knowing that it took the Mighty one time to gather momentum, he wagered Puce that if he could jump high into the sky and touch the skin of the sun, then he would let Saluee, daughter of the goddess Saluy, go into his custody."

"And if he lost?" Gregory interrupted.

"And if he lost, Emil the Bane demanded Puce's eye of the future."

"A heavy thing to lose," Greta said to herself.

Parnassus continued, "But what the trickster hadn't counted on was Puce's love for the people of the Shou-Earth. He took the wager and sauntered out to the center of the land. And with his heart filled with justice, Puce gathered all his strength and made an air-rending leap. Some say that the loudest thunderclaps from the most violent storms never matched what Puce had done!

"However, things didn't go entirely Puce's way. Perhaps his eye of the future hadn't seen what happened next, or he ignored it completely, but as he reached the sun and stretched out his arms, his hands missed. But not his head, smashing into it like a lumberjack's axe into a tree!"

"Golly," Gregory said.

"What happened next?" Greta asked.

"The force of Puce crashing into the sun was so great that pieces of it rained down on the Shou-Earth, falling like magma from a volcano. But the most miraculous thing happened. When the sun's pieces cooled, they became gold. Can you imagine, children? Gold as far as your eye could take you?"

Greta didn't respond and kept staring ahead towards the glittering river. "What happened to Puce?" Gregory asked, tearing off a corner of his bread roll and chewing loudly.

"Puce returned from his journey, much to Emil the Bane's displeasure. The trickster even tried to renege on the wager because Puce hadn't actually touched the sun. To which Puce, all three of his eyes turned on the trickster, declared that the wager didn't stipulate what part of his person needed to touch the sun. The game was up, and Puce was victorious. He took Saluee back to her mother, and there was much rejoicing. As promised, Saluy returned the fertility of the Shou-Earth and then some. All year round, the seasons were abolished, and the crops came up without blite, without frost. Food was so plentiful that no one needed to farm anymore."

Gregory looked at the half-eaten, slightly moldy bread roll in his hand and sighed.

"In time though," Parnassus continued, "the people's avarice and intemperance grew unbounded, especially in their children, and their children after them. When one part of the land was stripped of its gold and fruits, they moved on to the other, and so on. Puce disappeared, never to be heard from again. The goddess Saluy became so disgusted with mortals that she returned the seasons and the fragility of the crops to the natural order. And the people needed to learn how to work again to live."

"But that's just a story, isn't it, Old Parnassus?" Greta said.

Parnassus raised a finger in contradiction, "Ah, but it isn't just a story. While greed and gluttony did strip most of the wealth and *bounty brought by the Great Contest, there is still a valley on the Shou-Earth that was spared." She removed a gold locket from a pouch on her belt and held it up to the siblings, "My ancestors were what you call 'cynics.' They knew it would be a matter of time before the people ravaged the gifts Saluy and Puce bestowed and, through cunning and deception, managed to hide the last remains in the valley.*

"This locket was created to show the way, an eternal map. It was passed down from one generation to the next until it was given to me. I am the guardian of the Valley of Plenty, a privilege I hold dear."

Greta glared at the locket with green, lambent eyes. "To whom will you pass the locket down to, Old Parnassus? You don't have any family."

"Ah, that is correct. I don't have any kin. My family line dies with me. But I don't mourn it. I believe it wasn't right for my ancestors to hide away the treasure and plenty like a gaggle of misers. The valley should have been plundered to leave nothing for avarice's temptation. But it is not for me to decide.

"Before I dance off this mortal plain, I will cast this locket into oblivion. The Valley of Plenty will remain hidden for all of eternity."

Greta picked up a large, jagged rock near her foot and hefted it. It was cumbersome in her hand, so she gripped it hard. She caught Gregory staring at her, affirming the plot formulating in her head...

"Excuse me, ma'am?" the flight attendant asked Harriet. She was pleasant, but annoyance tinged her voice.

She lowered her book, "Yeah?"

"Is that your poltergeist in the back of the plane?"

Harriet stood up from her seat and turned in that direction. The Ghost of Warren G. Harding stood near the aft restrooms; his face melted in horror. He repeatedly wailed,

"What is this thing?" while the nearby passengers grimaced angrily.

"Oh, I'm sorry," Harriet said. "He's my buddy's ghost. Hold on."

She stretched over to Rab's seat across the aisle from her, where she was napping, a sleep mask over her eyes and earplugs firmly in place. She shook her shoulder. Rab jolted awake, ripped the mask off, and knitted her brows close. "What's up?"

"Warren's having a fit in the back."

"He's never flown before. That's normal."

The flight attendant interrupted, "But he's disturbing the passengers."

"How far are we from San Diego?"

"About another hour. You're not suggesting that our passengers put up with that, are you?"

"No, no. I'm not. Hold up, I'll go get him."

Rab stood up and headed to the Ghost of Warren G. Harding. Harriet saw them talking amicably, then walked back to their part of the cabin, a relieved sigh coming from the passengers.

"Alright, Warren," Rab said, "you just hang here and behave, and you'll get to watch your programs at all times, like I promised."

"That's a sacrifice," Harriet said.

Rab shrugged, "I can enjoy *Ninety-Day Fiancé* when I'm in the right head space, no problem."

They sat down. Harriet opened her book and continued reading. Rab crossed her arms over her chest. The Ghost of Warren G. Harding stood in the aisle, whimpered, mumbling, "Noise... height... Noise." Rab turned to Harriet, asking, "How's your book?"

"It's alright. Entertaining enough. I'd like it more if it wasn't so loaded with twenty-dollar words."

"Isn't it supposed to be ten-dollar words?"

"I'm adjusting for inflation."

THEIR FLIGHT LANDED in San Diego. A liaison from SDPD brought them to their headquarters building. The detectives met the captain of the homicide unit, a tall, former military man with a thick, broad nose and dark, incurious eyes. He stretched out a mitt of a hand to Rab and Harriet. "Name's Mol Lolly," he growled. "Thank you both for coming on short notice."

"No worries, Captain Lolly," Rab said. "I understand the federales are holding our suspects?"

"What's left of them, Sergeant."

"Is everything alright?"

"From what I was briefed on, the shadow boys completely tore apart the male of the equation."

Harriet asked, "He resisted?"

Lolly snickered, "The damn fool tried. He didn't last long. It would've been comical if he hadn't pulled that same stunt on my boys when he and his *heina* were on this side of the border."

"He fought your men?"

Lolly nodded angrily. "Lucky for them, the male's magic was more flash than substance. He's lucky my guys didn't put a couple of rounds into him when they had the chance."

"They had their guns drawn?"

"Drawn and ready. A few even said they had a bead on them before they jumped the border."

"But they didn't open fire?"

He smirked at Harriet but didn't answer.

"When can we pick them up?" Rab asked.

"As soon as we get you two to the border."

Mol Lolly and his team drove Harriet, Rab, and the Ghost of Warren G. Harding to the border station between Tijuana and San Diego. There, they met with federal agents, who escorted them to the Mexican side.

Six officers greeted them. Four were in army fatigues, glistening black boots, and the Mexican flag proudly displayed on their shirt sleeves. The last two wore pristine black suits, matching green and white striped ties, and aviator sunglasses. On their lapels were pins of the Mexican flag and the seal of the Shadow Secretariat, a silhouette of Quetzalcoatl holding the flame of knowledge in his hands.

"Here, I'll talk to them," Harriet said.

"How's your Spanish?" Rab asked.

"Pretty good."

Harriet showed her badge to the officers. "*Buenas tardes, camaradas,*" she said. "*Soy Harriet June, con mi compañera, la Detective Victoria Rabinowski y el fantasma de Estatos Unidos presidente Warren G. Harding.*"

One of the suited men, older and handsome, with thick black hair, brushed back and held up a hand. "It's okay, Detective June," he said. "Our English is good."

"Oh!" she smiled embarrassingly. "Got it."

"It's good to meet you both. I'm Inspector Cayo, and this is my partner, Sergeant Inga."

Sergeant Inga, a younger man with a thin mustache, bowed slightly.

"I hope our guests didn't give you much trouble," Rab said.

"No, ma'am. No trouble," said Sergeant Inga. "The male

tried to resist, but Inspector Cayo and I were able to secure him."

"His magic was paltry," Inspector Cayo said. "It did more damage to himself than to us—just as we prefer." Cayo and Inga chuckled.

"Well, thanks for your help. We'll take them off your hands if you don't mind."

"By all means," said Inspector Cayo.

Inspector Cayo and Sergeant Inga led Harriet and Rab to a holding cell where Tad Collinson and Monica Benavidez sat, handcuffed. Collinson looked worse for wear. Black scorch marks cut across his face. One eye squinted nearly shut while the other was open wide. A corner of his mouth was parted open ghastly, showing off his bloody teeth. Benavidez's face was hard. Her long hair was cropped into a bob. They looked up when Sergeant Inga opened the cell door, wincing when they saw Harriet and Rab enter.

"Well, look at what we have here," Rab said. "Feeling alright, Collinson?" He didn't answer.

Harriet crossed her arms. "You two have been giving us all kinds of trouble," she said.

"Get fucked," Monica said.

She feigned shock. "Such attitude! I wonder if it'll hold up once we get you back to the city."

Inspector Cayo, Sergeant Inga, and their officers loaded Collinson and Monica into an SDPD van and escorted them to the airport. Within three hours, Harriet and Rab had them back in San Francisco.

22

THE INTERROGATION

In their respective interrogation rooms, Tad Collinson twitched in his chair sporadically, moaning, lolling his head from side to side. At the same time, Monica Benavidez sat with her legs and arms crossed, staring intently at the table in front of her.

Rab, Harriet, and the Ghost of Warren G. Harding watched them from a monitor across the hall. "What's wrong with Collinson?" Rab asked.

"Cayo and Inga must've stunned him stupid," Harriet said. "Mexica magic is one of the most ancient and powerful disciplines. It's nothing to fuck with." She pointed to Collinson, "You want to start with him?"

"No, let him stew a little longer," Rab said. "Let's hit Benavidez first."

"Sounds good."

Harriet and Rab entered Monica's interview room and sat beside her. The Ghost of Warren G. Harding lingered in a corner. Monica stared at them coldly. "How are you, Monica?" Rab asked.

"Lawyer," Monica said dully.

"Look, we're not going to waste time. We know Tad Collinson murdered his colleague and her girlfriend. And we have a good idea that he is responsible for the deaths of your uncle and your husband based on his connection to you. That's four counts of first-degree murder he's looking at. That's death row.

"As for you, Monica, we know you provided the means for the murders, the Lacuna Mazda…"

"*Leabhar Cogaidh*," Harriet corrected.

"That. You remember your cousin, Tiny McDaniel?"

Monica glared hotly at Rab; her lips pressed together tightly until they blanched. Rage burned clearly in her eyes. An imperceptible growl came from her throat. "Lawyer," she hissed.

Rab continued, "He's willing to talk. Last I heard, his public defender and Oakland's DA are banging out a deal. All you have to do is bring the dots together, Monnie. You tell us everything, you and Collinson, the murders, all of it, and you'll probably get the low end of murder solicitation. That's years and not a life sentence."

Monica still glared at Rab and then at Harriet. She gestured with her middle finger, "Lawyer."

"You know, I get the feeling Collinson will take the sweetest of the sweetest deal to save his ass from the needle. That means he needs to throw you under the bus. His desperation will net us you two, no matter what."

When Monica didn't respond, Rab shrugged, "Come on, Harriet. Benavidez won't play nice with us."

They left Monica's interrogation room and shut the door. Harriet asked Rab quietly in the hallway, "Where did you hear that Tiny's working on a deal? That's new."

"I didn't," Rab said. "I made it up. Mostly to see if that got Benavidez going."

"Isn't that unethical?" asked the Ghost of Warren G. Harding.

"You, of all people, should know the value of lying to get a positive result, Warren."

"But we didn't get one," Harriet said.

"Yeah," Rab drawled. "Benavidez might think she has room to maneuver around us. Let's box her in. Collinson could give us everything."

Rab and Harriet entered Collinson's interview room. He twitched as they sat down, his lips still parted from a corner. "I won't ask how you are, Tad," Harriet said. "Our colleagues in Mexico gave you a good working over."

Collinson slumped in his chair, nodding his head vigorously.

"They sure don't take kindly to *gringos* causing mischief in their country," Rab said. "Honestly, I don't think they gave you enough of a spanking."

He moaned.

"We know what you did, Tad," Harriet said. "Did you think I wouldn't put everything together?"

"It was a lot of boneheadedness on your part," Rab said. "A lot of dumbassery. And that sloppiness is what's going to put you in the death house."

He responded with more groaning.

"Your girlfriend in the other room is lawyering up, Collinson," Rab continued. "That tells me she will put the whole thing on you. It'll be easy. You had an illegal grimoire, a very dangerous one. One that is connected to the deaths of four people. And there's not enough evidence to fully connect her to those deaths. Sure, her cousin was the dealer, and he'd give her up. But a good lawyer can put a lot of doubt in a jury's mind. I'm not her lawyer and already have a solid defense."

"You murdered her uncle, Theo De Lyon," Harriet said, "her husband Edward Cedillo, Molly, and Elysia. I can easily pin the magic used on you."

Collinson choked back a sob.

"No hump jury likes a murderous witch, Tad. You and I know that. They're going to see it Monica's way. She'll probably get a mistrial, a possession charge, or maybe an acquittal. But you'll head to death row no matter what. That's how I see it."

"Please!" he mumbled.

"How involved was Monica Benavidez, Tad? Start from the beginning."

Collinson mumbled through their shared conspiracy to the best of his ability. Monica's uncle, Theo De Lyon, was well-off, owning several rental properties in San Francisco. Unmarried and childless, he took in Monica as a child when her mother died young, and her father was nowhere to be found.

"But... she implied... that there was something wrong with their relationship," Collinson said.

"Implied?" Harriet asked. "Like?"

"She wouldn't say. But I got the feeling he was inappropriate with her."

"That he abused her?"

"That's what I thought."

"Did the family know? Her cousin also implied something was wrong with De Lyon and Monica."

"She told me her family never had her back, never came to defend her. That they abandoned her to her uncle."

Harriet and Rab turned to each other, both sighing.

"Continue, Collinson," Rab said.

Monica became rebellious as a teen, partying hard

nearly every night and causing enough trouble with the law countless times. But De Lyon always bailed her out.

However, their relationship was severely strained in time. Then, he caught her one night taking anything of value in his house, including his great-grandmother's prized silver pendant. He held her at gunpoint while he called the cops.

"That was the final straw?" Harriet asked.

Collinson nodded slowly, "He cut her off completely after that."

"And what happened after?"

"She struggled, man! What do you think? Like, she was couch surfing with friends, working all these shit jobs, and... and... trying to go to City College or something! She was trying to make something of herself! But... nothing was going her way."

"Look at him," Rab said slowly, "practically defending her, even now."

"What about Edward Cedillo?" Harriet asked. "What did he do to put a target on his back?"

Collinson looked surprised.

"You knew she was married to him. Otherwise, why did you target him?"

He lowered his gaze. "Eddy was causing trouble," he said. "He always was."

"Okay, so we have an estranged uncle, an ex-con husband, and your co-workers. When, why, and how were the murders planned?"

"It was about six months ago when I started at the Palace Hotel. I don't know, Monnie and I became friends. Then, one day, she came to me, like, raging. She was so furious. It was scary how mad she was."

"What was she mad about?"

"Her uncle. I didn't know the details then. Monnie wouldn't share them with me. But I dug into it myself. I learned that he got into trouble with a younger cousin of hers and that the law was involved, but he was let go. Like, the cops didn't even look into it. They just took his word, and his family didn't come to her cousin's rescue."

Harriet leaned closer to Collinson, "Was Monica the one who reported him anonymously?"

He looked at her with his good eye, "Yeah. She was the one who called in the cops."

"Is that when the murder scheme came up?" she asked.

"Yeah," he mumbled.

"What I don't get is why you got involved, Tad. Theo De Lyon didn't do anything to you. Why did you agree to murder him?"

Collinson ran his tongue around his deformed lips. "I wanted to help her. She was the only one who got where I came from and treated me with respect."

"What do you mean by that, Collinson?" Rab asked.

"I'm not going to sit here and explain. You two probably have enough dirt on me to know."

"That you're a fuck-up witch?"

A flash of anger crossed Collinson's face. Rab stared him down, unconcerned. He calmed down quickly.

"Monica Benavidez didn't treat you like a dud," Harriet said. "And that was enough to kill the old man?"

The Ghost of Warren G. Harding stepped toward the interview table and said, "There's one thing I would like to ask. It's been bothering me."

Rab and Harriet turned to him. "What you got, Warren?" Rab said.

"You've committed these murders, young man. That's

not in dispute. But I don't understand how you could when you had that Vermonter curse lording over you."

Harriet arched an eyebrow, "That's right." She returned to Collinson, "I'd studied enough of the *Leabhar Cogaidh* to know it has no countermeasures against such curses. How did *you*, of all people, get around the Winooski Protocol, Tad?"

"I found a loophole in one of the spells."

"Oh, this I have to hear!"

"There's this spell in the book, kinda like *Personae corpus*. You can use it to take over anybody if they have the bridging talisman. One of the side effects is temporary ego death. That's the trigger for the Winooski Protocol: ego. Ego leads to desire, and desire goes into intention, ending in effect. The curse's simple mathematics. But if there's ego death, the protocol can't detect desire or intention, preventing it from activating."

Harriet sat back in her chair, crossing her arms. "So, when you took over Elyria True to turn her into your murder weapon, both of your egos died in the process?"

Collinson winced. "Yeah. That's it. At that point, intellect took over."

"Intellect, meaning?"

"Using my mind to create the Desanguis curse without the ego. Using the skill of reading. If you look at it like conducting a mental exercise, then it's simple."

"Is that how you learned to live with yourself, Tad? You were just reading and not brutally murdering people with Desanguis?"

He choked back a tiny sob.

"The bridging talisman, that antique doll, you gave it to Elyria?"

"No. She would've been suspicious if I had given it to

her. She and Monica were work friends, though. Monnie was the one who gave it to her. She said it was her grandmother's or something, that it was a gift."

"Why her?" Harriet continued. "Why Elyria?"

He shrugged his shoulders pathetically. "She didn't like me. And I fuckin' hated her."

Harriet's impatience was growing. She nearly shouted, "Alright, so. Monica got you a copy of the *Leabhar Cogaidh*; you used it to take over Elyria True to kill Theo De Lyon. What about Edward Cedillo, Monica's hubby? You said earlier that he was causing trouble. What do you mean?"

"He..." Collinson hesitated. "He was the reason we had the *Leabhar Cogaidh*."

"How did he pull that off?"

"He knew Arturo McDaniel."

It took the two detectives a minute to remember the name. "Tiny McDaniel?" Rab asked.

"Yeah, I think that's what she called him. Eddy told her that Arturo was the Oakland connection for the grimoire."

"How did Cedillo know Tiny McDaniel was the connection?"

Collinson shook his head. "I don't know. Maybe they were partners? It wasn't explained to me."

"Did you off him to keep him quiet?"

He nodded gently. "I need you to speak up, Collinson," Rab said.

"After De Lyon's death was reported, Eddy knew it was Monica. He wasn't stupid. He knew she was responsible, but also, she wasn't a witch. So, he followed her around until he found me. One night, he cornered me, threatening to go to the police if he didn't get a payout. He thought I was some alchemist. I tried telling him that it was a myth, that there was no such science, but he wouldn't listen.

"I talked to Monica about it. She tensed up, looking very nervous. But then, she calmed down fast—like, real fast. It was almost scary how quickly she shifted. She told me Eddy wouldn't stop with his idiocy, that he would mess up our plan..."

Collinson stopped, stared at the two detectives and the ghost, and averted his good eye.

"Was she the one who gave the blessing?" Rab asked.

He rocked in his chair.

"Was she the one, Collinson?"

He slumped in his chair and slurped back some saliva, "Yeah. I didn't want to do it. I really didn't. But I was in too deep. It was going to be me or him."

"Who was responsible for stuffing him in the suitcase?" Harriet asked.

"Monica. She was there when I hit him with Desanguis," Collinson said.

"Shit, man," Rab said. "that's cold."

"Alright, we're two of four," Harriet said. "I need you to explain why you murdered both Molly Alay and Elyria True. Did Elyria know what was happening to her at any point?"

He didn't straighten up from his slump, staring out to nothing. "I don't think she did. But I caught parts of some conversation she and Molly were having once. She was concerned about losing parts of her memory but didn't investigate it further."

"What about Molly? Did she suspect something was going on?"

He shook his head. "I hit Elyria with the *personae* whenever Molly was on a shift and she was off, always made sure they were separated."

"Smart, that's smart, Tad," Harriet said. "You could still be a witch yet."

"When did Elyria stop being useful to you?" Rab asked. "And when did you decide that Molly had to die?"

He sighed deeply. "I knew I was in trouble when I tried to kill Jackson..."

Harriet straightened up in her chair, "Jackson? Jeremiah Lucian Jackson?"

"Yeah. He suspected something was going on at the hotel. At least that's what he told everyone there. And that he was doing his investigation. But it wasn't until Archambeau's robbery that I found out he discovered the *Leabhar Cogaidh* in my locker and made a copy."

"You kept your copy at the hotel?"

"Yeah. I used my workstation to conduct the spells. But when Jackson was sniffing around, I moved my book and the doll back home. I wasn't sure what he was going to do next. I worked fast to try to neutralize him."

"You attacked Jackson outside of the hotel?"

"Yeah. When I found out he was talking to you and his voodoo friends were closing in on me, I had to do something."

"But it didn't work."

"No. It was rushed, so rushed. I tried to link up with Elyria that day, but she resisted. I don't know how." He hesitated before going on. "I had to... brute-force the spell."

Harriet and Rab sneered at him. "You forced yourself on her?" Rab said.

Collinson was about to answer but stopped himself.

"Elyria resisted," Harriet snarled. "You forced yourself on her. You tried to attack Jackson with Desanguis?"

He nodded slowly.

"Say it out loud, Collinson!"

"I did! But I fucked the spell. It was a goddamn mess! My ego kept creeping up. I had to back off because I felt the protocol starting up in me."

"Is that when Elyria and Molly became suspicious?"

"Yeah. They were both on the hunt after that. They took time off work, had their little esbats. They spent nights... searching..."

"Searching for you," said the Ghost of Warren G. Harding.

"But they never suspected the porcelain doll?" Harriet asked.

"The magic I imbued it with only comes alive during the *personae*," Tad said. "When the spell is at rest, it's just another doll."

"How close were they to finding you out?"

Collinson stayed in his slump; saliva seeped from the deformed corner of his lips. The saliva globule wet his shirt. He flexed his scorched, filthy hands lazily. A glint of pride appeared in his eye, then died away. "Not even close," he said. "They never suspected the fuck-up standing behind them."

"If that's the case, why did you decide they had to die?"

"Loose ends. Monica was getting antsy. You guys were swarming. We both knew it would be a matter of time before you connected everything to us. That's why I decided to kill them both. Hit Molly first during her shift, so she didn't see it coming. Have Elyria kill herself."

Collinson touched the side of his neck and winced. "She tried to resist. I felt her resist. Like, you know that animalistic need to survive? The terror of death? I felt it. I felt her feeling it. But only for a second. In that one instance, as the blade went into her flesh, I knew what death felt like."

Harriet and Rab looked at each other again. Rab leaned

back in her chair. "What a mess you got yourself into, Collinson," she said.

The detectives and the ghost left the interview room. Rab then ordered Monica and Collinson to the county jail.

Rab briefed Lawrence Matt about the conclusion of the Desanguis cases, which he signed off on. She and the Ghost of Warren G. Harding went to her desk. Harriet rested her head on her own, the alewife hat pushed back.

"You alright, buddy?" Rab asked.

"I think I'm going to be sick," Harriet said, sitting up and taking a deep breath. "This Collinson and Benavidez business gave me the worst skeeves."

"I hear you. But hey, those two are going to spend the rest of their lives behind bars. And knowing Collinson, the humps are going to eat him alive."

"But Benavidez will probably run the prison."

"I don't doubt that."

Harriet started cleaning off the top of her desk, organizing papers into folders, and stacking them in one corner. She stopped and read the notes on some of the documents. "Huh. I forgot about the Dionysus heist," she said.

"Yup," Rab answered. "That case fell by the wayside, didn't it?"

"Not like it mattered much. There was hardly anything to go on."

"I'm sure Archambeau and the rest of her people got a nice insurance payout for the cup. They won't be hurting."

"But a precious artifact connected to their worship is missing."

"It'll turn up, Harriet. Probably in some European auction house. When it does, it'll be up to the Feds and the EU to figure out what to do with it, not us. We did our part."

Harriet placed the papers into a manila folder and stacked them. "For sure," she said, sighing. "It would be nice to find out how the thieves got away with it, though."

23

FUNNY RUNES

The offices of the San Francisco branch of the Coronado Detective Agency were in a corner of the Flood Building overlooking the Powell Street Cable Car turnaround. It was Beaumont Hart's favorite thing to look at when he needed to think. Something about the turning of the cable cars from one direction to the next and preparing a century-old vehicle to go up one of the steepest hills of San Francisco filled him with hope. The crews easily kept the operation moving, maintaining the delicate dance of the conveyance. It was skill and feeling, the two essential things a detective needs.

Beaumont was staring down at the turnaround, his head buzzing with thoughts. Early that morning, a UPS man dropped off a very rare copy of *The Law of the Fiskikarlar: Explorations of, and Meditations on, the Viking runic magic tradition from 640 AD to 1020 AD* by Professor Benedict Saint-Phineas, Coronado's go-to runic expert in North Carolina. Beaumont's attempts to reach him for help with the etchings on Selene Archambeau's trunk went unanswered, and feeling time's pinch, he figured he could do the work himself.

He searched for the professor's only known book, finding a single used copy on the Powell's Books website. He ordered it and paid extra for expedited shipping from Portland, knowing Coronado had a generous reimbursement policy. He went through the book at his desk, leafing its pages the whole morning. When he got to the history of Pfluegr and his work on compounded runes, Beaumont had to pause. It was noon, his head ached, and there was cable car traffic down on Powell Street.

Standing by the windows, Beaumont held a cup of black coffee, taking periodic sips as the crews spun a cable car around on the track heading up Nob Hill. The sound of the revolving turnaround echoed off the surrounding buildings, followed by the tracks' click. At that sound, a thought came to him.

Beaumont returned to his desk and pulled out enlarged photographs of Archambeau's trunk. He studied the etchings, especially the ones on each corner. He then took out a piece of paper and a pencil and copied them. When he was done, he returned to Saint-Phineas' book and reread its section on Pfluegr. An idea struck him.

He ran to the agency's resource library with his paper and pulled out a runic reference book, following the characters piece by piece. After meticulously breaking them down, Beaumont Hart discovered they were compounded runes. One corner of Archambeau's trunk had *Fehu* and *Gebo*, wealth and gift. The other had *Berkanan* and *Hagalaz*, new beginnings and transformation. At the bottom corner were *Isa* and *Jera*, concentration, and rewards. Opposite of those were *Mannaz* and *Peorth*. *Mennaz* was usually translated as intellect. But *Peorth* had a few translations: magic, mystery, secrets, or hidden.

Beaumont stared at the formula, feeling he was on the right track. But something was off.

He needed to talk to Saint-Phineas to clarify his hunches. Instead of calling his personal number again, Beaumont called the University of North Carolina, Chapel Hill, where the professor taught. When his extension went unanswered, he called the faculty department, waiting until an administrative assistant answered.

"My name is Beaumont Hart, and I work for the Coronado Detective Agency. I was wondering if I could be connected to Benedict Saint-Phineas. It's urgent."

"Oh! I'm sorry, Mr. Beaumont," the admin drawled charmingly, "but Professor Saint-Phineas is no longer employed with the university."

"Oh? When was this?"

"Some time ago. You weren't informed?"

"No. Any reason why he's no longer there?"

The admin hesitated momentarily, then continued, "Unfortunately, I'm not at liberty to say."

"Is there any way to contact Professor Saint-Phineas?"

"Have you tried his personal number?"

"I have. But he's not answering his calls. And he hasn't set up his voicemail inbox, so I can't leave a message."

"I'm sorry, Mr. Beaumont. Professor Saint-Phineas didn't leave any other contact information with us before his departure."

"I understand. Thank you."

Beaumont continued with his ad-hoc research, finding a YouTube video of a lecture led by Saint-Phineas that was sparsely attended. He clicked on a set timestamp:

"Our forebearers were truly clever when it came to concocting

new magics using their own ideographs," he drawled like a Kentucky colonel. "*As I've pointed out earlier in my lecture on Pfluegr, his discovery of the power of compounded runes, especially during a celestial event, was a game changer in the practice of philological psychokinesis. But his work was merely the beginning.*

"*What I recently discovered in studying the manuscripts of Luvdimir, the Tenth Century Baltic scholar, long thought lost until a cache was discovered in a Vilnius library, is something truly spectacular. He found that if compounded runes, accompanied with complimentary phrases, told the intention of the conjurer as if telling the story of his true heart's desire, the results would be astonishing. I've experimented with Luvdimir's work to see for myself.*"

Saint-Phineas turned towards the blackboard behind him and wrote down various runes. He cleared his throat. "*Now, I decided that my experiment would amount to nothing more than a simple prank, as the next proper celestial event was nothing more than the constellations of Gemini and Scorpio aligning with a full moon at twelve degrees, thus not inherently powerful. My colleague, Professor Natalia Smit, was my intended victim, from whom I purloined a precious casserole dish.*"

He pointed to the runes, "*By compounding these runes together, Fehu and Gebo; Berkanan and Hagalaz; Isa and Jera; Mannaz and Peorth, along with a few select phrases denoting my intention of taking her dish into my possession and writing them onto strips of masking tape, to which I secretly adhered to the insides of her kitchen cabinet, I was able to spirit away the crockery from Professor Smit's kitchen and into my office...*"

Beaumont slammed the stop button on his laptop so hard that his colleagues turned to him. He had found it, the means of the theft. His mouth was dry; his heart palpitated. He started developing a hypothesis: whoever carved the runes on Archambeau's trunk had the same knowledge as Saint-Phineas. He just needed to know who did the carving.

He called his contact at the North American Society of the Dionysian Faith, Mark Yarn. "Why, hello, Mr. Hart," he answered. "To what do I owe the pleasure?"

"Hi, Mr. Yarn, sorry to bother you. I think I found something in the Cup of Dionysus case..."

"Hold on, Mr. Hart." He was quiet; the clomping of his shoes in a hallway reached the receiver, followed by the squeaking of a door's hinge and the gentle latching of a lock. "Okay, go on."

Beaumont explained what he learned in the *Law of the Fiskikarlar* and what he found on Selene Archambeau's trunk.

"Are you accusing one of our own?" Mark Yarn asked.

"I'm not until more evidence comes forth. Do you know who might've had access to Ms. Archambeau's trunk?"

"Other than Madame Archambeau and Ms. Hemlock, I don't know. Have you tried reaching out to them?"

"I will. Is Ms. Archambeau around in the NASDF building, by any chance?"

Mark Yarn hummed in thought. "I don't think so. She hasn't been around a lot." He stopped for a moment. "Come to think of it, I haven't seen her since she returned from Frisco."

"Do you have her number, Mr. Yarn?"

"Business or personal?"

"I'll take both."

He gave Beaumont the phone numbers. "Thank you, Mr. Yarn. I'll contact you when I have more information."

"I'd be much obliged, Mr. Hart. So far, you're the only one still taking this theft seriously. We've stopped hearing from Captain Matt and the SFPD a spell ago."

The evening had come, and Beaumont left his ninth voicemail message on Selene Archambeau's cellphone. Her business line kept ringing until he gave up. The Coronado's offices were deserted. The street lamps of Market and Powell streets had come on. Beaumont yawned deeply in his chair and decided to call it a day. But his head was still firmly in the case. He decided to get a nightcap before heading home.

THE BAR WAS on Linden Street, near Gough. It was a tiny place with enough room to comfortably seat ten or twelve people. It was decorated with Belle époque-inspired wallpaper, soft lighting from delicate Spartan bronze fixtures, and a hand-made, well-varnished showcase that held a variety of top-shelf liquor. A record player spun in one corner, playing a sensuous Nina Simone LP.

Beaumont was sitting at the bar; an empty stem glass stood near his hand. He was slumped over his cell phone, going through a dating app. He landed on the profile of a man in his forties, who was subjectively handsome. His long, unctuous brown hair was tied in a messy knot behind his head. He was obviously fit from the look of his skintight polo shirt. But he relied too heavily on his photos to do the talking for him, as he didn't write much about himself, a clear red flag. That, and he was born on May twenty-fifth. Gemini, Beaumont reflected, absolutely not. He scrolled past very quickly.

Beaumont was about to exit the app when he received a DM. Curiosity compelled him, and he opened it. A single emoji of a waving hand greeted him. Usually, these poor, lazy attempts at flirting pushed Beaumont's patience to the edge, but the profile picture caught his attention. The subject was not just handsome but utterly beautiful, with lush, curly golden-brown hair and shimmering green eyes. Beaumont couldn't tell the subject's gender: were they male or trans? Either way, he felt a deep attraction. He opened the profile where, unlike most single men, they had a lengthy bio:

I was born of lyres, away from white-armed connivers, near a deep-eddying river where he who delights in thunder made love. He who knows us well, untamed ambrosial mane down to the unshakable mound, nodded approvingly of the fate of my mother.

My many nursemaids, with the sweetest voices, nurtured me in the dells of my homeland, Nysa, of the cloven fields. They were clothed in ivy and laurels as I haunted the wooded glens, echoing with my din.

And standing on the shore of a barren sea, a young man in the first bloom of manhood, I was taken by Tyresenians with evil in their hearts, leading me to chained captivity. And in my august fury, turning them into mindless dolphins, I took over their ship, vine-strewn, saving only the kindly helmsman, the first of mine...

Another DM from the subject appeared, this time asking to meet. Beaumont was thinking about it when the bar door opened. A shadow in an alewife hat entered and stood near the end of the bar. Beaumont turned and saw Harriet. She looked exhausted. She saw him, smiled, and approached, placing her hand softly on his shoulder. He grinned. "How are you, Detective June?"

"Tired, so tired. How're you doing, Beaumont?" she asked, sitting beside him.

"You know how it is."

"Is this your usual stomping ground?"

"Sometimes. Whenever I want to be alone."

She was startled and embarrassed. "Am I bothering you?"

"Oh, no! Not at all. I think a little company might be good for me."

"Well, that's good." Harriet caught the bartender's attention. "What do you want?" she asked Beaumont.

"Oh, I'll have the same."

"One Vesper," said the bartender. "And you, miss?"

Harriet scanned the case. "Oh! You have Saint Germain? I'll have a French Gimlet."

"You got it."

"You come here often?" Beaumont asked as the bartender went to work.

"I live up the block," Harriet answered. "It's hard not to drop by all the time."

He smirked at her, "Not to talk business, but I had to hear from NASDF that you guys dropped the ball on the Dionysus case?"

She slumped down on the bar top and sighed roughly. "I know we have. It's been a weird and rough one. Me and Rab had four goddamn murder cases drop on our laps all at once!"

His eyes widened. "Four? What the fuck!"

"It'll all come out soon."

"What happened?"

"You heard about the Palace Hotel employing clandestine witches?"

"I read about that in the newspaper, yeah." Beaumont looked at her, disturbed. "Were they the ones..."

"Just one of them. He murdered a girlfriend's uncle and husband with Desanguis before killing off his coworkers."

He shuddered. "Ew! Desanguis! Good god, I saw a

picture of a Desanguis victim once, and it skeeves me out to this day!"

"At least you didn't have to see two up close."

The drinks were placed in front of them. They brought the glasses together. "Oh well," he said, holding his glass up in a mock toast, "To another day of crime fighting."

Harriet sipped her gimlet, smiled briefly, and placed her glass back on the bar top. "Yeah," she sighed, "the good citizens are safe for another day." She looked at Beaumont. "Speaking of, how's your side of the Dionysus case?"

Beaumont sipped his Vesper, then leaned closer to Harriet. "I think I got something," he whispered.

Her eyes grew. "Yeah? What's up?"

He told her what he learned from *Fiskikarlar*, the Saint-Phineas lecture, and the runes on Archambeau's trunk. Harriet gasped, "I read the same book! Not long ago. But I couldn't make any sense of it."

"It's very dense. Saint-Phineas is one of those guys who has to prove how smart he is."

"Totally. I can see him being insufferable. It only makes sense then that his one blurb is from Archambeau and no one else."

He looked at her inquisitively. "What do you mean?"

"Didn't you notice her blurb in *Fiskikarlar*?"

"No, I didn't. She wrote one for the book?"

"Yeah. I saw it immediately. They're cousins!"

"No way! I didn't know that. God, small world, huh?"

"You think the person who set up the runes on the trunk might've been inspired by Saint-Phineas?"

"Maybe. I'm not sure. I have a lot of digging to do."

"What was your next step?"

"I tried calling Archambeau to find out who had access to her trunk all day today. But she wasn't answering."

Harriet contemplated. "It's strange," she said. "I've been having the same luck with her personal assistant, Holly Hemlock."

"You have her number?"

"Yeah. NASDF gave it to us at the beginning of the investigation. But she never answered when I called and hasn't returned my messages."

As Harriet was talking, something caught Beaumont's attention. High on the top shelf of the showcase was a pristine bottle of Isidoros Arvanitis Ouzo. Above the bottle, a fiery golden shimmer floated and undulated with a hypnotic radiance. His eyes were fixed on the phenomena as it danced and pulsed. Then, something came to him. No germ of knowledge, phantasmic voice, or whisper influenced it, but an idea was suddenly born in his mind.

"Maybe you should call her again tomorrow," Beaumont said.

Harriet looked at him strangely. "Holly Hemlock?"

"Yeah. Try again."

"You think I should?"

"Why not? What could hurt?"

24

THE SCENE AT ARCHAMBEAU'S

It was early morning when Rab and the Ghost of Warren G. Harding entered headquarters. Rab's head was burdened with the details of the Collinson case that the district attorney wanted to discuss later in the day. They arrived at the elevator bank, where Harriet awaited a car. She looked sick. Pale, dark shadows bloomed underneath her eyes.

"You okay, buddy?" Rab asked.

"Yeah," Harriet drawled. "Late night."

The Ghost of Warren G. Harding studied her. "You look kah-nackered, Ms. June. If you don't mind me saying so."

She turned to him, "Kah-nackered?"

"You had ridden the white lighting."

"Huh?"

"You've been drinking."

"Oh. Yeah, I was. I was hanging out with Beaumont last night, and time got away from us."

"Beaumont Hart?" Rab asked.

"Yup. It was a spontaneous thing."

Rab grinned and teased, "Did something happen during that spontaneous thing?"

Harriet shook her head. "He doesn't swing that way, Rab."

"Oh."

"But he did give me his piece on the Dionysus heist."

"Yeah? Has he found something?"

When the elevator reached their level, they boarded. As they approached their floor and headed toward their desks, Harriet told them about Beaumont's discoveries and hypotheses. Rab stood at her desk, thinking. "It's something," she said. "If circumstantial."

"That's what we thought, too," Harriet said, opening a desk drawer and pulling out a bottle of aspirin. She popped a couple of tablets into her mouth.

"And that's where he left off?"

"Yeah. He's hit a brick wall until he can talk to Archambeau about her trunk."

"But we did that, and she couldn't tell us anything about the thing."

"Maybe something will shake loose now that time has passed? I don't know."

"What about her PA? What's-her-name? Hemlock?"

At that, a sudden look of revelation came to Harriet. She stared ahead past Rab and the Ghost of Warren G. Harding. "Everything alright, Ms. June?" he asked.

"Call her," she mumbled.

"What's up?" Rab said.

"That's what Beaumont told me to do last night. Call Holly Hemlock."

"Wait. Didn't you try that at the beginning? She wasn't answering."

"He was really insistent that I try again."

Rab placed a fist on her hip. "Any reason why?"

"I'm not sure. He didn't elaborate."

"Maybe you should give it another go, then."

Harriet pulled out her cell phone and dialed Holly Hemlock's number. She set it on speaker and waited for an answer. After the eighth ring, someone picked up. Their voice trembled, "Hello?"

"Oh, hello! My name is Harriet June. I'm a forensic witch with the San Francisco Police Department. Is Holly Hemlock there?"

The voice on the other side pulled away, quivering. An aggressive man's voice took its place, "Who's this?"

"I'm Detective Harriet June, SFPD, badge number five-two-five, calling for Ms. Holly Hemlock. Who am I speaking with?"

"Detective June," the voice sighed. "I'm Greg Hemlock, Holly's father."

"Mr. Hemlock, good morning. I hope I'm not bothering you."

Greg Hemlock choked back a sob and composed himself. "No bother, Detective June. I'm sorry I didn't catch your department. What was it again?"

"San Francisco Police, Mr. Hemlock."

He repeated what she said in a whisper. "What's Frisco PD doing calling this number?"

"NASDF gave us Ms. Hemlock's number. We're investigating the theft of the Cup of Dionysus from her employer, Selene Archambeau, when she was visiting here."

"Oh. I see."

"Is Ms. Hemlock available to take questions?"

A sharp wail pierced the background, followed by the thud of a collapsing body. "One moment, Detective June," Mr. Hemlock said. His pleading voice retreated from the cell phone. After a moment, the wailing became softer until it ceased. Harriet and Rab looked at each other, bewildered.

They heard the sound of a cell phone being picked up. "Hello? Detective June?" Mr. Hemlock said.

"I'm here. Who was that earlier?"

"Oh, Denise. Holly's mother. She's overwhelmed."

"Overwhelmed?"

"Holly was found dead a week ago."

Harriet pulled back from her phone; Rab retreated a pace. The Ghost of Warren G. Harding stared out in sorrow.

"Oh my god, I'm so sorry, Mr. Hemlock! Our condolences."

"It was devastating to her mother and me. She was our only child, Detective June, a miracle."

"What's the state of the investigation, if I can ask?"

"Holly was found in a field outside of Savannah. SPD is still going through the evidence. They can't say what caused her death."

"They can't say?"

"The detectives are leaning towards suicide. But it doesn't make sense. There was nothing wrong with Holly. She would've come to us for help."

"Were the detectives at your home recently?"

"Yeah. They dropped off her personal stuff to us. That's why we have her cell phone."

Mr. Hemlock paused and gathered himself before continuing. "We opened her phone to see if we could find anything that could help with the investigation. That's when you called."

"Did you find anything from Selene Archambeau on Holly's phone?"

"No, nothing from work. Just her usual stuff."

"Alright. Thank you, Mr. Hemlock. Again, I'm sorry for your loss."

Harriet ended the call. The detectives and ghost stood in silence. Harriet broke the solumnity, asking, "What do we do now?"

"We have some calls to make," Rab said. "Savannah police, NASDF, Archambeau. We have to get Beaumont up to speed and on task."

A fearful revelation came to Harriet, "We have to make sure Archambeau is safe!"

Rab's face hardened. "That's if she's not responsible for the killing."

"You think she's involved?"

"How can someone not be involved when their PA is found dead?" She pointed to Harriet, "You call Beaumont and clue him in on what we learned."

"What are you going to do?"

"Wait."

Rab went to her phone, dialed a number, and waited. "Captain, we need the local cops to go to Selene Archambeau's residence. It's important." She held the receiver to her ear, an electrical voice tingling. "We just learned that her PA was found dead this morning. It might have something to do with the Dionysus heist. Okay, cool. Thank you."

She hung up. "Captain Matt is going to contact Savannah PD to check on Archambeau. He'll contact us when he hears from them."

Some time passed after Rab called in the request to Lawrence Matt. She tried to reach anyone with authority at the North American Society of the Dionysian Faith, with no luck. Harriet was having her own issues trying to contact Beaumont Hart. She tried reaching him on his cell phone. But a strange, unearthly tone kept coming up before the call ended. When she tried the Coronado Detective Agecny's San Francisco office, his supervisor informed her that Beaumont was off for the day.

Rab's cell phone rang. It was Lawrence Matt. "What's up, Cap?" she answered. Her eyes widened; her brows furled. "Seriously? Holy fuck... okay. Are they gonna loop us in? Okay. Thanks, Cap." She ended the call, put down the phone on the desktop, and stared at it. "I think our job just got more complicated, Harriet."

"Why?"

"Savannah PD found Selene Archambeau's mummified corpse in her bedroom closet."

"I'm sorry, 'mummified'?"

"That's what Captain Matt said to me."

"Was it Desanguis?"

"I'm not sure. They have their forensic witch at the scene now. They'll loop us in when there's more information."

AFTER A FEW DAYS, the Savannah Police Department emailed their preliminary findings of the Archambeau case to Harriet and Rab. Archambeau was murdered by blunt force trauma to the head. Traces of advanced necromancy were prominent on the corpse. She had been dead for nearly a month, according to the medical examiner.

"Wait," Rab said, staring at her computer monitor. "A month? Who the hell were we talking to back in the Palace Hotel?"

"Something isn't right," Harriet said, scrolling on her cell phone.

"What do you have, Harriet?" Rab asked.

"I'm going over my astrological app. Four weeks ago,

there was a rare planetary event. Uranus, Saturn, and Jupiter aligned perfectly with Earth, with Cancer at twelve degrees. Such a thing occurs once in a century."

"Okay, so?"

Harriet slapped the Saint-Phineas book on her desk. "Planetary events are weapon-grade uranium for these runic spells. You can do a lot of things during such a time. But this is where something doesn't make sense to me. The event happened around the time of Archambeau's murder, right? So that could account for the necromancy."

"Right. Whoever murdered Archambeau tried to get more out of her corpse. Maybe information about the cup. There's our suspect for the heist."

"But there were no planetary events at the time of the robbery. Whoever our killer thief is, they wasted a very good event on Archambeau."

"They still could've used the runes. That kind of magic doesn't always need the planets and the stars, does it?"

"I'm not sure. Beaumont has more knowledge on the subject."

"Have you had a chance to talk to him yet?"

"No! Every time I called him, it never went through. And I keep trying his office, but he's always not there. I think the staff are very annoyed at me."

"Shit. Jesus, we're stuck again, aren't we?"

"Yeah. Nothing short of divine intervention will probably help us at this point."

It was late at night when Rab and Harriet left the headquarters building, with the Ghost of Warren G. Harding following. "I'll drive you home, buddy," Rab offered.

"Thanks, Rab. I don't have it in me to take the streetcar."

They got into Bruiser and peeled out of the parking lot,

making a speedy turn on Mission Street. "Where did Beaumont go? Did he tell you?" Rab asked.

Harriet shook her head sadly. "I hope he's okay."

Rab glanced at Harriet and turned back to the road. "The Cap's going to put us on another case soon," she said. "We'll pass the Dionysus case to the next guys down the line."

"Yeah." Harriet stared into the distance past the windshield, "We were so close, though."

"So close and so far. Think of it this way, buddy. We laid the foundation for solving this thing on top of solving four murders. That's some hot-shit detective work."

"For sure. It's just... this case took one hell of a dramatic turn. What happened to Archambeau? Who did we meet at the hotel? What happened to Holly Hemlock? What about the cup? I have many more questions, and it's driving my little Libra heart crazy!"

Rab shrugged as she turned onto Fell Street, zipped up the hill, and turned onto Buchanan Street. She pulled up to the entrance of Harriet's apartment. A lone shadow sat on the stairs leading to the stoop of the upper flats. It was slumped, rocking back and forth, and cradling something on its lap. "Who the hell is that?" Rab asked.

"I don't know," Harriet said.

The detectives got out of Bruiser and approached the shadow. It stood up and descended the stairs, where a nearby street lamp illuminated Beaumont Hart's pale face. His eyes were mad, his hair eschewed. "Hey guys!" he shouted, his lips stretching into a bizarre, frightening grin.

"Are you alright, Beaumont?" Harriet asked, horrified.

"Dandy! Just... just dandy. I think. I don't know. Boy, I had a night, y'all! Let me tell you..."

"You've been gone for days!"

He looked at her curiously as if she had gone insane. "No! No, I haven't! Why do you lie, Harriet? I thought we were friends!"

"What are you holding?" Rab asked.

"Oh! Yeah!" Beaumont lifted the object in his hands. It was a tarnished bronze bowl painted with strange, faded figures, delicate hoop handles on each side, and a long stem ending at a large, intricate base. "It's what we've been looking for!"

25

THE DIONYSUS HEIST

The Cup of Dionysus stood on Harriet's kitchen counter. The three detectives stared at it from the dining table while Ditzy sauntered from chair to chair, whining and trying to make friends with Rab and Beaumont. "It's... not as spectacular as I thought it would be," Harriet said.

"Yeah," Rab agreed. "It's almost like a piece of junk."

"Three thousand years," Beaumont mumbled, rocking in his chair. "Three thousand years! You wouldn't look good either after three thousand years!"

Harriet stretched out her hand and took Beaumont's. He looked at her, trembling. "Okay, honey, what happened?" she asked. "Please tell us."

Beaumont swallowed and gathered his thoughts. He closed his eyes tightly. "I got a DM from a dating app."

"Who?" Harriet interrupted.

He shook his head, "Some... person. It looked like a catfish account. They only had one profile picture. This *really* attractive person, with a full, beautiful face, dazzling green eyes, and perfect locks!

"I felt drawn to them, wanted to meet them. Their beauty didn't seem real, almost like it was AI, you know? So, we message, they want to meet. I'm thrilled! They offer a location, and we set up a date."

Beaumont stopped and glanced past Harriet and Rab's heads toward an illumination only he could see. "Are you okay, buddy?" Rab asked.

"Yeah. Yeah," he said.

"Can I see the conversation between you two?" Harriet asked.

He opened the dating app on his phone and showed it to her, but there were no messages. "When did you talk to this person, Beaumont?" she asked.

"Today," he sounded exasperated.

Harriet refreshed the app and looked for the messages. But nothing came up. She looked up to Rab.

"So, you go to meet them," Rab said. "What happened? Where did you go?"

"It was this sushi place on Taylor, near Sutter. It's a nice, intimate place. I found a table in the back and ordered some appetizers. I was right on time at six p.m. And I waited for what seemed like an eternity. Just as I was about to leave, out of the shadows, they appeared. They didn't come through the entrance; I could see the entrance. I had a perfect line of sight of the entrance! It was, like, they materialized right next to me.

"And girl! They were just as beautiful as in the profile picture. Masculine and feminine, you know? They wore this form-fitting black suit that moved with them and shimmered in the light. I thought, 'They look like a panther walking.' They sat down in front of me. A plate of sushi suddenly appeared next to them, and they smiled. And... that smile! I don't know how to describe it, but it was pure ecstasy!"

"Did you get a name?" Harriet asked.

Beaumont thought for a minute, rubbing his hands together, "Maybe? It's right on the tip of my tongue, but I'm drawing a blank. It's the weirdest thing."

"Okay, this mysterious stranger appears and sits down with you. Then what?" Rab asked.

"They cut to the chase and say, 'I have a story I want to tell you.' Oh, their voice sounded like music! So, I'm entranced and go, 'Tell me.'"

Beaumont's demeanor changed. He straightened up into an almost rigid stance, his eyes becoming bright like glass reflecting points of brilliant light. Suddenly, the kitchen's air was fragrant with a perfume of rich earth and blossoming trees. His voice changed, becoming terrifyingly ethereal as if possessed by an inhuman force, "This is the story of a pitiful little man who had gone his whole life pursuing fame as a great magician, only to discover much too late that his sparse talents could not save him from a pauper's fate and memory's oblivion.

"After decades of vanity and arrogance, he was forced out of his beloved scholarly career with absolutely nothing. His one achievement, a book of *barbaros* tricks, was out of print and forgotten. He had not one penny of money saved, and his only source of income was paltry consulting work that came sporadically. This man raged deeply and despaired painfully, for he knew no one in the world cared about an impoverished, forgotten, elderly magician. He almost convinced himself that going the way of an antique Roman, opening his wrists in a hot bath, would be his only salvation. That is, until Infamy's temptation called to him.

"You see, his only remaining family, a cousin, Madame Selene Archambeau, a particular favorite of divine

Chthonois, blessed with remarkable intelligence and charm, had been honored with a legendary task."

Rab leaned closer to Harriet. "Who the hell is Chthonois?" she whispered.

"The Subterranean," Harriet answered, her eyes shone with wonder. "It's one of the names of Dionysus!"

Beaumont, his head now bathed in an illumination of unknown origin, continued, "After years of dutiful service, Madame Archambeau was named custodian of a precious, invaluable object, the personal cup of Chthonois himself, a position very few mortals were given. When news of her appointment came to him, this man burned with an unquenchable jealousy of her talents, favors, and accomplishments. His impotent fury grew in intensity. However, when the passions cooled, he saw the opportunity to save himself from financial ruin and eternal irrelevance. After all, look at Herostratus, he thought: why earn fame through great deeds when villainy is easier?

"This man was determined to steal Chthonois' cup, was obsessed with stealing it. He had a simple trick, a *barbaros* spell learned from Luvdimir of Vilnius, and knew that a once-in-a-century planetary event was fast approaching. It was more than enough to bypass the cup's protective wards and not leave behind evidence. In his arrogance, he plotted the theft of Chthonois' cup from its tabernacle in the Bacchaes' citadel. Every step was perfect, he thought. But there was one thing in the way: Selene Archambeau."

Rab and Harriet turned to each other.

Beaumont's countenance darkened, his voice low, "This man needed to surround Chthonois' cup with his barbaric runes before the planetary event. But how could he when his cousin was keeping her watch? The solution was easy, he thought. Cousins are family, yes. But not by much. The furies would not care, he believed. He slew her in the chamber of the cup, using her own *skeptron*. And as the planetary event was reaching its zenith, this man hastily laid his runes around the tabernacle and waited for his magic to complete the work.

"But nothing ever goes according to plan, does it? For at midnight, the *barbaros* spells worked their magic, and Chthonois' prized vessel vanished from its tabernacle. This man saw it happen. But it did not land in his hands."

"Oh... What?" Harriet whispered.

"This man went over his work repeatedly, retraced the lines of his spells, and everything pointed to the cup being in his hands! He could not understand how it had simply vanished. But he was not able to dwell on it longer, as he needed to flee the Bacchae's citadel. Before he did, though, he stared at the corpse of his cousin, Madame Selene Archambeau, on the floor. He knew that he still had the planetary event's power until dawn. And he needed answers. He brought her corpse back to her house and performed abominations, dragging her soul back from the pits of death to interrogate her."

Beaumont smiled and giggled, his voice taking on a high mischievous tone. "Oh, how I love her! Even in death, Archambeau refused him, taunting him furiously, 'Oh, what's wrong, Benny? Your magic couldn't cut it again, like always? Come on now, Dicky - her mocking nickname of him - why not use more of your runes if they're so perfect?'

"Benny-Dicky was angry and afraid. Angry that the cup evaded his grasp and afraid of his guilt. He swore he heard the furies circling above, their screams descending closer, madding guilt tightening around his neck." Beaumont stopped, then settled, "His panic was a thing of marvelous beauty!"

"What happened next?" asked the Ghost of Warren G. Harding.

Beaumont continued, "Benny-Dicky was desperate to find the cup. In life and death, Madame Selene Archambeau thwarted him. Yet, he believed he had a card to play and continued the game. He believed one other knew what could have happened to the cup because of her closeness to his cousin."

"The PA!" Harriet called out.

"Yes! Holly Hemlock kept Archambeau's diary, helped organize her life, and minded her magicks. How *could* she not know how Archambeau defended Chthonois' cup? Much like dear brother Hades, Benny-Dicky kidnapped young Holly on her way home one night and absconded with her to the dark realm of Selene Archambeau's basement to question her. But she had no knowledge of what happened to the cup. How could she have known? She wasn't involved with the cup, had no knowledge of what her mistress did to protect it. To him, she was worthless. Holly saw the malevolence in his eyes and begged madman Benny-Dicky to let her go."

He stopped, his brilliant eyes clouded with tears. He choked back, "Her pleading fell on deaf ears as the poisonous thought infected his mind: I'm on the hook for one death, why not another?"

He swallowed, his throat constricting. "The gods are not heartless," he murmured. "They are impulsive, yes, but not heartless. They mourn the deaths of their faithful and burn with terrible anger when injustice is done to them. The gears of vengeance ground forward."

Harriet, Rab, and the Ghost of Warren G. Harding stared at him, mouths parted in disbelief. "What do you mean, Beaumont?" Rab asked.

He held his arm up, his pointer finger out, shouting, "*Choiropsalas oide!*"

"What?"

"As Benny-Dicky worked to cover up his crimes and find Chthonis' cup, something strange and eerie happened. Word came to him of an announcement from the North American Society of the Dionysian Faith that Ms. Selene Archambeau was going to San Francisco for a lecture on its most sacred rites. With the cup as its showpiece!"

"I'm so confused," Harriet said.

"So was he! His confusion was limitless, and so was his fear! He thought it was an old story or a sick joke. Until he saw an online interview published days after the murders with Archambeau – alive and very much well – holding the young god's cup in her hands. He was seized by a maelstrom of emotion that paralyzed his intellect, tore his sanity apart, and turned him into the baying, drooling, helpless animal that man is!

"Numerous times, he nervously checked on Madame Archambeau's corpse rotting away in the closet he stored her in. As he poked and prodded at her decaying flesh, so too did his sanity begin to rot! Benny-Dicky used his scant money to buy an airplane ticket and flew to San Francisco. He wanted – no, *needed* – to see this Selene Archambeau for himself.

"He tracked down where this Selene Archambeau was staying and lingered in the hotel's lobby, anxiously getting drunk at its bar. On the Palace Hotel's CCTV footage, you will see a small, insignificant man with frizzy white hair and one eye larger than the other haunting the place for an entire day."

Beaumont grinned, showing his teeth, "On the night of the 'robbery,' Benny-Dicky finally saw Selene Archambeau.

She breezed on through the gilded entrance of the Palace Hotel, the very picture of life and health. He stared at her, mouth hung open, eyes twitching, hands quaking so much he needed to hold on to his knees to control them. She turned her gaze in his direction, dark green eyes firmly on him, and moved on like she hadn't seen him. He choked and sputtered, but he eventually gathered the fortitude to chase her down to the elevator bank, missing her car by a second. He kept an eye on the floor indicator until it reached the sixth floor. And then he followed.

"When he reached the sixth floor, it was dim. Shadows had overtaken every corner. The only sound came from the traffic outside and his raspy breath. Benny-Dicky walked slowly and cautiously, measuring each step of his feet. Then, he saw her shadow rounding a corner of a hallway. Caution be damned! He ran after her! He flew around that corner... and saw nothing there.

"Lights were burning low. The moonlight shone through the windows. He moved forward once again. And then he saw her running! From one hallway to the next, one after another, he ran after her. Her swift feet disappearing around a corner were the last thing he saw as he came closer. He was panting, his chest heaving painfully, spinning around disorientated, groaning pitifully as the chaos of his guilt crashed against the shoreline of his intellect. And there she was, standing in the middle of a nearby hallway, Selene Archambeau, the favorite of Chthonois! She *looked* at him, those shimmering, alien, green eyes cutting through the gloom.

"Benny-Dicky held out a hand, calling out unintelligibly. He stumbled towards her. She turned around and, like a ghost, headed towards the open door of a suite, vanishing through it. He walked into the darkened sitting room and saw a shadow fly across the open bedroom door. He rushed in, and there he saw it. An antique traveling trunk, one that reminded him of what his glamorous mother used when she traveled across the nation. It yawned open. He approached it. He noticed etchings that ran around the interior and inspected them. Runes, compounded runes. He recognized them. By then, he knew he wasn't alone and turned around. Selene Archambeau appeared before transforming into a youthful god of indescribable fury. The runes activated on their own, turning the trunk into a portal, into which Chthonois himself kicked our pleading, whimpering Benedict Saint-Phineas through."

"Benedict Saint-Phineas," Harriet whispered in disbelief. "Him?"

"Yes, him."

"Golly," said the Ghost of Warren G. Harding.

Harriet stood from her chair and turned to the Cup of Dionysus on her kitchen counter. "It was a trap," she said.

"What?" Rab said.

"It was a trap all along! Dionysus vanished his *own* cup before Saint-Phineas' runes had a chance to work. He disguised himself as Selene Archambeau, lured Saint-Phineas to San Francisco, and then ambushed him with his own magic!"

"But. All that trouble, why?" asked the Ghost of Warren G. Harding. "And why here in Frisco?"

Beaumont's eyes were no longer bright but obscured by some dark, twitchy film. He lowered his still-illuminated head as if held down by weight. "To prove that a crime happened," he said, "you need evidence. Compelling evidence. But what if that evidence cannot be obtained so easily? What if the criminal can cover his tracks so brilliantly that you police officers miss the trail? The laws are to deter man from his evil actions, but how do you prevent the criminal from circumventing them? What are the laws, then, if not suggestions?" He glared at them, "The young god knows how your laws work, how ineffectual they can be without... some help. He took it upon himself to offer this help."

"Where is Benedict Saint-Phineas, Beaumont?" Harriet asked.

"He's where he needs to be until the right time."

"How come Dionysus didn't punish Saint-Phineas himself?"

"Why should he? Look at Pentheus, detective. Did Dionysus punish him himself? No. Saint-Phineas is your responsibility."

Rab stood, went to the cup, and picked it up by its stem. "You have to tell me, Beaumont. If this was Dionysus' doing, and he had the cup the whole time, how did you get it?"

He said, "When my date finished their story, they were swirling a straw in a glass of water. I was mesmerized by it, and there was a rushing sound, like a violent hurricane, but only for a few seconds. And in a blur of shadow and light, they vanished. I blinked. The restaurant was fine. Nothing looked out of place. I blinked again and saw the cup where the water glass was!"

"But... how did you know it was the Cup of Dionysus?"

Beaumont rocked back and forth. "Past the lip," he muttered.

Rab tilted the cup towards her, looking into the blackened bowl. Harriet asked, "What are you seeing?"

"Nothing," Rab said, transfixed. Her eyes glazed a milky white, her voice taking on a resounding tone. "Nothing but a verdant field, surrounded by craggy mountains and skeletal trees, the young god's handmaidens, standing, dressed in bassaris, brandishing long, leafy thyrsus in their hands, snakes like diadems in their hair, shaking leopards madly in their hands, drums a-pounding in a circle, rhythmic and ecstatic, chants of something I can't make out, '*Eleutherius, Eleutherius, theos erchomai.*' Dancing, mad dancing. A fattened ox being led to sacrifice. The revelers are starving, sleep-deprived, thirsting, crying out '*Eleutherius, Eleutherius, theos erchomai*', louder and louder. The bloody revelers, each shouting something blurring together, '*Aesymnetes-phugasaeymnestesphugas!*' Approaching them, a gigantic glowing figure towering above the craggy mountains, face soft like feminine and hard like masculine, eyes like gold and steel, mammoth hands raised above, and ivies and vines growing from nowhere, mygodmygodmygod!"

Rab had collapsed on the floor, muttering and convulsing violently, tears streaming from her eyes and a wide grin on her face. The cup was still clutched tightly in her hand. Ditzy ran up to her, whining with concern, and started licking her cheek. Beaumont jumped on his chair, crouched, and screamed incoherently while clapping rhythmically, the sound reverberating horrifyingly throughout the apartment, trembling the walls and quaking the floor. The Ghost of Warren G. Harding ran to Harriet. "What is going on, Ms. June?" he demanded. "What is happening?"

Stricken by a chest-seizing dread, Harriet looked at her friends, both gripped by frenzy, glanced around the shaking apartment and returned to the Ghost of Warren G. Harding. "I think we're dealing with possession!" she screamed.

"What?" said the Ghost of Warren G. Harding. "How?"

"It's the cup! Beaumont and Rab touched the cup. Now they've become vessels for Dionysus!"

"What can be done?"

"We need to practice a divine expulsion! You keep an eye

on them, Warren. I'm going to gather supplies... this is going to be messy!"

THE FOLLOWING DAY, Harriet was in her disheveled kitchen; the eerie smells of last night's labor lingered heavily in the air, making her ill. She poured Ditzy's breakfast into her bowl. "Kibbies, baby," she whispered, setting the bowl on the soiled floor. Ditzy whined cautiously, sniffed the bowl, and ate.

Harriet stood straight and stretched her back. "It's going to take me forever to get this place back in order," she groaned. She sighed deeply, knowing she didn't have the energy to tackle the task, and decided to make herself breakfast to bring a little normality back to her life.

She made a pumpkin spice latte and went to her refrigerator to take out a loaf of sourdough bread and apricot jam. The coffee was delicious, as was every bite of her toast. Looking through the shattered kitchen window, she saw a bright, sunny day with a vibrant blue sky. With the mystery of the Cup of Dionysus solved Harriet decided to request some time off.

26

ALWAYS ON DUTY

When she returned from work throughout the week, Harriet worked on her apartment. Every inch of floor space was washed and sanitized. Broken window panes were repaired. Walls were replastered and painted, and any furniture that wasn't salvageable was replaced. By the time her vacation started, her home was decent again.

She was in the living room, straightening the framed singed photograph on her altar, when she heard her cell phone buzz nearby. She looked at the screen, and her face softened. It was Rab. "Hey, buddy," Harriet answered.

"Hey, buddy. How're you doing?" Rab sounded tired but livelier than the last time they saw each other.

"Chilling. I'm thinking about going over to Alamo Square for a little bit, get some air." Harriet let the quiet hang momentarily before continuing, "How about you, Rab? How are you holding up?"

Rab hummed softly, "Better. Way better, actually. I think I have the last of the ickiness out of my system."

"That's good. Where are you now? Captain Matt didn't say where you went."

"I'm down in Pacifica with Warren. It's the place for some good R&R, especially after what we went through."

"No kidding."

"I heard you still went into HQ to wrap up the Dionysus case, Harriet. Why didn't you let some other guy take it, give yourself some time off? You earned it."

"I had a few loose ends that needed tightening. And thanks to Beaumont's possession tips, we were able to bring together the evidence against Saint-Phineas. He'll be charged with double homicide when he's found."

"Oh! No one told you? Our peeps back east found Saint-Phineas."

Harriet sat in her leather chair. "No way! Where did Dionysus dump him?"

"They found him on the side of a road near the Georgia-North Carolina line. He was naked and filthy, had torn his hair out from the roots, and ripped his eyes out with his bare hands. He was practically confessing the robbery and the murders and begging to be arrested."

"Geez! Guess that's what you get for crossing an Olympian, huh?"

"No kidding. But he got off easy, unlike some I've heard about."

Harriet smiled. "So, when are you coming back to work, Rab?" she asked. "Everyone's asking about you."

"In a day or so. I got the all-clear to return to the force. I want to go back to work. Warren's whining is driving me crazy."

"Oh, I bet!"

"Yeah. Hey, listen, I won't keep you, buddy. We'll see each other soon."

"For sure. See ya soon, Rab."

They ended their call. Harriet picked up Ditzy's harness, leash, and her copy of *The Phantasmagoria of the Shou-Earth*. She shook the harness, its clasps jingled. Ditzy ran up to Harriet, dancing on her hindlegs, and whined excitedly. Harriet slipped the harness on her, and they went outside.

Alamo Square was peaceful. The typical groups of tourists congregating on its hills, attempting to photograph the Painted Ladies, were largely absent. A few families sprawled on blankets on the grass, playing in the sunlight. Women in athletic clothes jogged or practiced yoga. A line of customers stood near Lady Falcon's truck, waiting for coffee. Harriet found a spot on a mound and settled her and Ditzy down. She looked towards the Painted Ladies, towards the mountainous skyscrapers cleaving the skylight of San Francisco. A cool gust from the Pacific cut through the treetops, scattering leaves and rich earthy scents around the Square. Harriet sighed and was about to open her book when someone called to her. She turned toward Lady Falcon's truck and saw a young woman dressed in a light jean jacket, dark knit sweater, and tights walking toward her, a cup of coffee in her hand. Her jade necklace gleamed in the sunlight. "How are you, Yolanda?" Harriet greeted.

Yolanda stood near her. Ditzy had come alive, trying to get her attention. Yolanda bent low and started playing with Ditzy's ears and cheeks. "I'm good, Detective June." Yolanda focused on Ditzy, who had settled on her back, exposing her belly. She gently scratched the soft fur. A moment had passed before she looked at Harriet and said, "Thank you for letting us know about Brother Jeremiah's assailant. *Manbo* Kind was pleased."

"It was nothing," Harriet said. "If it weren't for you and

the Tranquil Mawu Society, we wouldn't have been able to solve these crimes."

"Hm." Yolanda continued scratching Ditzy's belly.

"How is Mr. Jackson?" Harriet asked.

"He's better," Yolanda said. "We got the last of that curse out of him when he was discharged from the hospital. But he's still a bit weak. Brother Antonio is helping him get his strength back."

"That's good."

Yolanda became stern, "Is it true that Jeremiah's assailant's going to cop a plea?"

Harriet leaned back on her arm. "It's sounding like it. The DA wants an easy slam dunk on the whole thing, and Tad Collinson is willing to talk for a lesser sentence and throw Monica Benavidez under the bus, too."

Yolanda scoffed, "Some justice."

"I know. It isn't enough, especially after everything Collinson did."

"Some justice is better than no justice. At least, we'll always know where he is." Yolanda's tone was malevolent. Harriet picked up on it: "Yeah, true. And who knows? Many things happen in jail—things we can't account for, right?"

"Hm. Yeah. Strange things have been known to happen." She smiled at Harriet, "May he have a long, long life."

Yolanda stood up and said goodbye, walking down a path towards a tree grove. Harriet scratched Ditzy's ears when she settled back into her lap and opened her book:

Dirty and aching with exhaustion from his travailing journey, Peter accinged himself and entered the nave of the unfathomable tower. The low flames of the flambeaus hanging from its columns paled compared to the illumination beaming from the gargantuan stained-glass windows of the faraway apse. Vibrant, rebarbative murals depicting the deeds of unknown figures surrounded Peter as he walked through on unsteady feet. An intoxicating aroma, wafted by phantom hands, filled his nostrils. As he neared the transept, Peter saw a titanic shadow standing on an intricate pulpit near a wing. "Piotr K!" the shadow roared, stopping him cold. The shadow descended the pulpit, shrinking into the form of a man. He was dressed in a glittering but senescent robe. His long, billowing silver hair dragged along the floor, and his eyebrows were as wild and delicate as monarch butterflies. A faint glow radiated from the edges of his body. His fiery eyes fell on the quivering boy. "You've sought me," he accused.

"Astronomer," said Peter.

"You've traveled far, through many hells and trials, endured many indignities to appear before me. Why?"

Peter gathered his courage and voice but failed to perform. The Star-lighted Astronomer considered him. "Imperfect," he said.

"It's not my station, Astronomer."

"Is that so?"

"Yes. I've proven myself to you, shown what I can do."

"Trivial violence and deception are not evidence of strength, cunning, nor determination."

"I've come seeking you, Astronomer!"

"And you've wasted your efforts."

"Astronomer! I want to know why I'm here!"

The Star-lighted Astronomer studied Peter, turned away from him, and ambled to the apse. Peter followed him. They continued in this manner, not speaking, until they approached the mammoth windows. Their illumination blinded Peter and made him feel vastly insignificant before the stained glass, and he trembled with animalistic fear but burned with terrific awe.

"There are many philosophies," began the Star-lighted Astronomer, "and many theologies in the Shou-Earth, striving to

explain its nature and our place in it. Each one combats the other, their adherents desiring to slit each other's throats to prove their infallibility. It makes me think of the one thing that unites them all."

"What is it, Astronomer?"

"The governing force, a parable."

"A parable?"

The Star-lighted Astronomer turned back to Peter, washed in an ethereal glow. He said, "On the edge of the barren world lays an oasis, lush and rich. From the outside lands came two children. They ran into the oasis, laughing and giggling, breathing in the heavy scent of the flora and soil. They enjoyed the sensation of the tall grass against their knees and the cool-ness of the trickling streams. The animals who long called the oasis home skittered from their tormentors and watched from the shadows with covetous eyes as the children easily broke fruit from the trees and took esurient bites, the juice running down their chins.

"Then, from the sky came a lone thunderbolt. It crashed into the largest of the trees, bringing it down and igniting it. The chil-dren, at first afraid, approached the inferno. It mesmerized them, and they thought of nothing else. From the corybantic flames came whisperings, soft and mellifluous. The children did not know if the whisperings were real or not. But they were taken in.

"In time, under the influence of the whisperings, the children became facinorous, taking the fruits of the oasis until its trees were barren, drinking its waters until nothing was left. They killed any animals that strayed into their paths, causing the rest to flee. A purulent sickness descended on the oasis. With nothing of their former lives left, the children turned on each other, causing violence until one lay dead on the ground. The survivor looked upon their dying world, feeling like a prince."

Peter asked, "What does it mean?"

"Whatever you want it to mean," answered the Star-lighted Astronomer...

Harriet's cell phone buzzed in her pocket. She took it out and saw Lawrence Matt's number on the screen. "Yes, captain," she answered.

"Sorry to bug you on your time off, June. But I need you right now."

"I understand. Is it a new case?"

"Yeah. Don't forget your kit."

"Will do. Where do you need me?"

"Meet me at the medical examiner's office. Rab's on her way."

CAPTAIN LAWRENCE MATT was leaning against his car in the medical examiner's parking lot when he saw Bruiser drive in and park. Rab stepped out, followed by the Ghost of Warren G. Harding. She was very pale, making her red hair more vibrant. They approached Matt. "How's it goin', Cap?" she said.

"It's going," he answered. "Thanks for coming in on short notice, Rab. Are you sure you're ready to return to the force?"

"Trust, I'm ready." She looked around the parking lot. "Where's everyone? Shouldn't there be more people around?"

He shook his head slowly. "It's just you, me, and Harriet on this one. I made sure of it."

Her brows knitted closely. "That serious?"

A taxi drove into the parking lot and stopped near them. Harriet stepped out, shouldering her messenger bag. "Morning, everyone," she said.

"Good morning, Ms. June," said the Ghost of Warren G. Harding.

"Okay, we're all here," Lawrence Matt said. "Come with me." He led the group into the medical examiner's building, where they met a man in the reception area. He was dressed in scrubs, stout, with a round face and harsh eyes that softened when the officers approached. "Dr. Salazar," Matt said in a salutatory way.

"Captain Matt," Dr. Salazar said, his voice harmonious. "Thank you for coming on short notice and for being discreet."

"Of course."

Dr. Salazar turned to Rab and Harriet, "And one of you is the forensic witch?" Harriet raised her hand. "Good, very good. Everyone, please follow me."

Dr. Salazar led the group into the examination room, where the smell of raw, wet meat and chemicals was pungent. The officers' horror struck them deeply. Dr. Salazar brought them to a covered examination table. "Peel it off," Lawrence Matt ordered. Dr. Salazar obeyed.

The victim was a man in his mid-to-late twenties. There was hardly anything left of the corpse. His chest and torso were torn open, the rib cage broken apart jaggedly. The organs were missing. His limbs were ripped from him by the joints. Only his left arm remained somewhat intact; its hand was shredded and sliced in half between the ring and middle fingers. What was left of the face was bulging eyes; all that remained of the nose and jaw was ragged meat.

"Jesus," Lawrence Matt whispered.

"Holy. Fuck," Rab muttered slowly.

Harriet said nothing. The Ghost of Warren G. Harding stared at the blood pools hungrily.

"Were you able to identify the victim?" Matt asked.

"I was lucky to have found a finger with a viable print," Dr. Salazar said. "Carlos Adolphus Kim, age twenty-seven. His last known address was in Noe Valley. Not married, no family."

"Thank god."

"Any priors we should know about?" Rab asked. "Does he have a record?"

"No, nothing," said Dr. Salazar. "He was a pretty quiet, average guy—so average that you could miss him."

"Whoever butchered him sure didn't miss."

"No kidding."

Dr. Salazar put on a latex glove and lifted the left arm, showing the hand to the group. "These appear to be defensive wounds," he said.

"Yeah, no shit," Rab said.

"He didn't stand a chance," Lawrence Matt said, his tone harsh, barely concealing his disgusted fury. "What kind of animal would do this?"

"An animal indeed," Dr. Salazar said. He went to a stainless tray near the examination table and picked up a long, broken, jagged yellow tooth. "This was found near Mr. Kim's body when it was discovered. It's the cuspid of a *Canis lupus*."

"What's that?" Harriet asked.

"A wolf. Particularly, a gray wolf."

The officers were stunned. "A wolf in San Francisco?" Rab said. "But that doesn't make sense. Wolves haven't been spotted in California for decades."

"And was he attacked by a pack?" Harriet said.

"Here's the thing," said Dr. Salazar, "both of you are right but also wrong. This is why I reached out to y'all privately."

"How so?" Lawrence Matt asked.

"Something about this tooth didn't sit right with me

when I first saw it. I don't know; call it my instincts kicking in. So, at the start of my investigation, I sent it to a friend to help identify it. She was the one who found out the species it belonged to, but she said it was highly unusual."

"Why, Salazar?"

"It's a grey wolf's tooth, yes. But the size and dimension indicate that it is also humanoid."

ABOUT THE AUTHOR

Born and raised in the shattered light of Los Angeles, California, Shanon Erami was educated in Santa Barbara, California, majoring in history before moving back to the *Pueblo*. After working odd jobs at even odder companies, Shanon turned to writing, first short stories and then novels that would never see the light of day. His first novel, *The Black Demiurge*, was published in 2024 and features the amateur detective Icky Taylor. Shanon Erami lives with his beloved wife and dog in Oakland, California.

To reach Shanon Erami:
    Instagram: @_sha_rami_
    Email: shanon.erami@gmail.com
    To read Shanon's short stories, go to www.sharamix.com

ALSO BY SHANON ERAMI

The Black Demiurge